"EXPERT ... EBERHART"

—*Best Sellers*

"She doesn't let her readers down in this one. There's a good measure of suspense, action, excitement and romance in the adventures of Sarah ... It is definitely one of those 'I'll read one more chapter and stop.' Only you don't ..."

—*Winston-Salem Journal*

"After a wild and secret journey to her husband's plantation ... Sarah finds herself involved not only in awkward family situations (including indecent proposals from the bridegroom's relatives) but in mysterious deaths as well ..."

—*Oakland Tribune*

Mignon G. Eberhart

The Cup, the Blade or the Gun

POPULAR LIBRARY · NEW YORK

© Copyright, 1961, by Mignon G. Eberhart
Library of Congress Catalog Card Number: 61-6244

Published by arrangement with Random House, Inc.
Random House edition published in July, 1961

Published simultaneously in Toronto, Canada, by
Random House of Canada, Limited.

All persons and events in this book are entirely imaginary.

Author's Note

The author wishes to make special acknowledgment to Gordon Carroll for his informed interest and advice, also for making available to her his collection of books on the Civil War, including the complete Official Record; to the staff of the New York Society Library; to Bruce Catton for his various books, especially *Grant Moves South;* and to Dee Brown for his *Grierson's Raid.*

To
EDNA AND ALBERT DORNE
in friendship and gratitude

CHAPTER ONE

Someone scratched lightly on the door.

Sarah Hugot spun around from the window. She then realized that it was too soon for the message she expected to arrive, and that this must be a maid. She called, "Come in," remembered that New Orleans through all its changes of government still remained a French, and bilingual city, and said, "*Entrez*." The room had grown dark while she stood at the window; she made her way through crowding shapes of tables, settees, chairs and trunks. As she reached the door it opened.

A middle-aged Negro woman, in a dark dress and a snowy white apron and *tignon* slid into the room and closed the door behind her.

"Madam Lucien Hugot?"

"Yes."

"I am Calista. I belong to Madam Fautier. There is someone who wishes to see you, madam."

"Oh!" Sarah said. So soon! "Is he here?"

"No, madam. He is waiting. He sent me to make sure that you are Madam Hugot."

"Oh, yes, yes. Tell him at once . . ."

"Yes, madam. *Merci*, madam." Calista slipped out the door again so gently that there were only the sounds of the crisp rattle of her starchy apron and the light click of the door as it closed.

So soon, Sarah thought again, with deep relief. She wondered who had watched her arrival. She had seen no one who seemed to take any particular interest in her.

She had landed that morning, a warm muggy morning in early April. She had followed her husband's directions to the letter, first accomplishing the landing formalities with a minimum of difficulty, then seeing to it that her trunks and the big black moiré bag she carried herself were deposited safely in a room at the St. Charles Hotel, then going to the

Provost Marshal's office, where again she encountered a minimum of difficulty.

She had then returned to the hotel.

The trunks contained contraband gold; the black moiré bag contained contraband medicines. It was April of 1863. She had been required, on landing, to take an oath of loyalty to the United States of America, and had done so willingly. She was thankful, however, that the blue-coated soldiers at the pier had barely glanced at the contents of her trunks and not even looked inside the big moiré bag over her arm.

She had had a moment's qualm while her papers were being examined but if anyone had ever heard the name of Lucien Hugot, Captain in the Confederate army, there was no sign of it; she registered at the hotel as Mrs. Lucien Hugot and while she fancied there was a flicker of recognition of the Hugot name in the eyes of the clerk, still he had said nothing and indeed was very likely to be a staunch Confederate, in spite of the fact that the hotel was now taken over, as everything in the city was taken over, by the Union army of occupation.

She had settled herself to wait. She had not heard from Lucien but the mails were irregular, often lost; her only course had been to follow the plan he had laid out for her. If he did not succeed in sending some friend in New Orleans to tell her of arrangements for her trip to Honotassa, Lucien's home and now her home, then she had intended to find a way herself, with or without escort, Union army or no Union army.

But clearly Lucien had contrived to send word to a friend to keep an eye on passengers arriving by boat from Cuba and the friend was already on his way to see her, after prudently sending the Negro woman Calista to arrange a meeting.

She was sure now, too, that Lucien had arrived safely at Honotassa. She had not known how tense and anxious she had been until now, when her spirits soared.

She knew that no Confederate officer could enter New Orleans; Lucien himself could not meet her. But he must be as he had planned to be, at Honotassa, waiting for her.

She pushed aside the stiffly starched lace curtain and looked down at the street again. With the dusk the scene was changing; it was as if a transparent curtain had been dropped in a theatre which had its own color and subtly altered the scene behind it. There were still groups of blue-coated soldiers but instead of marching briskly along as if intent on military errands, they were strolling in twos and threes, lounging, making for a saloon which was now brightly lighted. The colors in the street seemed mysteriously brighter, too; there were girls, usually alone, in red and blue and yellow dresses with elaborately puffed and curled hair; they strolled a little too slowly and invitingly.

A lamplighter, an old Negro with grizzled hair, adjusted his ladder just below her window, climbed up and touched a cluster of gaslights to bright tongues of flame.

Down in the street a soldier, half drunk, lurched up to a passing girl; the girl giggled and the two disappeared, arm in arm, among the rapidly growing crowds along the banquette.

General Butler had imposed stringent rules upon a conquered city, most of them hated by the Orleanians, and indeed by the entire South, especially after his famous (some said infamous) "woman order." The "woman order," which was to the effect that any Southern woman who insulted a Union soldier should be considered to be and accorded the dubious status of a street woman, had such a shocking impact that even in England a speech had been made in Parliament. England, however, did not come to the aid of the Confederacy.

General Butler also, however, had made rules for his own command and those rules were still in effect since General Banks had replaced him December twenty-fourth, Christmas Eve. There was little outright disorder. And while General Butler by then was known in the South as Beast Butler, still his regime had accomplished at least one very important result: the streets and the banquettes were clean and there had been less yellow fever in New Orleans during the late summer and early fall of 1862, when the plague as a rule struck with the most deadly persistence, than in previous years.

Sarah did not know that. She did know that she was a stranger, an outlander, one of a hated race in New Orleans that spring—and that since she had married a Southerner and a soldier, once she arrived at Honotassa she must draw even more heavily upon her self-control and tact because all his people, like Lucien, were devoted to the Southern cause and were not likely to welcome his marriage to a Northerner.

9

In another day, or several days, however long it would take to make the journey to Honotassa, she would see Lucien, and suppose—suppose they had been separated for too long a time! Suppose their acquaintance and the short two weeks of marriage had been too short!

She turned away from the window. Lucien could not possibly change and certainly she had not changed. The wall sconces were now dim blurs along the walls. She hunted around for matches.

In Paris a *femme de chambre* had lighted the gas jets—that is, in the formal salons, designed to impress visiting parents; a candle apiece thriftily had been allotted *les jeunes filles* in their bare little bedrooms. In Wilton, Connecticut, there had been no gaslights, only kerosene lamps.

She was fumbling along the marble-topped table for matches when again someone scratched lightly on the door. Calista's white *tignon* appeared as it opened and a man was with her.

His figure was outlined against the lighted hall. He was tall, with broad shoulders and a narrow waist; he wore a dark coat, light trousers, a ruffled white shirt and a wide black cravat. He carried a black hat in one hand. He had dark hair and dark eyes and Sarah's heart leaped. "Lucien!"

She rushed to his arms, she had her face up against his when he said, "I'm sorry, madam. I am Reverdy Hugot."

There was the hint of laughter in his voice.

She drew back sharply. "Reverdy!"

"Yes, madam. I'm sorry—Calista, perhaps we should have some light."

"But you—but I—"

"My brother and I resemble each other. It is very pleasant to receive such a warm greeting, madam."

She felt a hot flush coming up into her face. This was Reverdy—Rev, the gambler; Rev, the duelist, who yet had little stomach for fighting; Rev, who was bitterly jealous of his half-brother, Lucien.

Calista had found matches; she touched a gas jet which hissed and then flared brightly. She touched another gas jet and another; the room took on color and shape and Sarah stared at Reverdy.

He did resemble Lucien with his crisp black hair, his tall figure, his dark eyes which now danced with laughter.

"Perhaps my brother has told you of me."

"Yes."

A little smile touched his lips. "And nothing good, I'll venture."

"Nothing good," she said shortly, ruffled by her precipitate embrace and disappointed.

"That is candid." He limped heavily as he came nearer. "An old friend of my father's, Jules Lamoreux, lives in the hotel and saw your arrival and your name on the register. He went at once to tell my cousin—and Lucien's—Cousin Elise Fautier. I happened to be there at the time so I came to see you after sending Calista to inquire."

"Oh—but then Lucien didn't send you!"

"Lucien?" he asked politely, watching her.

"Lucien told me he would send someone to arrange for me to go to Honotassa."

"Honotassa!" There was a flash of blank surprise in his eyes. He turned to Calista. "Monsieur Jules is in the gallery of the rotunda, watching. He'll give me warning if anyone —but it might be better for you to stand outside and let me know at once."

"Yes, Mist' Rev." Calista went out quickly and closed the door softly again.

"Now then, madam," Rev said, "where is Lucien?"

"Where is—oh, I hoped he would be at Honotassa by now! He *must* be there . . ."

"No. I came from there only yesterday."

"But—why, it's been nearly three months since he left Cuba. Where is he?"

"That, madam, was what I hoped you could tell me. There has been no word from Lucien since last fall, after the second battle of Manassas. Then it was only a letter to the effect that he was missing, believed wounded and captured by the Yankees."

"But he wrote home. He told me. He wrote from Richmond and he wrote from Cuba. Why—why, then you didn't know of our marriage!"

His eyebrows lifted slightly. "No, madam."

"But—then where is he?" Captured again? she thought. Sent on some other military chore? Perhaps again in combat?

"I don't know. Did you say he was in Cuba?"

"Oh yes. He was sent to inventory and evaluate a shipment of arms."

11

"Arms?"

"They were manufactured in Europe, intended for the Confederacy. They were sent to Cuba. He went by blockade runner from Wilmington to Cuba. That's where we met and—and were married."

"Oh. You live in Cuba?"

"No, no. We—my father and I—went there from England."

He waited. She said, briefly, "I've been at school in Paris. My father had business in England and required me to join him there. Then we went to Cuba. That was in December. Lucien and I were married in January. He got passage home by a blockade runner again—that is, he was to go to Richmond to make his report, but then he had a furlough coming so he intended to go home to Honotassa. I am to meet him there."

"You arrived only this morning?"

"Yes. Lucien said I was to wait until March, and then I couldn't get a passage until now. But he intended to have a friend watch for my arrival and—and perhaps take me or at any rate tell me how to go to Honotassa. I thought the maid, Calista, was bringing Lucien's friend."

"Who is this friend?"

"I don't know. Lucien didn't know. He only said that he would manage to get a letter to someone here. . . . Do you think Lucien—he couldn't have been sent back to his company without having a furlough, could he?"

"Well, he could," Rev said noncommittally. "Anything can happen in the army."

"If this is the first you've heard from him since last fall—why, you didn't know whether he was alive or dead!"

"We believed he was in a Yankee prison."

"No—he escaped after he was captured. He had a fever and then he escaped and got back to Richmond. He was then sent to Cuba."

"Madam—there is something about your accent—may I ask where your home is?"

She put up her head; now it was coming. "I was born in Wilton, Connecticut."

"Oh! Then you are in a city conquered by your countrymen." His eyes still smiled but his voice was soft and cold.

"My father said that war did not change people. We are —we are all Americans, North and South."

12

"I'm afraid we Southerners can't quite concur in so Olympian a viewpoint." He turned toward the door, listened for a second and then looked at her again. "I'm interested, madam. You were born in Connecticut, you went to school in Paris, you then went to England and then to Cuba. You've had an interesting life even if so short."

There was something in his voice which flicked at Sárah's temper. "That is true. Now, will you tell me how to go to Honotassa?"

"With the country crawling with Yankees!" He laughed shortly.

"Lucien expects me to go there."

He leaned on the table a little wearily. "Madam, I take it that your father was a staunch Union man. Did he approve of your—marriage to Lucien?"

"My father . . ." She had schooled herself against grief; it was an easier lesson because in fact she and her father had been separated for so long. Yet in another way they had been close. "My father went to visit a sugar plantation he owned in Camaguey province. It was a bad season for yellow fever in Cuba. He died."

"I'm sorry. I didn't know—you are not in mourning."

She was wearing the moss green bengaline dress in which she had landed from the ship that morning. "My father detested mourning."

"I see. . . . May I ask how you met Lucien?"

"He was staying at the same hotel. He met my father. My father introduced him to me."

"A Confederate officer!"

"My father felt that the time will come when we are again a united country."

"In short, that the North will win."

"My father was not the kind of man to permit war to affect his regard for a friend."

"Then he and Lucien were friends?"

"Yes. That is briefly. My father died so soon."

"And then you and Lucien were married?"

"Lucien was very kind to me, very helpful. But this is wartime. Lucien had to return to Richmond. It seemed impractical for me to remain in Cuba. He said we should be married at once and then—after giving him time to report and to reach Honotassa, I was to come to New Orleans and then to Honotassa."

13

"Your father knew of course that Lucien is an officer in the Confederate army?"

"Certainly. Lucien made no secret of it. Besides he was in uniform. Cuba is friendly to the South. There are many refugees from Louisiana in Cuba."

"You say he left Cuba in January. Did he buy the arms?"

"Oh, no. He wasn't empowered to buy them, only contract for them, provisional to the approval of the Ordnance Department."

There was still a kind of reservation in his face; yet it was, too, slightly warmer and more friendly.

He said slowly, "I am very grateful to you—more than I can say—for giving me news of Lucien. . . ."

Calista scratched on the door, opened it and slid into the room. "Mist' Rev—Monsieur Jules say he is in the hotel, down at the desk. He say hurry . . ."

"Ah!" Rev snatched up his hat and bowed to Sarah. "Thank you, madam . . ."

"Wait—where are you going?"

"Back to Honotassa if I'm lucky. Good-bye, madam . . ."

"Hurry, Mist' Rev," Calista whispered.

"I'm going with you," Sarah said.

"You—" Rev gave her an astonished, half-laughing look. "That's impossible!"

"I'm going with you. Lucien expects me to go to Honotassa. If he's not yet at Honotassa it may be weeks, why, it may be months before he can send for me. I'm going with you now."

He waited a moment; the flare of the gaslight was full on his face. Then he said, "My dear madam, this has been a most interesting story. Indeed I believe part of it—you must have seen Lucien in Cuba. I do not believe in your marriage, permit me to say. And I don't intend to take Lucien's fancy lady to Honotassa."

Sarah's temper snapped. "Fancy lady, nothing! Now then, get a carriage or a wagon for my trunks."

Reverdy's dark eyes suddenly danced. He glanced at the array of trunks. "These? Through Yankee patrols!"

"I don't intend to leave all that gold here!"

His face sobered. "Did you say gold?"

"Lucien told me to bring it."

"How much gold?"

"Twelve thousand—"

He stared at her. "Dear Jesus God," he said softly, "I didn't think there was that much gold in the whole Confederacy!" Suddenly he made a sweeping bow. "Madam, I apologize. You are Lucien's wife. And I'll take you and your gold to Honotassa or die trying. And it may come to that," he said a little grimly and turned to Calista. "Calista, help madam put the gold in that small hand trunk. I'll send Uncle Tip with a carriage. Show her the back way out of the hotel. Now then, madam"—he looked at Sarah—"I've got to get a horse for you. I may not be able to manage a sidesaddle. Can you ride?"

"Certainly."

"Well, then, this may take a little time. If you had a pass—"

"Oh, I have a pass."

"You—what?"

"Lucien explained to me that the Union forces control Natchez but there is a sort of understanding, so once I get to Natchez I can go on to Honotassa."

He stared; then unexpectedly and softly he laughed. Calista tugged at his arm. "Mist' Rev, Monsieur Jules say, hurry. Once that man see the name on the register he sure to ask to see Madam Hugot. . . ."

"Yes, yes . . ." At the door he made another sweeping bow to Sarah, his eyes still dancing, then he opened the door, glanced into the hall and vanished.

Calista said, "It is very dangerous for him here. You understand, madam. He is not in uniform."

Chapter Two

Sarah looked at Calista without actually seeing her. So this was Reverdy, she thought—and certainly he had given her no welcome.

Whether or not he was in uniform did not concern her. Lucien had told her that Rev was in the Confederate army at the beginning of the war; but then Lucien had said something about the conscription law and the loophole it gave planters: anybody who owned twenty or more slaves was exempt. The purpose of the law was to promote the production of food and supplies for the army but it did naturally give rise to some discontent; the saying "a rich man's

15

war and a poor man's fight" rose partly from the exemption provided by the conscription act.

Lucien would not have taken advantage of that loophole; she had had an impression that Lucien rather expected Rev to do so. Strictly speaking, Rev didn't own the slaves of Honotassa; he owned no part of Honotassa, it belonged to Lucien, but there were ways.

The important thing was that she was going to Honotassa, now, immediately, with Rev as her escort.

She wished that Lucien were already there. She wished she knew where Lucien was and why he had been delayed.

If Sarah looked at Calista without seeing her, Calista scrutinized Sarah so closely that she did not miss a seam of her tight and stylishly revealing bodice, nor a ruffle of the snowy undersleeves which fell around her wrists.

She was taller, slimmer than the fashion of the day, which approved a round little dumpling of a woman, yet, eyeing her, Calista did approve. She had thick red hair, done in a roll, high on her head; that was not fashionable either, yet it caught Calista's interested gaze. Green eyes—no, blue—green and blue. Lips that were slightly pinker than was entirely natural. Calista's own lips tightened. A nose which was far more definite than, again, the beauty standards of the day favored.

Calista shook her head and unconsciously shared the view of Sarah's teacher of deportment (which covered a wide field, including the light but skillful use of cosmetics), "*Mais votre nez,*" Sarah's teacher had said gloomily. "*Votre nez n'a pas un futur,* mademoiselle.*"

Whether or not Sarah's nose had a future, it barely escaped the shrewd and decisive lines of her father's, James Salter's nose, the sight of which alone had been known to vanquish a financial foe.

Sarah's dress, moss green, full-skirted so it displayed to advantage her small waistline, interested Calista, too, for at a time when a woman's dress was festooned to the last inch with laces, ruffles and bows, Sarah's dress was simple. A narrow edging of lace demurely circled her throat; her sleeves ended in a froufrou of white but there was no other ornament. Yet to Calista's experienced eyes there was a certain elegance.

"Madam," she hinted, "there is not much time."

Sarah stopped thinking of Lucien and flew to the trunks.

They emptied first the small hand trunk. Sarah searched out the bags of linen in which she had placed the gold; she had distributed the bags among her trunks so as not to arouse unwelcome interest by its weight. Calista avidly, if swiftly, examined the dresses, the silks, the laces, the velvet cloak which Sarah had worn to the opera or the ballet and with less interest the plain schoolgirl dresses. They wedged the bags of gold into the little hand trunk, surrounding it with clothes, any clothes.

"I'll take my bag—the black bag," Sarah said.

The big moiré bag was a carpetbag but on a de luxe scale, made of heavy silk with great amber handles. Calista put aside Sarah's feverishly active hands and methodically chose a dress, a change of lingerie, some black Moroccan slippers. The bottles of medicines clinked. There were not many of them; yet she had felt that even small amounts of drugs would be welcome on an isolated plantation, where the supply of medicines must have been exhausted long ago.

"*Les cosmétiques*," Calista said mistakenly. She had obviously assimilated, in New Orleans, some French phrases which however were slurred and soft. "*Alors*, madam,—*un peignoir, peut-être*."

"Here," Sarah dived into a trunk and found a thin puce-colored wrapper.

"Your costume," Calista reminded her.

"Oh, yes." Sarah searched out her black tailored riding habit. Calista helped her into it. The black broadcloth was too thick and hot for the warm spring night. She struggled into riding boots. She found heavy riding gloves. She thought of a hat and forgot it, for at the same time she thought of her marriage certificate and her marriage contract, sealed with red wax in an envelope. It was still in a pocket of the moiré bag along with some money.

"The trunks! My room—I've got to pay for it."

Calista's eyes flashed with alarm. "No, no! Not in the foyer, madam."

"Calista, who is it? Who came into the hotel? A Union officer, a patrol . . . ?"

"The hotel is full of Yankees! This is a man who knows Mist' Rev and would have him arrested. Write a note. Leave some money here."

Sarah scribbled a note to the manager of the hotel, asking him to send her trunks to Natchez to be called for; she didn't know what else to say. She put some gold on top of the note, hoping it was enough to pay for her room and for sending the trunks to Natchez.

She had barely done so when Calista, at the door, whispered, "Here is Uncle Tip, Madam Fautier's coachman."

He came into the room; he was an elderly Negro, his hair white.

"That trunk," Calista told him. "*Prenez garde*, madam."

Sarah took care. She followed them cautiously into the hall, past the main stairway, along narrow halls, down a little back stairway. They met no one, not even a maid.

A carriage waited across the banquette; she heard the whiffled breathing of horses and the slight rattle of harness. The old man heaved the trunk into the back. It was dark; Sarah groped her way into the back seat.

Calista whispered, "Good night, madam."

"Thank you . . ."

"Yes, madam."

The horses started up and the carriage rolled over cobblestones. In a moment the hotel and Calista were lost in the velvety darkness. After a while the old man turned. "Mist' Rev say when the patrols stop us, show them your pass and say you on your way to visit Miz Carroway."

"Yes—yes . . ."

The carriage turned and turned again. She guessed that the coachman was purposely avoiding the busy, still lighted streets. They were nearing the outskirts of the city when first they were stopped and a soldier, a boy really in a blue uniform, held up a lantern and asked for her pass. There were other soldiers with him, dimly seen in the yellow light from the lantern. She had not expected to feel any sense of fear; how could she be afraid of a boy who spoke with a familiar New England twang?

She was tense with apprehension, just the same. She took a long breath of relief when the horses jingled and clop-clopped on.

It was a dark night, cloudy, with only an occasional glimpse of stars, which seemed very far away. After a long time she sensed that they had turned into a narrow country road, for the black shapes of trees seemed to come nearer and there was a fragrance from the close, crowding shrubs along the side of the road which smelled like honeysuckle and carried her back to Wilton, in the summer. A faint gleam of

18

red light showed ahead and the coachman leaned back. "Sentry post ahead," he whispered.

This time it took a little longer. They scrutinized her pass by the light of a flaring red pine knot; they lifted it to scrutinize the coachman, too. But in the end they were satisfied with her pass to Natchez and her explanation that the coachman was taking her to visit Mrs. Carroway, on her way to Natchez. They let the carriage pass and the flaring red light died away behind them. A chorus of distant frogs multiplied until the night seemed alive with their croaking. At last they jolted into a narrow, dark and deeply rutted lane and came to a halt. Rev's voice came at once out of the darkness. "Have any trouble, Uncle Tip?"

His tall figure came up beside the carriage. "No, Mist' Rev," the old Negro replied. "Sentry boys stopped us but Missy talked to them."

"Good. How are you going to get back to New Orleans? Better not pass the sentry post so soon again."

"Oh, I know a way back. You get another horse?"

"I did."

Uncle Tip slapped his thigh and chuckled. Rev, too, seemed to be amused. "If a Yankee officer leaves his horse tied to a hitching post while he goes visiting he deserves to lose the horse. This one is not right bright and he's got a back as wide as a barn door but he's a horse."

"Get rid of his saddle. Likely got United States mark on it."

"I will. Bring up the horses, will you, Uncle Tip?" He moved to Sarah. "Now then, madam, where is the gold?"

"Here, in the trunk."

"Open it. We can't strap a trunk to a horse's back. We'll divide it, put it in the saddlebags. It ought not to weigh more than about sixty pounds, that's thirty pounds extra on each horse. They're up to that."

In the darkness she dug into the trunk and handed the little linen bags, a few at a time, to Reverdy. She heard the thud of horses' hoofs as Uncle Tip led them nearer the carriage. "Uncle Tip," Reverdy said, "put this trunk in the Carroway kitchen. They're gone, but I broke open a window. Now then, madam, I'm sorry but I couldn't get a sidesaddle. I'll put you up on my horse. I hope it's not too difficult."

"I had a pony when I was a child," she said shortly. "I think I can stay on a horse's back."

"What's that you've got?" He had detected the big moiré bag in her hand.

"Some clothes. I've got to have something to wear."

"Give it to me."

The bag was packed so tightly that there was scarcely more than a subdued clink of the bottles of medicines. He said, "I've shortened the stirrups. His name is Vampa. If I tell you to be quiet just touch his shoulder: he'll stand like a rock."

He gave her a lift up from the palm of his hand. Vampa did stand like a rock although he turned his head back and snuffed at her knee as if surprised. The saddle seemed enormous, like a rocking chair, nothing like the flat pancake of an English saddle which she was accustomed to in Paris. As a child she had ridden her fat old pony astride and often bareback. The skirt of her riding habit was full; she hitched it up and knew she looked absurd, her legs sticking out below the hunched-up folds of broadcloth, but then it was dark and nobody could see her.

Uncle Tip said, "Good luck, Mist' Rev."

"By God we'll need it. Thanks, Uncle Tip."

Rev swung himself into the saddle of the other horse. "Now then, madam. The roads are crawling with Yankee patrols. For the next few hours my life will be in your hands. I don't know how you feel about hanging but personally I don't wish to be at the wrong end of the rope."

The unexpected apprehension she had felt when the Union patrol and the Union soldiers at the sentry post stopped her rushed back. There was a deadly seriousness in the soft voice coming out of the darkness. "You mean that!"

"I do, indeed."

"But why should they hang you? What have you done?"

"For one thing, I'm a Mississippian. For another, I'm not in uniform."

"Then you're still in the army?"

"Of course!" He sounded surprised. "I'm at home on furlough. We'd better get started."

"But I thought . . ." She had been so sure that he had taken advantage of the loophole offered him by the conscription law. "Wait! If that's true, I mean about hanging you if they catch you, I can't let you risk your life for me."

"I'm not risking my life for you."

20

"Well, for Lucien then."

He laughed softly. "Nor for Lucien. It's the gold in these saddlebags."

Well, that was frank, she thought with a flicker of anger. Rev's horse started up and Vampa followed. They jogged through the black tunnel of trees. She said, "I hope Uncle Tip gets back safely."

"Don't worry about him. He's a smart old boy."

"You seem to have many friends in New Orleans."

"Well, I have. I've known Uncle Tip ever since I can remember. Cousin Elise Fautier was a Hugot. Calista was born at Honotassa. . . . I left my horse in Cousin Elise's stable."

"But what a risk! Why on earth did you go into the city?"

There was a pause. Then he said, "I had business there. There are ways of getting into New Orleans and out again— if you know the ways. If you want the story of my life, madam, you can have it. There'll be plenty of time. But just now we'd better cover as much distance as we can before daylight."

They turned in the narrow country road again, which shortly became a mere lane, pitchy dark.

The mosquitoes were merciless.

The frogs dinned so shrilly and monotonously that the sound began to rasp nerves Sarah hadn't known she had. The brush along the way scratched her legs. They turned into invisible byways, paths that were scarcely paths. There was more mire, more water, there were more sludgy little streams to cross than she would have thought could possibly exist in what was supposed to be dry land. Occasionally, cautiously, Rev led the way for a short space along corduroy roads, or over a bridge, the horses' hoofs thumping dully.

Twice when they took to what seemed to be traveled roads, which gave at least firm footing for the horses, Rev gave her low-voiced warnings and drew the horses into thickets at the side of the roads and waited while distant hoofbeats and the murmur of men's voices came nearer, jogged along close to them, passed by. Vampa, when she touched his shoulder, stood still. The other horse once threw up his head to snort and in the darkness she could see Rev's swift motion as he leaned forward, caught the horse's nose and held on until the night riders were well past.

21

They rode by night and rested by day. The first day at dawn they stopped at what Reverdy told her was a trapper's cabin. It stood nestled amid great trees hung with gray and wispy Spanish moss, on the very edge of a still and slow-moving bayou. Rev and the trapper spoke a French patois which Sarah's Parisian-trained and sleepy ears could scarcely understand. At sunset they went on.

They spent the second day in a house, which loomed up indistinctly amid the grays of dawn at the end of a long avenue of trees. Here a woman came cautiously to the door, opened it wide when she saw Rev, was introduced as Rose Tiller, a cousin (how many Hugot cousins were there? Sarah wondered, tiredly), and tucked Sarah into a big bed. When in the dusk they rode away again Sarah knew that Rev had told her of her marriage to Lucien, for Mrs. Tiller called her Cousin Sarah.

The first two nights Reverdy had talked very little. Certainly he had not told Sarah the story of his life, there had been little chance to talk of anything.

Gradually, though, she began to revise her estimate of Rev's character. She had, naturally, adopted Lucien's estimate of his brother; she realized that Lucien, knowing Rev so thoroughly, could not be mistaken. Yet Rev was unfailingly kind and considerate; he was polite and once or twice he seemed genuinely friendly. One of those times was when a strip of good road permitted them to canter and she later remarked on Vampa's easy gait.

"He's a single-footer," Rev said and leaned over to fondle Vampa's lovely, small head. There was pride and affection in his voice. "He knows all five gaits. But by nature he's a singlefooter."

Another time he spoke of Honotassa. "It's not one of the great plantations but"—there was pride and love in his voice again—"but it's beautiful. Prosperous, too. But then Lucien has told you of Honotassa. Lucien owns Honotassa."

And that she thought, almost unwillingly, is why you are jealous of Lucien.

CHAPTER THREE

The year of 1863 was a crucial and a climactic year for both North and South. In the spring Confederate hopes were riding high. The battle of Second Manassas, ending September first, 1862, was a costly yet indisputable victory for the South, leaving Eastern Virginia in its possession; the battle at Harper's Ferry, September fifteenth, was another victory. Two days later Antietam took its terrible toll from both sides but General Lee was successful in withdrawing from Maryland into Virginia and saving his armies. In December the battle of Fredericksburg was a victory for the South.

New Orleans had been captured by Union forces, in June of 1862, but Vicksburg was still in Confederate possession. And in December, at the very end of the year, hope in Mississippi rose high again for there were two more heartening victories at Chickasaw Bayou and at Holly Springs, in northern Mississippi.

No one doubted, however, that attack would come. So in Mississippi the burning question, the urgent, immediate focal point, was the defense of Vicksburg.

They told each other that Vicksburg was impregnable; Vicksburg could never be taken. It was high above the river; guns on its bluffs could control Yankee gunboats passing along the river below. Its outer rim of defense lay in the twisting, treacherous curves of the great river itself, and the maze of streams and bayous, along which no Union boats could maneuver.

At the same time it was known that General Grant was a stubborn, patient fighter—and he had men. Effectives in the Confederate army were growing almost as scarce as everything else in the Confederacy except hope and courage.

Along the river and in lower Mississippi a peculiarly uncertain and dangerous situation had developed. New Orleans was in Union hands; Vicksburg was in Confederate hands; the long, winding stretch of river between was in dispute. Natchez had surrendered to the Union forces; it had little in the way of defense and was not a point of vital strategic importance. Union raiders in legitimate search of supplies—and in some instances in illegitimate search of private looting—were all too likely to fan out across the country. Private looting was forbidden; nevertheless no isolated planter in that section could go to sleep at night secure in the belief that by morning his livestock and food supplies might not be raided, his valuables carried off or his house burned. It was not a common practice; neither was it outside the realm of possibility.

There were also many small bands of guerrillas, Southerners, harassing Union supply lines when and as they could; they, too, needed supplies and were likely to take them willy-nilly when opportunity offered.

All this was an inevitable result of war now within the state. Another result, perhaps as inevitable in the unsettled times, was the sporadic existence of bands of outlaws, renegades, thugs, who sprang up mysteriously, scattered as mysteriously, were wholly outside the law of both North and South, who struck and slid away like snakes and who constituted, literally, a terror by night.

The main danger during the first two nights of that roundabout journey, made longer by the necessity to take bypaths and forgotten lanes, was the danger of encountering Union patrols. By the third night Sarah knew that somewhere they must have crossed the Mississippi line, so she was surprised when Rev drew the horses again into a thicket near the road and again waited while a little group of riders jogged past in the darkness.

"Who were they?" she whispered when the blur of passing figures, the jingle of bridles, the creaking of leather and the muffled thump of horses' hoofs had died away.

"Might be Yankees. Might be friends. Might be bushwhackers. Might be outlaws, just plain thugs out to turn a dishonest penny. We can go on now."

They went on. That night Rev seemed more inclined to talk. Certainly he had long ago dropped a stilted and distant manner of speech. There was no more madam this, and madam that. But it would have been very silly, Sarah thought, for him to say, "Pray duck, madam, here is some brush," or "Pray hang on hard, madam, here's a slippery stream to ford."

He still didn't tell her the story of his life, if there was one, but he led her on to speak of her own life, her childhood in Wilton, her school days in Paris, her father—that rugged, gray little man with his steely eyes, his hard intelligence, his kindness to her, his natural reticence. "He wasn't at home very much," she told him. "I was brought up by Granny Salter."

"Don't you have any brothers or sisters?"

"No—I have an aunt in the north of England."

He gave her a startled look. "Well, you've come to a land of big families. The Hugot connection spreads over all of Mississippi and half of Louisiana. The house is always full of relatives."

"Yes, Lucien told me." The prospect of a large family connection was welcome; she only hoped that eventually this new family would welcome her.

But then Rev said, "You say that your father was away from home a great deal?" And she knew that a moment and a disclosure she had dreaded were upon her.

Well, she couldn't hide it forever; besides it was nothing she should be ashamed of; her dread was due to the almost certain view her new relatives would take. She said flatly, "My father's main interest and source of income was in Pennsylvania. A foundry and rolling mills."

She didn't look at Rev but she heard his saddle creak as he turned toward her.

"Do you mean that he manufactured arms for the North?"

"Not directly. It comes to the same thing. He"—she swallowed—"he had some contracts with Mr. Eads."

"Eads! Why, he's building those Union ironclads!"

"Yes."

There was a long pause. Finally he said, "So in effect, since your father's death—I take it you have inherited his property —you are manufacturing supplies to be used directly against the Confederacy?"

"Yes. Except that my father's will has not been probated. I wrote to his lawyers in New York at the time of his death. I haven't yet heard from them."

"Did Lucien know this?"

"Why, yes, of course."

"Yes, of course. There was your marriage contract—lawyers in Havana must have drawn up your marriage contract."

"Yes, but that was very simple."

"What were the terms?" he asked bluntly.

"Why, only to provide for the death of either of us. If or when that happens the property belonging to one of us goes

25

directly to the other. We can alter or change our agreement later if it seems advisable. Everything was hurried. There wasn't time for the lawyers to haggle over terms."

"Then that means that Lucien is now in fact owning and operating a Union foundry and rolling mills."

"Oh, no!" she said sharply.

"But"—he reverted to the distant, chilly form of address —"madam, don't you realize that in the South when a man and a woman marry they become one person and that person is the man?"

"But Lucien wouldn't—he doesn't . . ." She took a long breath. "We couldn't come to any conclusion about the mills because right now there is nothing I can do about them. I can't stop their operation. I can't sell them, even if—"

"Even if you want to?" he finished dryly. "Doesn't it strike you as inconsistent? Marrying a Southern officer—and manufacturing arms to be used against him and his people at the same time?"

She said shortly, "My hands are tied. Lucien said that time would settle it. As a matter of fact, he said there was no reason why any of you should know about it."

"Then why did you tell me?"

"Because—well, it's the truth. Besides you'd find out sooner or later."

He gave a short laugh. "Spoken with true Yankee prudence. May I give you a word of advice? Nail your colors to the mast if you must but there's no need to flourish them in our faces."

"I don't intend to." Now that every hoofbeat brought them closer to Honotassa she was beginning to wish with all her heart not only that Lucien would be there but that he had had time to tell his people of his marriage—and his marriage to a Northerner.

And perhaps by now Lucien *had* arrived. Perhaps he would come laughing, to take her in his arms.

She hadn't talked to Rev of Lucien; she had almost a superstitious feeling that fears unspoken were the more likely never to become facts. She said though, "Do you think that Lucien may have come home since you left?"

"He might have. I hope so. But he might have been delayed in Richmond. You mustn't worry about it."

"No."

She felt him look at her. "You *are* worrying."

"I'd like to know where he is and—and it's been so long since he left Cuba. I haven't even had a letter from him since he left. But he would have to send it by a blockade runner. . . ."

"He could have sent a dozen letters and all of them lost. You've been very brave and courageous about the whole thing."

It cheered her, coming like that, unexpectedly and in a friendly way. She laughed. "You wouldn't believe that I was married to him! You called me his fancy lady."

"I'm sorry. I didn't mean it that way—I—" His voice was still friendly yet there was a slight evasion in his words. "You see, naturally, not having heard from Lucien in so long —well, it was hard for me to believe, that's all. I was wrong and I was a damn—I beg your pardon—fool. If I'd had any eyes in my head—"

"I could have shown you my marriage contract," she said lightly.

They rode on for a little before he said, soberly, "Only the French with their—our—practical ideas of money would cling so stubbornly to the old-fashioned forms of a marriage contract. Was there no discussion of paraphernal rights?"

"No." But the contract itself had implied that neither Lucien nor Sarah could exercise a control over the other's property. "Perhaps in the South the man is considered the head of the house—"

"Always in the South."

"Well, and in the North, too, in a way. But Lucien would never seek to use or control my father's money."

The horses' hoofs thudded softly. They went into the deep shadow of some trees and out again. Finally Rev said, "No. How could he? But marriage contracts—you see, that was how it happened that Lucien inherited Honotassa."

She turned in astonishment. She could see only the outline of his figure in the faint and misty starlight. He was looking straight ahead. "But I thought—that is, Lucien is five years older than you and—" She had also believed that Lucien's and Reverdy's father had left the plantation to Lucien because he felt that the family property and source of income would be safer in Lucien's hands than in Reverdy's. She didn't say it.

Rev said, "Lucien's mother and my father had a marriage contract much like your own with Lucien. When either died

27

the other was to inherit his—or her—entire estate. There was an added provision to the effect that when both died the estate was to go to Lucien's mother's descendants. This was not altered at the time of my mother's marriage to my father or at the time of my birth. So Honotassa belongs to Lucien."

She groped through her memories of the little Lucien had said of his inheritance and decided that she had drawn her own obviously erroneous conclusions. "But that wasn't fair!"

"It's legal. There are all sorts of odd quirks among some marriage contracts—especially the French contracts. This is one of them."

"Why didn't your father change it?" she asked, although her memory suddenly provided some casual words of Lucien's: "Of course my father knew that I would always see to Rev. I'm older and—he wouldn't have wanted Rev to gamble away the land—the house—everything."

After a moment Rev replied. "I'm sure he meant to change it sometime. But he didn't expect to die—not soon. He was that kind, full of life and vitality. As a matter of fact, he did die by accident."

"Lucien told me. He said a horse threw him."

"Stash, one of the boys, found Pa and held him in his arms at the last. . . . Speaking of friends in New Orleans, Stash is Calista's son. Pa gave him to me. He went with me, when I went into the army, my body servant."

She said absently, thinking of Honotassa, "But Mr. Lincoln's proclamation freed the slaves, beginning the first of January—"

"I reckon you're forgetting that Mississippi is a sovereign state. Mr. Lincoln does not make laws for us. Although I must say he's caused us some trouble. So many of our people have drifted away that if this goes on we'll get down to a two-mule farm. As a matter of fact, I freed Stash, long ago. He sticks with me because he wants to."

"Oh." She wished she had kept her mouth shut as she had resolved to do. And Rev began to tell her of Honotassa. His grandfather had come from New Orleans, had bought the land, had planted cotton and built himself a house. Rev's father, Lucien's father, had eventually come into possession of house and land and during the state currency and banking problems of the late thirties, when gold was also at a premium, he had had gold and had bought more land and more slaves to work the land. By 1859 there were perhaps three thousand big, producing plantations in the South. Honotassa was one of them.

"It's not a show place—but it's a good plantation. Or was when we had enough field hands. Shall we take a breather?"

They checked their horses in the shadow of a clump of trees and both horses stretched their necks to crop grass. Rev said, "Lucien told you that Miss Celie lives at Honotassa?"

"His aunt, yes. He said that she had lived there ever since his mother died."

"She came when Lucien's mother died. She stayed on after my father's second marriage. My mother was Martha Mc-Clung—a Mississippian. Then after her death Miss Celie brought both of us up, Lucien and me." He bent over to adjust a stirrup. "You'll have to get used to all the ramifications of family. Mostly we don't bother to figure out exact relationships, we just call everybody Cousin. And everybody who has the slightest connection has always been welcome at Honotassa. Lolotte, now—" He paused, busy with the stirrup.

"Lolotte?"

"Didn't Lucien mention her?"

"No, I don't think so."

"Well, her parents both died during a bad yellow fever epidemic in New Orleans. She's lived at Honotassa since she was a child. Lolotte Hugot. Then there's Cousin Maude and her husband, Ben Greevy."

"Lucien spoke of them."

"George Osborn is at Honotassa now, too. He's a second cousin. And Emile Trevant comes and goes." He drew up his horse's head. "That's the present lot of us. Only a few."

Only a few, Sarah thought with dismay. And not one of them had ever heard of her and every single one of them was devoted to the Southern cause.

Rev hesitated as if he had something else to say, but if so he said only, "Shall we be getting along?"

They went on.

There were fewer clouds that night. She could see now, open fields, stretching away on both sides. At last they came out upon a main road, and Rev said, "This is Honotassa land."

Honotassa! And perhaps, just perhaps, Lucien!

"The house is further on, where you see that black line of oaks. That's the driveway."

As they neared the black line of trees jutting up in the faint light, more trees and hedges showed themselves, clustering around what seemed to be a settlement of buildings, dimly outlined in the night. The oaks grew nearer and bigger, so huge that as they turned at last below them, their arching boughs shut off even the dim starlight. "Live oaks?" she asked.

"Water oaks mainly. Some of the oldest in this part of the state." She was already accustomed to the long wraiths of Spanish moss which dripped from the trees everywhere. They made now a kind of veil through which she could dimly see the outlines of a long white house at the end of the avenue of oaks.

Her home, she thought. And perhaps Lucien was waiting. Her heart beat faster. She tried to tidy her hair. Rev saw her gesture. "I doubt if anybody hears us," he said. "They'll all be asleep. You'll not have to meet any of them till morning."

He was wrong, however.

They emerged from the arching trees and she had her first sight of the house, a wide-winged house with white pillars going up past the second story, tranquil and serene in the night.

There was no light anywhere.

Rev checked the horses, slid out of his saddle and tied both horses to a hitching post. He came to her side. "Look here," he said abruptly. "I'll explain everything to them. But you do understand that your marriage is going to be a surprise. It may not be easy for you."

She had clung to the hope that Lucien would be there. Her spirits sank.

"You don't think Lucien is here."

"We'll soon find out. If he isn't, he'll come soon."

She hadn't expected a welcome; she couldn't have expected one when none of the people sleeping in the long, lovely house before her so much as knew of her existence, let alone her marriage. Yet all the same, in some deep, instinctive layer of her consciousness she had desired something like a welcome. "You mean—I'm a Northerner and nobody will like that."

"Well, that and—" He broke off as a dog gave a high-pitched yelp away off in the darkness beyond the house. Another dog took it up; the night was suddenly clamorous with sound. Somewhere a horse whinnied and Vampa, knowing he was now at home, shook his head and snorted. A light sprang up in the house.

"Hell's bells," Rev said. "Now everybody'll wake up and come downstairs and—well, just leave it to me." He put up his arms toward her. She slid down from the saddle and he held her for a moment, steadying her. Then he led her toward the wide porch.

It was roofed and, supported by white columns, rose to the height of two stories. Its roof made a heavy band of shadow on the porch but there were windows on both sides of a wide door and the flicker of a candle moved inside. Then the door was flung open and a woman, a girl, beautiful in the light from the candle she held in her hand, cried, "Rev! You're back—" saw Sarah and stared, her dark eyes wide.

Rev said, "Sarah"—and Sarah had a little twinge of surprise for he never till then called her Sarah—"Sarah, this is Cousin Lolotte. . . . Lolotte, has Lucien come home yet?"

"Lucien!" Lolotte was staring at Sarah. "No, of course not. Who—"

Rev said quickly, "Lucien is safe. He escaped. He was sent to Cuba. He is now on his way home probably, from Richmond. This is Lucien's wife, Sarah."

"Lucien's wife!" Lolotte dropped the candle. It rolled, guttering, on the floor.

Rev drew Sarah inside a big, shadowy hall and scooped up the candle. "They were married in Cuba. Now Sarah, I'll call Miss Celie."

"I don't believe you!" Lolotte cried in a gasp. She had a lovely, heart-shaped face, big dark eyes and a magnolia white skin. She wore a pale pink silk wrapper, flounced with Chantilly lace; dark, soft hair fell over her shoulders.

Rev said, "Lucien was taken prisoner but he escaped—"

"Rev!" A man's voice preceded another candle from a cavernous, dark room at one side. The light wavered and so did the man's voice and body as he came forward peering at Sarah. "Who is this!" he said, grinning, and Sarah caught a whiff of brandy across the small candle flame and realized that he was very drunk.

Rev moved between them. "Sarah, may I present Cousin Emile Trevant? Emile, this is Lucien's wife. She was in New Orleans."

Emile was young, fair, with a bulging forehead and chin

31

and he was so drunk that when he attempted to bow he all but fell over.

"No, no!" Lolotte caught at Rev's arm. Her eyes were enormous. "Lucien can't be married!"

"I'll explain later." Rev drew Sarah toward a stairway which rose in dim beauty of curving mahogany banister toward a landing with arched windows; he stopped as a woman came down the stairs. "Miss Celie. I've brought home Lucien's wife."

Sarah had drawn a picture of Aunt Celie—no, they called her Miss Celie—in her mind. She would be charming and vivacious, resembling Lucien, and in spite of her age, for she had to be at least in her fifties, still attractive. The woman coming toward them, a candle in her hand too, was short, solid as a rock, thick as an old tree trunk—thicker for she had small bones set in great cushions of fat. Her face was white as a blancmange; her dark eyes were like raisins; she had thick black hair, swinging in two great braids, and thick black eyebrows; she had a dot of a nose and a heavy, square jaw. She was formidable. The word shot into Sarah's mind with its finely shaded French connotation but Miss Celie was formidable in any language.

Sarah was swiftly conscious of her own tousled hair, her muddy riding habit, the bodice unbuttoned at the throat because of the heat. She made some kind of bow while Miss Celie simply stood, her flowing black wrapper blending into the shadows around her, and looked. Reverdy again instantly took command. "Will you take Sarah upstairs, Miss Celie? We've ridden from New Orleans. She is very tired. I'll explain everything later."

Still without a word or a change of expression in that blancmange face, Miss Celie turned around and started back up the stairs. Rev said, "Go with her, Sarah." Sarah followed the rustling, thick tower of black.

Suddenly in the hall below, Emile began to laugh. It was an ugly laugh which rang out shockingly in the quiet house. "Lucien's wife," he shouted. "In New Orleans!"

CHAPTER FOUR

They had reached the landing of the stairs and Sarah looked down. Emile was doubled up with laughter, his fair hair in locks over his bulging forehead, his face red. Lolotte was standing against the wall, one hand at her throat, refusing to look at Emile, her dark eyes blazing up at Sarah. Emile grasped Lolotte's arm and cried with derisive glee, "A pretty trick! What a joke! She's a beauty too. Trust Lucien for that. Oh, a pretty trick he's played . . ."

Rev's hand went out so swiftly that Sarah barely saw the motion, and clipped Emile's chin; Emile gave a startled grunt and sagged down, sprawling on the floor.

Miss Celie whispered calmly, as if it were no unusual thing, "Emile is drinking. Come with me. . . ."

It was a husky yet piercing whisper and it seemed to be Miss Celie's customary way of speaking.

She reached the top of the stairs and there was a murmur of voices from below, Lolotte's voice, questioning, Sarah thought, and Rev tersely replying. Miss Celie led Sarah along a wide hall, lined with doors; she held the candle high so Sarah could see. She was aware of other candles, two—no, three people, their staring, surprised faces looking white among the shadows of the hall. The other cousins, she thought, and followed Miss Celie's massive black figure, moving ponderously yet with agility too, into a large room.

Miss Celie put the candle on a stand. A huge four-poster bed draped with white mosquito netting cast enormous shadows. The room was in such exquisite order that it looked as if it had never been used and Sarah sensed that it was a guest room. A big mahogany armoire with a mirrored door stood against one wall. A stiff, small couch, covered in red velvet, stood at the foot of the bed. Miss Celie went across the room to open windows; she came back and began to remove the heavy white counterpane. She folded it and placed it over a chair. She turned down sheets and a thin coverlet; she plumped up a huge bolster and still did not speak to Sarah or even look at her. A current of balmy night air drifted across the room. The shadows in the corners and on the ceiling wavered.

There was a soft murmur of voices outside the room, voices downstairs, voices everywhere but no distinct words. Rev came briskly into the room, carrying the big, black moiré bag. He put it down and said, "Sarah's trunks are still in New Orleans."

It occurred to her that he emphasized the word "trunks" as if he wanted Miss Celie to know that Sarah, appearing with no announcement, no visible background, nothing, at least had trunks. He glanced at Sarah. "I'll bring up the other things," he said and disappeared.

The other things? Sarah thought. Oh, yes, the gold.

Miss Celie whispered, "Be sure to tuck in the mosquito bar when you go to bed. I'll send up water and something for you to eat." Her black eyes shot one look at the huge bag on the floor. Then she went away, moving very lightly and very swiftly.

Not a question, not a comment. Nothing.

But Lucien wasn't at Honotassa. They had heard nothing from him. Sarah looked at the great bed and had a tired and desolate impulse to put her face down in the fat bolster and cry.

Well, she wouldn't. She'd unpack the moiré bag and brush her hair, and wash and—as she turned she caught a glimpse of herself in one of the mirrored doors of the armoire. Her face was white and her eyes blazing green and blue; her hair was a wildly tousled mass of red curls. Her riding habit was stained with mud, wrinkled, torn by brambles. Her riding boots were muddy, too.

She pulled off her boots, first. Her stockings were torn to ribbons. She took up the black moiré bag. It was mud-splashed and smelled of horse. She dumped out its contents on a table. Thank heaven, there was at least one dress, a thin green and blue lawn. Thank heaven, there was the puce-colored wrapper, silk and thin, too. Thank heaven, Calista had crammed in one petticoat; it was crushed and limp but steam and a hot flat iron would restore some of its crispness. There was also a handful of crushed lingerie, hand sewn with lace edges, wedged around the cosmetic bottles which held the medicines.

She found her silver-backed brush. She yanked the pins out of her hair and was brushing it when Rev knocked and at her word came in. He was in his shirt sleeves, carrying a heavy load wrapped in his coat.

He opened the armoire, stacked small bags within it, said briefly, "I'll bring the rest of it—" and went away again.

She had finished brushing her hair and it lay in smooth waves around her shoulders when he returned with the second load. After it was deposited in the armoire, he closed the door and gave her a huge brass key with a red silk tassel on it. "Keep this. Now then—is everything all right?"

Everything was all wrong. She didn't say it but Rev guessed. "I'm sorry Lucien isn't here. It's a disappointment." He hesitated, then put one hand gently on her shoulder. "As to Miss Celie and—everybody—I'll explain everything to them. Now get some sleep. You'll feel better."

There was the clatter of dishes at the door. He turned. "Come in, Rilly. Oh, you've brought something for her to eat. Good. This is Rilly, Sarah, she'll see to you. Good night."

He went away again and Rilly put a tray down on a table near the bed. She must have been aroused from her bed, yet she was primly neat in a starched calico dress and a white *tignon*. She pulled a small chair up to the table. There was cold ham, biscuits and a carafe of wine on the tray. "I'm sorry things is cold—" She already knew Sarah's name and said, "Miss Sarah. Couldn't get up a fire fast enough and Miss Celie say you must be plumb starved." She disappeared and came back with a bucket of water, towels and a tiny cake of soap. "Best we can do about soap, Miss Sarah. We made it ourselves." She poured the water into an enormous china pitcher, decorated with red roses and gilt. Over it she shot a measuring glance at Sarah. She was obviously bursting with curiosity and surprise but had the good manners to restrain both. "Shall I put away all these things, Miss Sarah?" she asked, eyeing the litter of clothes Sarah had dumped from the black bag.

"No—thank you."

"I better take them away and have them washed and ironed."

"Oh—yes, please."

Rilly gathered up the crushed heap of white. She found a nightgown which Sarah had not seen Calista pack. She put it neatly on the bed. She took the dress, too. Then she looked around the room and finally, reluctantly Sarah thought, said, "Anything else now, Miss Sarah?"

"No. Thank you."

Rilly went away, softly closing the door behind her.

The cold ham and biscuits, the warmth of the clear red wine were heartening. It was a relief, too, to get out of the muddy, hot broadcloth riding habit and apply herself to soap and water.

She waited a moment, at last, glancing around the great, shadowy room. Then she blew out the candle, fell into bed, remembered to tuck the mosquito netting around her and went to sleep. On the very edge of sleep she thought that tomorrow Lucien might come home. Tomorrow things would be different.

She slept so long, in such utter exhaustion, that she did not awaken until late afternoon and was drowsy and confused, stared at the misty cloud of mosquito netting and wondered where she was. Then she saw the mirror of the armoire and remembered with a rush.

The room was dusky; the shutters had been closed and only a few streaks of sunlight danced across the duskiness. Someone had come into the room while she slept. Her muddy riding habit was gone; her clothes, freshly washed, and ironed, lay over chairs. Someone had brought fresh water and fresh towels. Someone had removed the tray which had held her late supper and brought another one. A silver pot of coffee caught a ray of sunlight and winked at her. Someone had picked up the great bolster and put it over the little red couch where it sat like a ghostly white presence, observing her. She dimly remembered having jerked its suffocating plumpness from under her head during the night and pushed it to the floor.

She felt refreshed, armored, ready to tackle anything, eager to see Honotassa, Lucien's home and now her home. Perhaps Lucien had come home while she slept!

She sat up, listening for some stir or commotion, half hoping she would hear his gay, laughing voice.

She didn't; she knew he wasn't there. But he might come any day, any moment. She thrust aside the mosquito netting and went to open the shutters. The late afternoon light, gold and rose, poured into the room.

She looked out upon an incredibly beautiful, quiet and tranquil scene. The room was on the south side of the house, directly opposite the front entrance, but here was another roofed porch with more tall white pillars and a band of shade. Beyond it lay smooth green lawns and masses of flowering shrubs, some camellias and flaming azaleas, which still lingered, and white magnolias, and climbing roses, which were already coming into bloom. All were framed by huge oaks, which already cast blue shadows across the grass and veiled themselves in the Spanish moss.

Off at the left there seemed to be a garden, hedged with lush, glossy green shrubbery. A small brick path led through an opening in the green wall and she saw the black points of a kind of circle of cedars or cypress trees. There was a languid afternoon hush over everything.

Honotassa, she thought, and looked for a long time at the white and red and pink masses of bloom; she smelled honeysuckle and watched the soft blue shadows lengthen—and realized suddenly that it must be very late in the day and hurried to drink her coffee and dress. The coffee had a curious nutty flavor; it was not really coffee but it was still warm, very sweet, and refreshing.

She dressed swiftly and was thankful that the one dress Calista had chosen was a becoming one, for its mingled greens and blues brought out sea colors of blue and green in her eyes. It was lucky, too, that it was of the very latest, if rather daring mode, indeed *le dernier cri*, barely introduced in Paris, for the skirt was draped up to a big pouf in the back and it required no hoops. She could not really have expected Rev to transport hoops, too, along with her bulging moiré bag!

The sleeves of the dress were tiny puffs; the neck was cut low; the bodice was tight and the waistline cinched in slenderly. She brushed her hair till it shone and pinned it up in the neat thick roll which—again *le dernier cri*—displayed her ears. In Paris women were displaying, too, curls in the back and curls above the forehead. After some experiments, Sarah confined herself to a smoothly waving pompadour and no curls at the back.

Once in the thin lawn dress, once her hair was shining and neat, she gave herself a rather approving glance; she might fall short of the rosy, round and dimpled standards of beauty of the day, the flutter of curls and eyelashes and fans, the frame of ruffles and flounces and laces, but she had been taught to make the most of what she had—and she knew that she had acquired some taste and elegance in dress and posture.

Of course, she was not beautiful as Lolotte was beautiful. She thought of Lolotte's lovely face, her great, dark eyes

with their long lashes, with a tinge of wistful admiration.
Her hands hovered over the tiny rouge pot and lip paste that
stood on the table amid the litter of toilet articles and the
bottles of drugs. A skillful use of cosmetics, a slight touch of
pink on cheeks and lips, a soupçon of shadow on her eyelids,
the barest touch of crayon around her eyes—all that was
customary in Paris. But what about America? What about
the South?

No. *Ce n'était pas comme il faut, pas ici.* In Paris, yes; in
New York perhaps; but a feminine instinct told her, not here.

She fastened tiny emerald earrings in her pierced ears—a
barbarous custom, piercing the ears, she thought, as she had
many times, but she liked the earrings—and went out of the
room.

The long corridor passed the stairwell and ended in the
distance with a door, apparently to some outside landing or
stairs, for a diffused light streamed in and green vines beyond
hung over a white railing.

There was light, too, pouring from the arched windows
above the landing at the stairs where she had turned the
night before on hearing Emile's drunken laughter and had
seen Reverdy knock him sprawling to the floor.

She went down the stairway, her hand sliding along its
mahogany banister, polished to satin smoothness by the passage of many hands.

The hall below was wide, like a lounge, and went straight
through the house from the front entrance to the south porch,
which Sarah had seen from her window; a stir of air drifted
through it rousing a faint fragrance of potpourri from some
vase. Through one arched doorway she caught a glimpse of a
dining room shaded by the porches, gloomy with heavy
sideboards and long table and chairs; ornate silver coffee
services, tea services, pitchers, a tantalus, loaded down the
sideboards. It was a formal, graceless room.

But on the other side of the hall, another arched doorway
led into a salon—no, a parlor, comfortable, a little shabby as
if it had grown with the needs of the house.

It had been originally furnished in the French manner.
A gilded mirror hung above a delicate pink marble mantel.
There were sparkling gilt and crystal girandoles on the mantel and one or two pieces of porcelain. There was a scatter-
ing of graceful, small French armchairs. There was a rose-
wood piano. Added at some time were other, less beautiful

pieces, deep and worn lounge chairs, a sofa, one or two chairs of carved walnut upholstered with horsehair, not so comfortable. There was a flowered Brussels carpet which looked as if it were made of iron, yet showed worn paths made to the fireplace, the piano, across the room to a door opening upon what looked like a small library; she had a glimpse of books on shelves and a black leather armchair. But altogether the room was a unit. There was something sturdy and full of character in its very lack of plan or studied arrangement. It was obviously the result of many years of living.

The room was shaded by the porch which shut out heat and glare but also shut out air. The whole house seemed oddly still. A huge breakfront cabinet along one wall had glass doors, behind which glittered small objects in enamel, silver-gilt, or clear porcelain colors. On another wall hung three portraits.

She went closer to look at them. The man in the middle must be Lucien's and Reverdy's father, for both Lucien and Reverdy resembled him closely, having the same crisp black hair and black eyebrows and black eyes. It had been painted probably when he was young; there was in the stiff portraiture a kind of arrogance and pride, yet she could see, or at least imagine, a gleam of charm in the painted black eyes. He was flanked, she was sure, by his two wives; it was not difficult to choose Lucien's mother for she was dark, too, faintly resembling Miss Celie but in her younger days, dimpled and rosy, with white shoulders and long dark curls. The other portrait was that of a young woman, too; no beauty, yet with a reticent face, an aquiline nose, smooth brown hair and a straight but rather wistful look in her gray eyes. The gray dress in which she had posed came up close around her slim young throat. It struck Sarah that it was not a happy face. She wondered flashingly whether or not Miss Celie's presence, the constant reminder of her predecessor in that house, had accounted for that.

But then, portraits were only portraits, often deceiving.

There was a rustle behind her and she turned. Lolotte was standing in the middle of her room studying her as intently as Sarah had studied the portraits.

"I was waiting for you," Lolotte said.

"Oh. Thank you." It was the first gesture of welcome in that house and Sarah's voice and heart warmed. Lolotte was even more beautiful than she had been in her pale pink silk wrapper the night before. Now her dark hair was parted neatly in the middle and netted into a chignon at the back of her lovely head. She wore a dress of white muslin, sprigged with pink roses; below her tiny, laced-in waist her skirts billowed out over her hoops. Sarah said, "I was looking at the portraits. I suppose that is Lucien's father."

The grandfather's clock in the hall ticked loudly for a long moment. Lolotte came a step nearer. "What did Lucien see in you?" she asked.

It was like a slap in the face.

She went on. "Lucien was engaged to marry me. He's in love with me. Why did he marry you?"

A slap in the face was nothing to the curious kind of blow which struck somewhere within Sarah and literally did take her breath.

"But he—but you—" she said blankly. "Why, he is your cousin!"

"Don't cousins marry in Connecticut? Our marriage was settled long ago. Everyone knew it."

So that, Sarah thought, was why Emile had laughed the night before. She had dismissed it as merely a drunken notion; she saw now that his taunting laughter was aimed at Lolotte.

Sarah made an effort to steady herself. "I'm sorry that Lucien didn't tell you. He must have written."

"I had no letter."

"Mail is irregular. I'm sure he wrote. Or he intended—yes, of course, he expected to come to Honotassa before I came and he intended—"

"I never heard of you until you came into this house last night and said you were his wife. None of us had ever heard of you. Lucien was engaged to marry me."

Sarah had no doubt whatever as to the truth of Lolotte's claim. But she was sure, too, that it had been, it must have been a youthful, perhaps childish romance—smiled on, even brought about by family.

Lolotte said, her small face hard, "Didn't Lucien tell you about me?"

"No." Sarah groped for a reason and found it. "He wouldn't have told me. He meant to tell you first. He would have told you before I came. I'm sure he intended to—to tell you, talk to you himself. That would have been better

40

than writing. He'd have wanted to make sure that you understood."

"You don't believe me."

"Yes, I believe you. But it was, as you say, an understood arrangement, you were both very young and—"

"You don't know a thing about it."

It was unfortunately true.

Lolotte's dark eyes veiled themselves in long lashes. "But then I know why Lucien married you. Rev told us that your father was a rich man. We need money here."

"Lucien married me because he loves me!"

"That's silly. He's in love with me."

She swirled around, her hoops swaying, and walked with assured and lovely grace out of the room.

Sarah felt weak.

Lucien should have told her of Lolotte. No, perhaps he wouldn't talk of one woman to another. Though he should have seen Lolotte, made sure that his engagement to Lolotte was broken off; but then he couldn't have seen Lolotte, he couldn't have talked to her; time had not permitted it. He should have written to her, but again Lucien would not have written, baldly, "I've fallen in love with another woman. I'm going to marry her at once." No; he couldn't have done that.

Lucien was too kind, too gallant. How could he have written to Lolotte: I've met Sarah; I love her, she loves me; she's the only woman for me; I'm the only man for her?

She longed for Lucien to come, walking swiftly, gracefully into the room—to laugh away her troubled sense of something like guilt (yet it wasn't guilt; she had known nothing of his youthful understanding) and put everything right.

If Lucien had come home sooner, if he had not been delayed, this would not have happened. It was going to be difficult.

Rev had known; he had tried to warn her, saying things may not be easy. Perhaps he had tried to tell her of Lolotte's engagement to Lucien. It would have been hard for him to do.

Lucien would settle everything as soon as he came. Oh, Lucien, she pled in her heart, please come soon.

There were voices in the hall, a man's voice, and Lolotte's in one sharp angry word. Then Emile came to the door. "Cousin Sarah, I've been looking for you. I must apologize for my behavior last night."

41

But it was not Sarah he had laughed at, it was Lolotte. He had taken a cruel pleasure in Lolotte's shock.

"I was not myself," Emile said and bowed. "May I show you around the place, Cousin Sarah?"

She would have preferred anybody's guidance to Emile's but her encounter with Lolotte left her in a numbed and troubled state of mind. She hesitated and then went with him through the wide hall, only refusing to take the arm he offered her with an exaggerated bow. He held open the door onto the shady south porch and she would have stopped there among the scattered chairs but he sensed her reluctance. "Please let me show you the gardens, Cousin Sarah. It will soothe my abject sorrow for my inexcusable behavior last night. This way—down the steps. Our gardens are not famous, not like the Clifton gardens in Natchez. They were famous until the owner, Mr. Sugret—at least that's the story, it may be gossip—but the story is that Mr. Sugret failed to invite a Yankee engineer to a party he gave and would you believe it, cousin, suddenly the Yankees were obliged to demolish Clifton for some mysterious military purpose. Perhaps it's all gossip. These camellias are Alba Plenas, Miss Celie's pride, past their best bloom now, regrettably."

They entered the brick walk she had seen from her window. The narrow brick walk was green with moss. The boxwood on either side was so thick and overgrown that it narrowed the path and sent up a bitter sharp odor. Sarah did not however see the gardens, for they came out suddenly in a grassy circle, walled in with pointed black cedars, which from Sarah's windows had looked like cypress. In the middle of the grassy circle a weather-stained marble cupid stood and simpered. A circle of roses bloomed and drooped around his feet. Thorny tendrils crept across the grass.

There was something oddly unpleasant about the little, hedged-in circle. For a moment Sarah did not listen to Emile's talk although she knew vaguely that he was talking of the cupid, sent from Italy long ago, and the marble bench which stood at one side of the circle. The shade was deep; there were mossy patches where the grass was thin. It looked as if no one ever came there but someone had come there for there was a half-smoked cigar on the marble bench. Behind it, almost hidden, a half-empty bottle of whiskey leaned against its carved marble base. Emile said quickly. "This is my retreat. Nobody but me ever comes here. They let me alone—do sit down, Cousin Sarah."

She felt suddenly very far from the house. "I think I'll go back now. . . ."

"Sit down," he said silkily. His eyes were peering and red-rimmed; his face flabby and smiling. "I have a word to say. I think you'd better listen. No, wait. I'll make it short. You're a rich woman. So, Cousin Sarah, I'm willing to be your friend."

She stared at him, perplexed and then angry.

"I don't know what you're talking about. I think you're drunk!"

"Wait!" He gripped her arm as she turned toward the path and spun her around to face him. "It's all plain as a pike staff. You're a Yankee. Lucien is in cahoots with the Yankees. So is Rev. You're all very smart—you'll see that you're on the winning side but you'll keep Honotassa, too. Well, I'll go along with you, I'll keep quiet about it. You're a rich woman and I need money."

It was so wildly unexpected, so utterly preposterous that for a second she simply stared at him. Then she blazed. "That is a lie!"

Emile's light, red-rimmed eyes went past her. He dropped her arm but not quickly enough, for Rev came from the path, crossed the little circle and his fist struck Emile again. Even in that moment, Sarah thought with a strange little quiver, like laughter, he did it in a businesslike way, as if it happened every day. As indeed, thinking of the previous night, seemed very likely to be the truth.

Emile glared up from the bench where he sprawled. "Sometime you'll do that once too often!"

"Sometime," Rev said, "you'll need it once too often and I'll break your neck and be done with you."

He saw the bottle, scooped it up and tossed it long and far above the pointed cedars. There was in the distance a muffled thud and shiver of broken glass.

Emile thrust himself up on one elbow and giggled. "You've hit Miss Celie's Empress Josephines. She'll have your hide."

Rev took Sarah's arm and led her out of the shaded, dank circle. As they went along the mossy brick path Emile's high-pitched giggle died away behind them.

"I didn't hit him hard enough to hurt him. It's the only way to shut Emile up. Don't worry."

She wasn't worrying.

Rev said in a matter-of-fact way, "I heard what he said to you. There's no truth in it, is there?"

CHAPTER FIVE

She turned around to face him. "What on earth are you talking about?"

"Lucien and you." His voice was soft; his eyes hard. "You *are* a Yankee."

"What do you—why, what do you think I am?" She blazed again. "A—a spy? Another Rose Greenhow—except for the North? What is there here to spy about even if I wanted to?"

"I don't mean that."

"What do you mean?"

"You are a Northerner. You make no secret of your views. A man can be influenced by a woman—his wife."

It was again so preposterous that anger went out of her. "Not Lucien. Besides, I couldn't influence him if I tried and I haven't tried and never will. He'll tell you that. Ask him when he comes home."

"I'm asking you now."

"Well, I've told you. And I told Emile. I told him he lied. He wanted money."

"Yes, I heard that, too. I was in the office and saw him bringing you out here. . . ."

"Did you know that he was going to—to try to threaten me like that?"

"Emile is a drunken lout," he said soberly. "He had a bomb-proof desk job in New Orleans till the Yankees came. Since then he's spent most of the time at Honotassa—drinking. There's no telling what he'll do or what he'll get in his head."

"This time it was the silliest nonsense I ever heard of! Lucien's as loyal a Confederate as you are. I wouldn't think of trying to get him to turn against his own people. Why, Emile said the same thing of you! He said *you* were turning Union."

"We call it deserting," he said mildly, gave her a long, thoughtful look and then suddenly genuine warmth and

44

friendliness came into his face. "I believe you. It *is* nonsense. Forget Emile. Somebody once said that there are only two kinds of Hugots, good Hugots and bad Hugots, no shades between." He started walking along the path again and she went beside him. "Emile is a bad one, no getting around that. Oh, he's not actively bad, I mean he doesn't rob, steal or murder. He's only weak and vicious."

"He laughed at Lolotte last night. You hit him for that, too."

"Oh. Did Emile tell you about Lolotte?"

"No. Lolotte told me."

"I see. I'm sorry about that. I tried to tell you myself, then I decided it would be better to talk to Lolotte first."

"It's true then, her engagement to Lucien?"

"Yes."

They walked on for a little, the acrid-smelling boxwood brushing her skirts. Finally she said, "Was it a long engagement? So the whole family knew and accepted it?"

"Yes. We're all very fond of Lolotte. She's lived here since she was a child. I told you."

"But Lucien couldn't have talked to her. Everything about our marriage was so hurried. He must have meant to talk to her himself—before I was to arrive. But then he was delayed and—why, that's why you didn't believe that I am Lucien's wife!"

"Sarah—" They reached the end of the path and the opening of the hedge. He paused and put his hand on her wrist. "You haven't had much of a welcome, have you?"

She looked up and met his eyes, which were so kind, so gentle that suddenly Emile's stupid, drunken accusations, Lolotte's attack, which she could understand, both faded into a proper perspective.

"I didn't expect a welcome. How could I when none of you knew anything about me? I'm not a child."

A light flickered deep in his eyes. "You're a very beautiful woman," he said, and instantly took his hand from her wrist and added in a polite and impersonal way, "Lucien is to be congratulated. Maude and Ben are on the porch, waiting to be introduced to you."

They emerged from the path and Sarah looked up at the house. Miss Celie, wearing black, sat massively in one of the chairs, her hands busy with sewing.

Another woman, who must be Maude, sat near her, sewing,

too. A man, holding a tall glass, watched them.

And then Sarah stopped involuntarily for she was caught by the beauty of the house, the tranquil serenity of the evening light across the lawn and the flowers, the long blue shadows under the oaks.

The house itself was a typical expression of Southern architecture, and of its times. The middle section, with its perfectly balanced lines, its white pillars and shaded porch, had obviously been well and graciously planned. An added wing to the east was as obviously an afterthought as was a small stairway climbing its outside wall, roofed only by a trellis and heavy vines. Toward the west there was a covered passageway to a kitchen, its chimney smoking, removed from the house. Beyond the oaks and the veils of Spanish moss there were clusters of small buildings, cabins, whitewashed and rather ghostly in the soft light. About it all there was a careless generosity, which did not mar the austere dignity of its central, pillared section.

Honotassa, indeed, and everything about it was characteristic of the times. For some years before the war, cotton had been literally king. A good year's crop amounted to a small fortune. Much of this had already been used up in production costs and was already pledged to the factor. But in a good year—and there had been many good years—enough money remained to supply not only needs but every luxurious fancy, every engaging whim. The rich planter sent orders to New Orleans, to France, to Italy, for handwoven silks and velvet curtains, tables inlaid in various semiprecious stones, marble statuary—anything that took his fancy. Some of it was lovely, some of it ugly, all of it found an enduring place in his home. But out of all that opulence there emerged a certain sturdy pride and harmony. Even the trees, the masses of shrubs, the heavy flowering vines seemed to have grown of their own will.

Sarah said dreamily, "Emile said Miss Celie's Empress Josephines. Did he mean yellow tea roses like those at Versailles?"

"He meant yellow roses. I don't know Versailles. Lucien and I were to take the grand tour. But then Pa died. And the war began."

"All those flowers!" She drank in their beauty, too; it was like an orchestra in color, pianoforte. In Connecticut, flowers marched in orderly bloom through the seasons. "Everything seems to bloom at once here."

"Well it was a cold winter and it's a warm spring. It happens like that."

"What's that sweet smell? Honeysuckle?"

"Yes. Or the Cape Jessamine. Or sweet shrub."

Something in his voice made her look at him and he was watching her again, smiling a little. "You like it?"

"Yes. Oh, yes."

Why, it's home, she thought. For a moment it was as if she knew the house in all its moods and had always known it. It was a strangely revealing moment, a moment of deep alliance, which even then her instinct recognized and accepted.

A flight of chimney swallows whirred up from the rim of trees in beautiful alignment, intent on some mysterious and urgent purpose. She watched their flight across the clear twilight sky. Somewhere a bird sang a liquid, lovely note or two. Rev said, "It's a mocker. There's a family of them in the wisteria. They come every year."

A star was out above the trees. The sun had gone. Yes, Sarah thought, this is home.

In that long and, to Sarah, significant moment the blue shadows had come nearer. The porch was deeply shadowed. Miss Celie put down her sewing.

Sarah was introduced first to Maude, and words of Lucien's darted out of her memory. ("Maude's father was an Italian count. Made quite a flutter in New Orleans. But he was a no-'count really." Lucien's disarming laugh erased any touch of cruelty in his words. "Got all the money he could out of the Hugots and then went back to Rome.")

She had pictured Maude as a slim, dark beauty; instead she was a blonde with thick, light hair, parted and looped in sleek buns over each ear, cold blue eyes, and a truly Roman nose, a nose which put Sarah's nose quite in the shade, for it rose between Maude's eyebrows in a perfect Roman arch; even her chin was like a Roman marble, tucked in under the lips and then curving out roundly. Her body looked small until she sat down again; then Sarah had an impression of thick, solid hips and thighs below Maude's spreading skirts.

Ben Greevy, her husband was perhaps in his forties, little with a baldish head, a rabbity face, sharp dark eyes and a paunch. He wore a white linen suit and an embroidered silk waistcoat; he bowed to Sarah and called her Cousin Sarah.

Maude and Ben Greevy, Sarah knew from Lucien, were more or less permanent members of the household; Ben owned a sugar plantation in Louisiana but their home was in Natchez; they had refugeed from Natchez to Honotassa.

Lolotte was not there. A little Negro maid in clean but faded calico brought a tall glass with a sprig of green mint thrust into it, for Rev. Here, apparently, the ladies took no apéritif.

Apparently, too, they had already talked over Lucien's marriage, and certainly Sarah; talk was now of the news Ben had heard in Maville that afternoon. Sarah concluded that Maville was the nearest town and post office.

"No mail," Ben said. "But I didn't expect it. They say though that the old Mississippi has finally licked Grant. No doubt about that. They had to give up on that canal, they got themselves stuck in Lake Providence, Yazoo Pass, Steele Bayou—couldn't get through there. By the last of March we had them as good as licked. So now they say Grant is just sitting there across the river."

Rev looked sober. Maude said, "That canal would never have worked."

"Well," Ben said, "seems it looked like a good idea to them. They thought they'd divert the river, leave Vicksburg an inland city, not important to anybody. But along came the old Mississippi and flooded them out. Yes, sir, the river's got Grant licked."

"I don't know," Rev said. "It might have worked. I don't like Grant being on the Louisiana side of the river. He'll have to cross somewhere."

"Rev!" Maude cried sharply. "Why, how can he get across the river right under the guns of Vicksburg?"

"There are other places." Reverdy swished the drink in his glass.

"Oh, that's silly," Maude said. "Why, he got such a setback when his stores were destroyed at Holly Springs, he had to run fast, his tail between his legs. He'll run again."

"Maybe," Rev said. "But somehow I don't think Grant is a running man." He turned as a man came out of the house, and rose. "George—" Rev introduced him to Sarah. "May I present Cousin George Osborn. . . . This is Lucien's wife."

George Osborn had been a vaguely familiar name to Sarah, too, and now her memory of it clarified as again words of Lucien's flashed to her mind. "George is a good-natured

48

fool," Lucien had said and laughed. "He'd lick my boots if I'd let him."

Looking at George now, Sarah could understand his admiration for anyone with Lucien's charm, his wit and grace. George was stolid, plainfaced; he had washed-out light hair and washed-out blue eyes. One arm was missing and the empty sleeve folded and pinned up. Later she learned that he had lost the arm at Chickasaw Bayou in December. He did not seem to see Sarah's extended hand and as he sat down on the porch and leaned back against a pillar, she caught a glance from his pale eyes which startled her for it was a look of icy cold hatred.

But then he knew that she was a Northerner, a Yankee, she reminded herself. Why shouldn't he hate her? Surely, though, hatred was too strong a word.

At once George earnestly entered the talk about Vicksburg. "Sure, Grant wants to get to Vicksburg. But even if Grant got his army through the swamps and bayous as far as a point opposite Grand Gulf, there're twelve big guns at Grand Gulf to keep them off. Grant made a mistake taking the Louisiana side of the river. He's licked right now."

Miss Celie whispered, "Supper is ready."

They sat around the long mahogany table, which was lighted dimly by a three-armed silver candelabra. The candles were tallow and smoked. Two places were vacant; neither Emile nor Lolotte came to supper but no one commented on their absence. The young Negro maid served and sent surreptitious and inquisitive looks at Sarah; her name was Glendora. The men talked of war; places and names hurtled around Sarah's ears. Rev said that since there was only one vulnerable approach to Vicksburg it seemed logical to conclude that General Grant would attempt an attack from the east. This brought forth a chorus of protest from George, Ben and Maude—although it seemed to Sarah that Maude's Romanesque face was a little thoughtful. In Maude she began to sense a far older and colder realism than her own.

Miss Celie served dessert from a Sèvres bowl with a silver ladle as big as a dipper, and apologized because it was stewed dried peaches. "We couldn't have a soufflé or cake. I put all the fresh eggs for the last three days down in water glass, just in case the commissary takes all our chickens the next time they come around." Her raisin-dark glance went to Ben.

"Whose place was raided at Maville?"

"The Otterbridge place. They didn't burn the house—just took all the livestock and food they could lay their hands on. Burned the cotton in the sheds."

George's face flushed. "There's only old lady Otterbridge and the boy there! Easy picking."

"Are they sure they were Yankees?" Reverdy asked.

Ben shrugged. "They burned the cotton. Took a shot at the boy, as a matter of fact, when he tried to stop them, but missed him."

George gave Sarah a brooding look as if Sarah herself, personally, had burned the Otterbridge cotton, taken a shot at the Otterbridge boy and ridden away with hens over her saddle.

Maude said, "That's only about ten miles from here."

"Twenty at least," George said. "They'll never get this far."

"Honotassa is way off the main road," Ben said comfortingly. "And they do say that the Union military command has forbidden looting."

"But it happens," Miss Celie whispered grimly.

Maude sighed. "I wonder who's living in our house in Natchez."

"Probably nobody," Ben said. The talk drifted to other things.

But the fading of the Otterbridge place remained in the back of their minds, for as they finished dinner a dog somewhere outside yelped shrilly and in a second Rev and George were on their feet and George had, like magic, a gun in his left hand. Glendora dropped a plate. Several other dogs yelped too but without any real zest and the noise died away almost as suddenly as it began. Ben put down the napkin he held at his lips, listening. "Rabbit," he said. "Possum."

Miss Celie's huge bulk heaved with a sigh. "Pick up the pieces, Glendora," she directed resignedly and Glendora gathered the pieces together in her apron and fled.

After supper they sat in the parlor, Miss Celie and Maude busy again with sewing. A big lamp was lighted. It had a huge bowl, painted with roses, and a big yellowish globe and it, too, smelled and smoked. "No kerosene." Miss Celie adjusted the wick.

Ben smoked a cigar and complained grumpily that his store was almost exhausted. Its fragrance blended stuffily with the smell from the lamp. Still neither Lolotte nor Emile ap-

50

peared. Rev went into the library, the small room beside the parlor. Through the open door Sarah saw the bookshelves, a few gun racks, all empty, and Rev's head bent over a book. After a while George followed him. "Find anything?" George said.

"Not a thing. This book is out of date. Printed in 1805! I'll try hot bran mash."

"Too bad old Tobias ran away. He was a right good horse doctor. I'll go with you and help."

Apparently some horse, worth his weight almost in gold now, was ailing. The two men went out by way of a door into the hall. Presently Ben rose and strolled out, too. Miss Celie caught Sarah in a stifled yawn, said Sarah was tired, rose and trundled with her remarkable agility into the hall where she lighted and gave Sarah a bedroom candle. Then she said good night firmly.

So this is my first day and first night at Honotassa, Sarah thought as she made her way up the broad stairs, her candle scarcely lighting her path. Well, Rome wasn't built in a day. Lucien would come home soon and then everything would be different.

Once in her room, with the candle casting shadows again in the corners of the room and on the ceiling, she began idly to arrange her small possessions. Her riding habit had been returned, brushed, cleaned and pressed. She couldn't remember for a moment what she had done with the key to the armoire which Rev had given her the night before and then found it, among the toilet articles on the table. She opened the armoire. The little sacks of gold were arranged in orderly ranks. She hung up her riding habit and her now ironed and crisp white petticoat. She relocked the door of the armoire simply because Rev had locked it, after placing the gold there the night before. She arranged her small stock of lingerie in a drawer of a huge carved chest; the drawer smelled of lavender. She looked over the little supply of medicines she had brought and discovered that two bottles were missing.

She had brought only calomel and quinine, opium and chloroform, in necessarily small amounts and only for family needs. Knowing that such were contraband, she had emptied cologne bottles, jars of face powder and cream, and refilled them with the medicines, in the hope that no inquisitive official at the New Orleans dock would look further than the labels. She counted over the bottles again; unluckily the missing bottles contained the drugs which were hardest to secure in the South and the most needed in emergency, opium and chloroform.

She had barely glanced at the bottles the night before; certainly she hadn't counted them. The possibility that someone in the house, Rilly perhaps or the maid Glendora, had taken the two bottles, believing them to contain colognes, crossed her mind and she rejected it instantly, not only because both drugs had distinctive and unpleasant odors but also because she did not believe that even so trivial a theft could possibly occur in a household managed by Miss Celie. Also it was obvious that the two bottles had dropped out of her moiré bag while the horses, with her and Rev clinging to their backs, had plunged and stumbled across some muddy stream or through some thicket. The bottles and jars holding quinine and calomel were ornately decorated and still bore their labels of Cologne and Orris Root and rice powder. She must give them to Miss Celie to add to whatever household store of medicines there was. Her bottle of Rowland's Kalydor Tooth Wash actually contained tooth wash; she put it on the marble-topped washstand. There were fresh towels and fresh water; she dimly remembered having heard Glendora's softly thudding feet upstairs sometime after supper.

She arranged her silver-backed brush with her few toilet articles on a big dressing table which stood in the darkest corner of the room and thought, half amused, that its position alone, far from the light of the windows, suggested that no guest at Honotassa was in the habit of using cosmetics. She went to the open windows and looked out into the velvet black night.

The frogs made a steady, antiphonal chorus off in the distance. Occasionally a bird rustled somewhere in the darkness. There were no voices, no other sounds, only a deep country quiet. Honotassa seemed divided from neighbors by wide-spreading acres.

She couldn't see even the darker rim of the garden hedges; she wondered if Emile were still down there in that vaguely sinister circle—having secured another bottle from somewhere and undoubtedly drinking himself into insensibility. She wondered if Lolotte, presumably behind one of the doors which lined the upstairs hall, had heard Sarah's own rustling skirt or had seen the faint glow from her candle as she moved along the hall.

She turned away at last and began to unbutton her bodice when without any warning a gunshot rang out through the stillness, rocked the night, rocked the house and everything in it.

It was again, for a long moment, perfectly still. Then a bird cried out shrilly and fluttered, a voice shouted from somewhere outside, footsteps pounded along the porch and Sarah ran to the window.

Someone—George, she thought—shouted, "This way—they're in the garden!"

Ben from directly beneath her shouted, "Maude, bring me my pistol!"

Maude gave a scream. "*Yankees*—"

Sarah could see nothing but the night was turbulent now with shouts and running feet. Then a lantern bobbed across the lawn; its yellow light illuminated running legs in light trousers. Maude's wide skirts loomed up dimly as she ran across the lawn too, toward the garden. Ben's white linen suit came into view; he caught Maude's arm, thrust her back toward the house and pounded across the lawn in the wake of the lantern. The lantern disappeared along the brick walk but it sent up a moving circle of light above the hedges against the blackness of the sky and shrubbery.

It stopped moving. The dark points of cedars were outlined in its yellow glow. She thought that Maude returned to the porch. Then she heard Miss Celie, below the window. "They've found something—"

Maude said, "Stay here!"

The lantern was moving again; it was coming swiftly along the brick path. It burst out, a yellow light, from the black hedge. Men were running toward the house. Rev cried, clearly, "They've shot Emile."

Ben puffed, jerkily. "Right through the heart. . . . He's dead. . . . Nothing we can do for him. . . . We've got to find them. . . ."

Instantly everybody was talking at once—Yankees, guns, get the men from the quarters, tell Stash to see to the horses, something about silver, something about Lolotte. The lantern bobbed off again toward the slave quarters, a door banged and there was sudden confusion now, all through the house, voices, running footsteps. Sarah's bedroom door was flung open and the candle flame wavered wildly in the draft from the windows. Maude ran in.

"Yankees have killed Emile. Hide your jewelry. Not in your dress, they'll search you. Not in your hair either, they'll make you take it down."

"Where are the—the Yankees?" Sarah's own voice sounded queer and stiff.

"Somewhere—in the woods—nobody knows. Hurry—" Maude flashed away, her hoops tilting. Downstairs something fell with a clatter.

Jewelry? But they wouldn't loot, they wouldn't search out jewelry. Or would they? Against orders, against military command? And then she thought of the gold.

Maude's panic had communicated itself. She was already hunting through the moiré bag, searching out her few jewels —two wide gold bracelets, a brooch set with sapphires and emeralds, a tiny necklace of pearls. The bracelets and brooch had belonged to her mother; James Salter had had a New England and Scottish dislike for ostentation but he had given Sarah the necklace of pearls. Downstairs there was the sharp clatter of running feet along the parquet floor of the hall. What could she do with all that gold?

She ran to the window again and now there were torches, lights, lanterns in the slave quarters and toward the stables. She heard the loud snort of a horse and shouts from men.

Simply because Maude had told her not to hide jewelry in her hair and it would have never occurred to her to do so, she contrarily yet absently did stuff the brooch and the pearls into her thick roll of hair. She shoved the bracelets under the mattress and as she did so thought, why that's the first place anybody would look for valuables.

She was no more inclined to let Union soldiers, looting secretly and under command not to do so, walk away with the gold than she would have been inclined to hand it over to a burglar. Besides these might be thugs, renegades.

She ran to the window again. There were fewer lights; the voices seemed distant now. The men seemed to have scattered toward the front of the house, past the fields, along the great avenue of oaks.

There were no more gunshots. There were no sounds, no thud and clatter of horses in the driveway, no shouts or shots from advancing—or fleeing—Yankee soldiers.

And all at once she thought, there are no Yankees. There are no stragglers or thugs. Someone else shot Emile.

CHAPTER SIX

After a long, long moment she left the window, took the key to the armoire and thrust it down among the cushions of the sofa, left the gold where it was, picked up her bedroom candle and went downstairs.

If she did not believe that there had been a Union raiding party, or even a surreptitious party of stragglers, then the others did believe it. That, or they gave very convincing evidence of believing it.

Candles were burning haphazardly, in unlikely places, on chairs, the steps, anywhere, tilting and dripping drunkenly. The massive silver was swept clean from the dining room sideboards.

In the parlor the lamp stood fantastically in the middle of the floor, smoking and smelling. Chairs were pushed haphazardly; one stood at the huge breakfront case. Its doors were hanging open and its shelves, too, were bare, swept of all their glittering ornaments. The portrait of Lucien's and Rev's father was gone, leaving a clearer, brighter patch of wallpaper, but the two young faces of his wives looked blankly at Sarah across the wildly disordered room.

Through the open door, looking north along the driveway under the oaks, she saw the red flares of pine knots and the yellow gleams of lanterns; there were shouts far away. At a patter of hasty footsteps behind her she turned and Lolotte, in her white muslin with its sprigged roses, came running along the hall; her face was white, some dark curls had escaped her netted chignon. Her hoops swayed as she ran and she held a long, flat box in her arms. The door to the south porch behind her quivered, softly closed and immediately was flung open again as Rev came running in. He cried, "I think they've gone! We'll make sure. What have you got there, Lolotte?"

Lolotte hugged the box; it was covered with green velvet. "Lucien's dueling pistols. I don't want the Yankees to get them."

"Where were they?"

There was an infinitesimal pause. Lolotte widened her eyes. "In Lucien's room, of course."

"But you came in from the porch just now. I saw you."

"Oh for goodness sake, Rev Hugot! Do you think *I* shot Emile? I was trying to find a place to hide them and couldn't think where."

"I'll take care of them." Rev took the box from Lolotte. "Where is Miss Celie?"

"In the smokehouse hiding everything. Maude and I got the silver put away."

"Go and tell Miss Celie I think they've gone."

Lolotte gave Sarah a sliding glance under her black eyelashes and put her hand on Rev's arm. "Rev, why can't Sarah tell them she's a Yankee? They'll not touch Yankee property. Make her tell them that she's Mrs. Hugot and a Yankee and a sympathizer. Then maybe they'll not burn the house."

There was a delicate, yet definite malice in Lolotte's demure face. Rev looked at her soberly for a second. "I don't think Sarah will do that. Besides they may not be Yankees."

"Who else would shoot Emile? Of course they're Yankees!"

"Go find Miss Celie. I think we've scared them away. They didn't expect to find men here—or guns."

"No!" Lolotte cried. "They thought they'd find only women, like the other places they loot." She went away, her skirts swaying, her little feet running along the hall and out onto the south porch.

Rev looked at Sarah. "What did you do with the gold?"

"It's—safe."

George shouted from the front entrance. "Rev—" His pale, excited face showed dimly in the light from the candles. "Rev, there's no sight or sound of them near the house! We'll have to search them out!" He carried his gun in his left hand.

Rev started out, remembered the case holding Lucien's dueling pistols, opened the door of the big grandfather's clock, slid the flat box tight against its back wall so it was behind the great swinging pendulum, closed the door, and ran out with George.

Sarah sat down on the bottom step of the stairs. The big pendulum caught lights as it swung back and forth, back and forth as if it said, "This will pass. This will pass. Time alone goes on."

Lolotte had known that Lucien had, and apparently prized, dueling pistols. It was a custom; men fought as if shooting

56

each other could settle a quarrel or a slight, fancied or real. It was not a Connecticut custom though. She wondered how many duels Lucien had fought, decided swiftly that probably he had fought none at all, and in any event it was not within her power or province to poke into an established custom or try to change it—not then.

Lolotte's suggestion that Sarah tell the raiding party (if in fact there was a raiding party) that she, Sarah, the titular mistress of the house, was a Northerner, was, she knew, a dagger thrust on Lolotte's part.

It suggested on Sarah's part a settled disloyalty to Lucien's people, who were now her people. It suggested a disloyalty to the house and land with which she had allied herself. There was no possible conflict between her heart and what was now her home, and her innate, strong belief in the right of the Union. Looting or burning a house could not advance the Union cause.

In a way it was true that she had been away from home and the immediate pressures and violent emotions engendered by war. She had never been face to face with war itself, or its inevitable accompaniment of violence.

In another way Rev was wrong. Something her father had written in one of his many letters came to her mind, almost word for word. "The North will win. We must win. Besides we now have the men and the arms to win. My hope is that out of this bloody conflict there will emerge a strong Union, one nation. When President Lincoln said that a house divided against itself cannot stand, he spoke a profound truth. If states are permitted to secede at will, what will we have in the end but a loose confederation of small principalities, weak enough to be gobbled up by any foreign country? It is a fair land, a great land, all one land, God willing, united."

She had brought gold, she had brought a little supply of medicine into New Orleans on the very day when she had taken an oath of allegiance to the Union—an oath which Lucien had called derisively the eagle oath.

But Honotassa was nobody's enemy. Honotassa was a part of that fair land.

It was no specious argument with which she supplied herself. She could love and, if it came to that, defend Honotassa because it was still and always would be a part of that fair land, that great land, her own land.

The candle at her feet smoked. It seemed strange that in so

turbulent and hurry-skurry a moment a profound and basic truth seemed to reveal itself to her.

She roused as Lolotte and Miss Celie, Maude and Rilly and Glendora came in, hurrying so their passage made the candle flames lower and rise and lower. They rushed together to the front door and stood, looking down the avenue under the oaks.

Sarah was still utterly convinced that no Yankee raiding party existed, yet their talk, their exclamations, their whole attitude of anxiety and fear almost persuaded her to believe that there *had* been men out there in the darkness, intending to loot the house, and driven off by the discovery that it was not a house where only one or two women waited and worked out the war but that there were men on the place ready and able to defend it.

The shouts of the men, the shrill yelping of the dogs seemed farther away. There were still no gunshots.

Unexpectedly a tiny, nagging question presented itself in Sarah's mind. If no Yankee straggler or renegade looter, no disgruntled servant, had shot Emile, then someone else had shot him. Her pulses seemed to stop and then raced, for that someone else had to be—who? Ben or George? Rev? Miss Celie or Lolotte?

No! She had to be wrong.

She went to join the women at the door. There was nothing to be seen outside except the occasional red flare of a pine knot or the gleam of a lantern. After a while the men came back, their feet crunching slowly along the driveway, their faces gradually coming into the light.

Everybody had an explanation and their explanations were all the same. Ben, wiping his rabbity face, was positive. "They've gone, no doubt about that. They knew we'd heard the shot—saw that there were armed men here and skedaddled. Must have been only two or three of them. Got scared out."

Rev was still on the porch. He called, "You boys can go back to your cabins. They've gone. But keep your ears open tonight. They might come back."

Maude said, "Why did they shoot Emile?"

Ben came into the hall. His white suit was rumpled and muddy. "Way we figure it they must have come in across the fields, circled around the house, wanted to reconnoiter, find out if there were any men here—or any guns. Met up

58

with Emile in the garden and he was likely just drunk enough to try to fight them. They figured he'd give the alarm—or maybe he just got them worked up and somebody with a nervous trigger finger shot him. Then they heard all the commotion, saw the lights, saw us—and got away across the fields again."

"I didn't hear any horses," Maude said. Sarah glanced at her quickly but Maude added, "We wouldn't, of course. They left their horses in the woods or somewhere. Heavens! We've been running around like scared chickens and they were more scared than we were!"

Rev came in. "I'm sure they've gone, Miss Celie."

Miss Celie whispered, "Emile."

"We'll see to that. Stash and some of the boys will make the coffin tonight." He glanced at Ben and at George. Without another word the three men tramped through the house and out toward the garden, where Emile lay in the sinister circle around the cupid, a bullet through his heart.

The women made a half-hearted attempt to restore some order; they gathered up candles, they pushed chairs back into their usual position. Maude picked up the big lamp and blew it out. No one wept for Emile, yet the unalterable fact of his death was now forcing itself upon them.

It would be easiest for Sarah to accept Ben's explanation—the explanation which all of them, even Rev, gave every evidence of accepting. She mustn't think about it. But she did think about it.

Miss Celie said with a sigh that there was nothing they could do that night, sent Maude and Lolotte and Sarah off to bed and told Rilly to stay with her. Sarah heard then the slow tread of the men and their low voices; they were bringing Emile back to the house.

Lolotte gave a little gasp and fled up the stairs. Maude said, "Come, Cousin Sarah."

The men were entering the hall from the porch when Sarah and Maude reached the landing. They carried Emile on an improvised litter, burlap stretched across two planks. Miss Celie's vast bulk floated to meet them. "Take him to his room."

The heavy tread of the men seemed to follow Sarah and Maude like a fateful echo up the stairs. Sarah did not look back again but once in her own room she closed the door, put down her candle and went to the windows. It was all

59

quiet now, as quiet as it had been the moment before Emile was shot.

There had been no Yankee raiding party, no band of looters. She'd have heard their voices. She'd have heard something in that night quiet. There was only again the murmur of frogs—and suddenly a regular tap-tap, as of hammers, somewhere in the distance. Hammers. The men were making a coffin for Emile.

The enormity of her own speculations struck her then with utter horror. She must be mistaken. It was wrong, unjust, wicked to permit her own mind to seesaw back and forth in dreadful argument. Rev believed in the Yankee raiding party. Rev had said to Emile, "Sometime I'll break your neck." No, she would not explore; she would not try to find motives for Emile's murder; she would close that door of speculation and keep it closed.

Something was pulling at her hair, the brooch, entangled. She removed it and the string of pearls. She got the two bracelets out from under the mattress.

When at last she blew out the candle and the room was in complete darkness, the tap-tap of the hammers seemed louder.

The next morning they buried Emile. The burial took place in the family lot. It was at some distance from the house, a quiet little plot of moss-covered and weathered headstones, shaded with oaks and overrun with myrtle and ivy.

Sarah's only dress, the thin blue and green lawn, would offend Miss Celie's, perhaps everyone's, sense of propriety. She wore her riding habit; the heavy broadcloth was stifling that hot spring day but it was black.

Several men, strangers to Sarah naturally, came to the house early, had a talk with Rev, George and Ben, and, she thought, with Miss Celie, and later took their places in neighborly and sympathetic decorum, behind the family during the short service. There was also a handful of other neighbors, several women and one or two elderly men to whom Sarah was later introduced, who all expressed surprise at the news of Lucien's marriage and were almost too polite to her, in a remote and coolly courteous way which suggested to Sarah that Miss Celie, or someone, had also told them that she was a Northerner.

That was after the service which Rev read, the dappled

60

sunlight falling upon his face and the book in his hand.

After he closed the book the Negroes, standing in the background, sang spontaneously and very low, "Swing low, sweet chariot—coming for to carry me home . . ."

It was the first time Sarah had heard the music of Negro voices; the low, beautiful harmony was indescribably moving, as if they were not mourning for Emile but for all the sorrow in the heavily laden world—and promising hope and peace. A mockingbird sang somewhere like a flute accompaniment.

Back at the house the neighbors and family sat in the small French chairs with the mirror over the mantel reflecting them. Rilly and a grizzled old Negro whose name was Uncle Jethro served sherry and small crisp cakes.

She did not distinguish the names of the neighbors, even when she was introduced to them. Their talk was sympathetic but mainly they were frightened and angry. "I wish you'd caught them and strung them up," one old gentlemen said, his white beard jerking with fury.

"Our place is so isolated," a woman they called Miss Kate said wearily.

There were no tears and no protestations of grief for Emile, for which Sarah respected her newly acquired family. Family ties are deep and strong, mysterious in their power, yet no one even pretended to grieve for Emile.

She wondered once how the news of Emile's death had gone so swiftly over the countryside. The little group of neighbors went away in buggies, or riding horses which had been hitched in front of the house.

She did fasten in her mind the name of the last man to leave, for Rev addressed him as Dr. Raymond and thanked him. "Is there anything else we should do?" Rev asked.

"No, no. Sorry it happened like this. Reckon we have to expect it." He was old too, white-haired, and wore square, steel-rimmed spectacles with thick lenses. He bowed to Sarah, got into his buggy, put a battered white Panama hat on his head, and jogged off along the driveway.

"He's the coroner," Rev told her. "That is, he's the acting coroner. The real coroner is in the army."

"The coroner! Why?"

For a swift second it occurred to her that Rev, too, had an ugly doubt as to the manner of Emile's murder. But he said, meeting her eyes quickly and directly, that he had sent a messenger to Dr. Raymond early that morning. "Reckon the boy stopped along the way and told Miss Kate and Grandpa Fant. I had to let the coroner know Emile was killed. It's the law. We couldn't wait long for the services, not in this kind of weather and in these days. Sarah, get out of that hot dress and come to the office. There are things you'll have to learn about the place. The office is right opposite the kitchen. Along the path to the slave quarters. You'll see it."

Later she guessed that Rev chose this hour and this day to launch her upon her new and in fact unexpected duties in order to distract her mind from Emile's murder. At the time she was only thankful that he had given her something to do.

In the dining room Maude and Lolotte were busy replacing some silver on the sideboards.

Miss Celie was whisking around in the parlor, brushing crumbs into a napkin.

Sarah changed into her thin, cool dress and went out to the office, a low whitewashed building with a chimney, which snuggled below the oaks and was covered with trumpet vines whose red-orange bells like everything else were in full bloom.

It was a single room, shaded by the oaks and the vines outside. There was the black, smoke-stained gulf of the fireplace, several pine chairs, a long table and a big cherry-wood cupboard. Its doors were open so she could see that it was stuffed with papers and ledgers.

Rev limped across to pull out a chair for her. "You see," he said, "I'll be leaving soon. George is going back to the army as soon as he can. Ben has been helping out here, but he hopes that he'll get some kind of post in the commissary—he's got a weak heart so he hasn't gone into the army. The point is you'll have to see to things."

She sat down, appalled. "But I don't know anything about cotton or farming or—"

"You'll have to learn."

"But—but Lucien will come home."

"Not to stay. Now then, we keep our records in this cupboard—"

"Rev, I can't!"

He gave her a straight look. "All over the South women are working farms and plantations. Plowing, chopping out cotton, picking cotton—swilling hogs, hoeing corn, doing anything that must be done. Honotassa's life or death will be in your hands. . . . You're going to need that gold of yours. What did you do with it last night?"

"I—left it where it was, in the armoire."

He was already turning toward the cupboard; he stopped, his black head up as if he were listening. The little room was perfectly still; off in the distance she heard the creak of wagon wheels, the soft murmur of Negro voices, birds murmuring lazily in the noonday heat, but there was nothing to hear in the office but her own thoughts, racing again along the course which she had forbidden herself to pursue.

Rev turned around at last. His eyes were hard and he knew exactly what she was thinking. "There was a cartridge from a Spencer carbine. Yankee cavalrymen carry Spencers. It's true," he lifted his shoulders a little, holding her with his eyes, "anybody could own a Spencer—pick it up on some battlefield. But nobody at Honotassa owns a Spencer." He added carelessly, as if as an afterthought, "I gave the cartridge to the coroner."

The point was, and she knew it, that whatever Rev believed or didn't believe about Emile's murder he didn't intend to do anything about it. He was also coldly and unmistakably forbidding any action, any speculation, anything at all on her part.

Anybody could own a Spencer carbine, anybody could pick it up, and anybody could use it. Rev himself.

A smile hovered suddenly around his lips and again he answered her thoughts. "I could have beat the daylights out of Emile but I wouldn't have wasted a bullet on him."

A whole army of invisible yet powerful taboos seemed to range themselves around Sarah. A catbird gave its hoarse squawk outside the window. She linked her hands together and the wide wedding ring gleamed. Rev was waiting, watching her. She said, "Show me what I have to learn."

CHAPTER SEVEN

The April days slid rapidly toward May and Sarah had never worked so hard in her life. When she wasn't in the office, poring over records as Rev explained the entries, or trudging with him through sheds, the blacksmith shop, the carpenter shop, stables, she was with Miss Celie, learning housekeeping, which on a plantation was itself a full-time job. "I'm getting old," Miss Celie whispered. "You are Lucien's wife. It's your place." She looked worriedly at Sarah. "Good heavens, child, is that your only dress?"

It was the third day after Emile's death, and Sarah's lack of dresses was already a minor but an exasperating problem. There was clearly no way of getting her trunks from New Orleans; she wondered now and then what had happened to them. But her green and blue lawn was washed and ironed, and washed and ironed and still was only briefly crisp and fresh. Miss Celie shook her head, gathered up a yellow poplin dress of Maude's and a faded but mended pink muslin of Lolotte's and brought them to Sarah. And she and Miss Celie, Maude and Lolotte came very close to a friendly, woman-to-woman talk.

"But they can't spare these," Sarah said.

"That lawn dress of yours is going to be in rags one of these days." Miss Celie eyed it with a spark of interest in her dark eyes. "Here are some hoops, too. I notice that that dress of yours doesn't require hoops. Are hoops going out of fashion?"

"No. But this dress of mine—the Paris designer was just bringing in this skirt. He thinks it's the coming fashion."

Miss Celie trundled to the door. "Maude—Lolotte . . ." she called down the drowsy, afternoon-lighted hall. "Sarah's going to tell us about the new Paris fashions."

She came back. "We haven't had so much as a glimpse of a fashion magazine for—oh, I don't know how long."

It was, even for Lolotte, irresistible feminine bait. She and Maude came; they and Miss Celie sat around in Sarah's room on the bed, on the stiff sofa, asking questions like girls. They, too, Sarah realized then, had eyed her one dress with keen but withheld curiosity.

Yes, she told them, ladies still wore hoops, enormous hoops, with skirts draped up to show vast petticoats, but there was a new and daring mode just coming in and her dress was an example of it; the skirts were draped up from the front to a huge pouf in the back, and one dress she had seen in the salon had had a big bunch of silk roses fastened to the pouf—it was a ball gown, ivory silk, and the roses were pink.

Lolotte's eyes glistened; for once her long eyelashes were wide open.

"No more bishops?" Maude asked.

"Bishops?"

"You know: that little pad just below your waist in the back."

"Oh, no. The material of the dress makes the pouf."

"Pantalets?" Miss Celie asked in her husky, yet penetrating whisper and Sarah told her no, pantalets had gone out.

"A silly fashion anyway," Maude said. "But I must say I like hoops."

Lolotte gave her a sliding glance; Maude was wearing a wrapper and her solid hips and thighs looked bigger and more solid below its betraying folds. Miss Celie said flatly, "They suit your figure, Maude."

"I'd never have caught a beau if it hadn't been for hoops." There was a sparkle of frank mirth in Maude's cold eyes.

Miss Celie gave a whispering chuckle. Lolotte's lovely little face took on one of its swiftly sullen expressions. "Oh, you made your market before the war," she cried. "What about the rest of us! All the men gone to war or—getting caught by some Yankee woman with money—"

"Oh, stop it, Lolotte," Maude said. "What's done is done. The way you do your hair, Cousin Sarah—is that a new style, too?"

"They're wearing it high, off the ears, but usually with curls at the back."

"Rev said you'd been in London. Did you see the Queen?" Maude's Roman nose thrust forward avidly.

"Yes. Once."

"What's she like? What was she wearing?"

"She was wearing black, heavy mourning, a little widow's cap. She's small and plump with full eyes that seem to go right through you."

Maude's eyes pinned Sarah. "Do you mean you were presented to the Queen?"

"Oh, no. That is—well, yes, in a way but not at court. I expect Rev told you my father had business in London." He had; there wasn't a flicker of question in any of the faces around her. She wondered whether or not Rev had told them that that business had to do with English foundries and new English methods of production. She felt that he had not. She went on. "The Queen somehow heard that I was with him. I think she knows everything that goes on. The Queen wished to talk to my father and she sent word that I was to come with him. That was all."

"But she spoke to you?" Maude asked.

Sarah laughed. "Honestly, I don't know. I was making my curtsy and afraid I'd fall."

There was a rather pleased silence on the part of Miss Celie and Maude. With a little wry amusement, Sarah followed the course of their thoughts; this new wife of Lucien's might be a Yankee, still she had been presented to the Queen.

Lolotte said, "When is England coming in on our side?"

"Never—" Sarah began and stopped. England never backs the losing side, her father had said. She couldn't tell them that. She said quickly, "My father said that no woman wants war. No woman wants to waste lives and money, certainly not Victoria. He said, too—well, he said that it wouldn't be a good thing for the South or the North if England got into the war because"—she saw she was getting into deep water but went on—"because England, France, any country coming to the aid of the South would expect to get paid. If, in the end, England's assistance would mean an English colony in the South, Canada in the North and the United States sandwiched in between—"

Maude's nose looked a good inch longer. "You are assuming that the North will win. You're wrong. Why, with England we'd lick the Yankees!"

Lolotte's eyes flashed. "Without England we'll lick them!"

Miss Celie whispered, "They say it's slavery the Queen hates. Yet the English—"

Maude picked it up. "Yes! Look at England's record. That uprising in Delhi—"

Miss Celie rose and her black silk rustled out of the room.

Lolotte said to Maude, "You shouldn't have said that. You know—"

"She'll get over it," Maude said coldly and turned again to Sarah. "I reckon your father told the Queen the North was going to win."

"I don't know what he said. I was taken to another room, all red plush and gold, and waited."

Still no one mentioned the foundries and the rolling mill. But the friendly, gossipy atmosphere was gone. Lolotte said, "You must have all sorts of Paris finery in those trunks of yours in New Orleans."

"Not much really," Sarah said. "A few dresses for the opera or the ballet. And when I left my father told me to supply myself with clothes."

"You don't need this then." Lolotte suddenly snatched up the faded pink muslin; then she flung it at Sarah. "Yes, go ahead and wear rags! The rest of us are wearing rags. See how you like it."

She flashed out of the room. Sarah disentangled herself from the folds of pink muslin, and almost lost her head and flung the dress back at Lolotte. Luckily Lolotte was gone. Maude said coldly, "She's spoiled. They've all treated her like a baby. But then Lucien—oh, well, pay her no mind. I wonder what's happened to your trunks. Likely some Yankee officer's wife is strutting around in your fancy new dresses!"

Sarah swallowed hard. "I don't think so. I left a note asking the manager of the hotel to send my trunks to Natchez."

"The same thing! There are Yankees there, too! Thieving and looting!"

"Thank you for your dress," Sarah said, exerting more self-control than she would have believed herself capable of.

"You're welcome, I'm sure," Maude said and left, too.

Sarah sat for a long time looking at the two dresses and unexpectedly thinking of Emile. None of those three women could have taken a gun, gone out to the garden and shot Emile. Yet it struck her, too, that in their separate ways each of the three women was formidable. Miss Celie had an authority, a will, and a suggestion of hidden ferocity. Lolotte's weapons were her beauty and her single-minded determination. In Maude there was certainly a cold realism, which might make no more of killing Emile than stepping on a bug. Ten minutes ago they had been chatting together like schoolgirls.

Presently Sarah started to put on Maude's yellow poplin and then defiantly put on Lolotte's pink muslin instead. It was too short for her; she untied the waist tapes of the hoops Miss Celie had brought her and their absence permitted the skirt to fall lower around the black slippers Calista had swiftly selected; the thin soles, she saw regretfully, were already wearing through. To her surprise the pink muslin was becoming; she had always been told she couldn't wear pink, not with that red hair.

The next day Miss Celie resumed Sarah's housekeeping instructions. There was the kitchen, the sewing room, the stores of linen. "The linens are greatly depleted. We've sent as much as we can to the hospitals. Any cotton or linen materials we can possibly spare go for bandages."

There was the smokehouse, the storehouse; there was the wellhouse, shaded with vines and cool, its dusky interior smelling faintly of sour milk, its shelves laden with milk and butter and clabber. Miss Celie told her of substitutes and makeshifts which the shortage of supplies made necessary; she showed her the "Doctor's Book," a shabby, leather-covered book with entries made in pale brown ink. Some of the early entries were dated in the seventeen hundreds. One of them began: "For the complexion, rose water, lemon juice . . ." Another read: "For scurvy, ten drops of vinegar, repeated . . ." Another: "For dysentery, Rice, beef tea, blackberry wine, blackberry roots steeped . . ." She gave Miss Celie her small store of calomel and quinine. "I had some opium and chloroform, too, but we lost them on the way from New Orleans."

Miss Celie opened the frivolous-looking jars and bottles, sniffed at and tasted the contents, gave Sarah a nod of conspiratorial approval and said that it was right smart of her to bring them in that way, that Sarah would find them useful. Sarah thought, with a wave of panic, so I'm to be doctor, too. Again she attempted a feeble resistance. "Miss Celie, I don't know anything about medicines and—"

"The mistress of the house—" Miss Celie shrugged. "It is the custom."

"Well," Sarah said tartly, "it's a custom that must have killed a good many people!"

A faint quiver, not a smile but like one, crossed Miss Celie's pudding white face. She said, however, "*Cela va sans dire*," and shrugged again.

That goes without saying. Good heavens, Sarah thought, does she mean that, doesn't she care?

Miss Celie put the quinine and calomel on a shelf.

The days were warm and for the most part sunny with more flowers bursting into bloom, and long rows of peas and beans, corn, okra and squash. There was some cotton, too, but as Rev explained to her, not much.

"For one thing, we haven't the field hands we need to work much cotton. Almost every night some of them drift away—some will come back but—" He frowned. "For another reason we've already got too much cotton baled and stored in the sheds. We're too far from Mobile or Wilmington to try to ship it off to Nassau or to England. The Yankees want cotton of course; Memphis and New Orleans are alive with speculators but—"

"Do you mean," she asked astonished, "that there's trade in cotton with the North?"

He gave a short laugh. "You're a baby, Sarah. The North needs cotton, mills are standing idle. The South needs—well, the South needs everything. So Northern speculators are buying cotton—sub rosa—and some Southern planters are selling it. The Northern speculators are making fortunes. Cotton is cheap in the South, high in the North. It's a waste keeping our cotton but I'd rather do that than sell it to a Yankee speculator. Besides—when the war is over cotton will go high. You may get a fantastic price for that cotton in the sheds. Unless the Yankees get it first."

"Here! At Honotassa! Why, Ben says—"

"Ben doesn't know. Nobody knows. If they come they'll either take the cotton and ship it north, or burn it. Cotton takes a long time to burn. You can't put out the fire. Just try to keep it from spreading. If," he said grimly, "there are any men left on the place to help you."

He leaned back in his chair, thoughtfully. "I was one of those who believed that we should send all the cotton we could to England and build up a reserve fund there, before the Yankee blockade closed down. Others put their faith in the power of cotton, the need of English mills. So we held onto our cotton. King Cotton—well, we put too much faith in King Cotton. It hasn't yet brought England or France into the war on our side. We're lucky though, here; we haven't gone hungry. We've still got plenty of food even though the commissary is asking for more and more. We've got hogs, chickens, turkeys, ducks—we can get fish and game. We've still got a few horses and mules and enough cows for milk. We're rich in comparison to some of the plantations and farms in Virginia. But you'll need that gold. Things break and have to be repaired. A mule can die and the price of mules is sky high."

The gold was by then hidden under the floorboards of the office. Rev had come to her one night quietly, after the house was asleep, and transferred it and later showed her where he had taken up planks directly below the long table and replaced them so carefully that they looked as if they had never been disturbed. "The house might be burned," he had told her. "But nobody's likely to bother with this little office." He had warned her, too, a curiously blank look in his face. "It's better not to tell anybody—anybody at all about the gold. Things get around. There's a grapevine. When you use the gold, use only a little at a time. No sense in starting a rumor that you have unlimited quantities of it."

She grew accustomed to the routine of the house. Glendora, the young Negro maid, brought coffee to her room early in the morning when it was still cool. The coffee was a substitute made, Miss Celie had told her, of ground-up nuts, dried peas and chicory, various different concoctions, sweetened with sorghum and on rare occasions sugar.

After breakfast downstairs in the dining room—ham and eggs; waffles and hot corn bread and more coffee—everybody worked. Miss Celie was a meticulous housekeeper; the smallest speck of dust, the slightest smear of tarnish on a silver spoon caught her raisin-dark eyes. She drove Lolotte and Maude as unrelentingly as she drove Rilly and Glendora and cook. Dinner was shortly after midday, after which the ladies retired for naps while the languid, hot afternoon hours drifted toward sunset. Supper was in the evening—after they had gathered for an hour or so on the south porch (which Miss Celie always called the gallery), the women sewing or knitting, never idle, the men lounging and holding tall glasses which were beaded from the coolness of water taken freshly from the well, for there was no ice. The green sprigs of mint in their glasses came from the mint bed, close to the wellhouse; the whiskey, Ben told her, came from a supply of good Kentucky bourbon he had contrived to bring from Natchez.

After supper they lingered on the porch again unless there was a south wind which brought mosquitoes. When that happened they sat in the parlor—and the women sewed and knitted. Miss Celie soon gave Sarah a big basket of mending, which somehow was renewed every day, and one of her precious store of needles.

They went to bed early. Rev and George usually made a kind of tour outside, carrying lanterns, satisfying themselves that all was well; yet, not every morning but often, there were one or two fewer people in the quarters.

Ben suggested keeping watch with a gun. Reverdy said no, those who were determined to leave would leave, there was no stopping it. Probably many of them headed straight for New Orleans; perhaps some tried to cross the river to Grant's army. Rev added, rather wearily, that it made that many

70

mouths less to feed.

He was troubled by it though. Once he showed Sarah the records of the slaves born, bought and sold; there were their dates of birth or purchase, the dates of death or sale. She thought she was prepared for it; but in fact the records, in black and white, of selling and trading men and women seemed to epitomize the whole sin of slavery. She only glanced at the book.

At the same time she had seen enough of the world to know that slave labor existed in far too much of that world. She thought of the miners in England—and in Pennsylvania. At Honotassa at least, the aged were cared for, the children were treated with indulgent kindness.

It was another thing she could do nothing about.

Day after day passed and Lucien did not return.

CHAPTER EIGHT

Gradually, by one almost imperceptible sign and then another, she began to believe that not only Rev but others in the house knew or refused to know, or only suspected something of the true manner of Emile's murder. Sometimes, too, Sarah was almost convinced that her own secret conjecture was wrong.

And then something would happen, some word would be spoken, some swift, half-communicative glance would be as swiftly broken. The indications were so slight that afterward Sarah could not be sure that they were indications.

If anyone spoke of Emile it was clearly inadvertent, and the conversation was swiftly turned. That alone, she thought, indicated doubts—or did it?

Once Ben questioned Rev minutely about the Spencer cartridge—where had he found it, when, was he sure that it was a Spencer? Miss Celie's busy white hands stopped dead still, her needle poised in the air. Lolotte's palmetto fan checked itself. Rev said easily that of course it was a Spencer cartridge; it was so marked. He added, looking lazily out over the garden, that it had been in the circle around the cupid the night Emile was shot.

If it was a lie, it was a convincing one. Miss Celie's needle began to flash again and Lolotte's fan stirred. Ben said that

71

he had thought of riding in to Maville the next day; there might be some mail.

There was never anything definite, anything Sarah could pin down and say to herself, yes, that's proof: they know that Emile was murdered and they know that someone here— someone in this house—killed him.

No Yankee raiding party, no straggling band of looters or thugs returned to Honotassa. One day the portrait of Rev's and Lucien's father was again hanging on the wall between his two young wives.

The small, glittering bijouterie in enamel, porcelain, silver-gilt returned to the big breakfront case in the parlor.

Gradually, too, Sarah began to observe slumbering little family feuds and not so slumbering idiosyncrasies. Maude and Miss Celie made no bones of what seemed to be not only a natural antipathy but a deep-seated mutual grudge. The antipathy was natural because they were both strong and authoritative and consequently clashed over a hundred small household decisions in a day. The grudge, she discovered, dated back to Miss Celie's opinion of Maude's father, which Miss Celie at some time or other appeared to have most eloquently expressed.

She discovered that Ben was almost obsessed by figures; he would spend hours calculating the proceeds he would have had that year, the next year, any year from his sugar plantation in Louisiana. Lolotte was as confiding as a kitten at one moment; she would snuggle against Miss Celie, or George, or Reverdy, who patted her little dark head absently. The next moment Lolotte could fly out with the claws of a beautiful young tiger, almost as reckless and savage, not caring what or whom she clawed. Everybody waited till the storm had passed and then indulgently Miss Celie would say, "There, there, *ma petite*." Ben might grunt but could not resist Lolotte if she kneeled down beside his chair and looked over his long columns of figures.

Many of Lolotte's flashes of anger were aimed at Sarah but they were only flashes—expressions, Sarah believed, not so much of hatred or even jealousy as of hurt pride.

George had two obsessions; he wore a gun at all times and spent much of his time cleaning and polishing it, holding it between his knees and working away with one hand. His other obsession was Lucien and when he talked of Lucien, which was often, his pale eyes went to Sarah. He never said,

"You're not good enough for Lucien." He didn't need to say it.

Once Maude laughed. "The way you talk about Lucien, George, you'd think he was a prince."

"Well, he is," George said, working lovingly at his pistol. "There was a time when you—" He stopped. Maude gave a cold little laugh. "A time when I thought so, too? But I was very young then, George. That was before I met Ben and set my cap for him."

Ben grunted. "You set your cap for my money and got it, too," he said, but good-humoredly, even a little proud.

Sarah thought, with a touch of dismay, another woman in love with Lucien? Maude said, "If the Yankees don't strip us of every penny— But Lucien's settled down, married, the head of the house, so don't get your dander up, George. Everybody knows you think the sun rises and sets in Lucien. I do wish we could get hold of some newspapers and find out what's happening in the world. Did you hear any news in Maville today, Ben?"

Ben made occasional trips to Maville; usually he came back with news but there was rarely any mail and no letter from Lucien. In a way the long hours of work made the days of waiting easier for Sarah. Every night she told herself that the next day, or the next, Lucien would come. Rev told her firmly that Lucien was safe, wherever he was; if anything had gone wrong they would have heard from his commanding officer.

Maude once said tartly, "Stars alive, Cousin Sarah, Lucien's too smart to let himself get a Yankee bullet. . . . Besides if he has to come home by blockade runner there's no telling where he's gone or how soon he can get home. . . . Will you turn the heel of this sock for me? Somehow I can't get the hang of it." It was lucky, Sarah thought, that Granny Salter had taught her to knit.

Whenever Ben went to Maville his news was awaited eagerly and talked over endlessly. Sometime past the middle of April, Ben came home with rumors that there was action of some kind in the northeast part of the state; nobody knew just what, but the talk was that it was a Yankee cavalry brigade. George said with finality that they couldn't get far; General Pemberton would send somebody to stop them. Besides General Ruggles had a force guarding the railroad up there, the Mobile and Ohio; nobody could get past him. Rev

73

listened, questioned Ben, who could tell them no more, and sat for a long time, looking out at the blue shadows of the evening in silence.

Nobody visited the garden. That, too, seemed to Sarah to have some kind of significance, especially when Miss Celie said airily one day that the garden, even her Empress Josephines, needed no care and the crops did need it; they couldn't spare hands for cultivating roses.

From Sarah's window she was always aware of the black points of the cedars rising somberly above the green hedge. The hedges themselves grew tall and lush; the little brick path leading to the marble cupid was almost hidden with box-wood and ferociously growing honeysuckle. Nobody suggested that they be pruned.

There were days which were so fully absorbed with what seemed to be a perfectly normal and undisturbed routine of life that it was easy, too, for Sarah to put Emile—and his murderer—out of her mind. Those were days which all but denied murder and certainly denied a murderer, walking, talking, sitting at the supper table.

A murderer should show some sign of having crossed the forbidden barrier civilization has set up. Perhaps the next day another slight, small hint of murder and shared but secret knowledge of it would show itself, like the faint cat's paw of a pending storm ruffling the yet calm surface of the sea.

It was something more than a cat's paw the evening it developed that Lucien's dueling pistols had disappeared and no one knew or admitted knowing what had happened to them. George brought it up. Having almost regretfully discovered no spot or smear on his own gun, he said, "Where are Lucien's dueling pistols, Rev? I'll clean them, too."

Lolotte's dark eyelashes lifted and dropped.

"I put them in the hall clock the night Emile was shot," Rev replied.

Maude's Romanesque head lifted from her knitting. "They're not there now. Lolotte told me you had put them there and I looked—"

Lolotte snipped the frayed edges of the seams of a dress she was turning. "I looked for them, too. The morning Emile was—the next morning. They were gone then. I thought someone had put them away."

Miss Celie's black dress rustled; she said, "They're not in Lucien's room. We were cleaning it this morning. Usually he

74

kept them on the table by the window."

There was an abrupt silence, almost tangible, as if it could be felt and touched. Then Lolotte put down the dress and said it was getting too dark to sew. Ben said it would be a pity if the pistols were lost but he reckoned they'd turn up somewhere. George got out his own spotless pistol, blew on it and polished.

That night the door of ugly conjecture which Sarah had closed swung wide open. She tossed and turned beneath the ghostly white mosquito bar, tried to remember the sound of the shot which had killed Emile, but there was no possible way she could know whether it came from a Spencer carbine, one of Lucien's pistols, or some other firearm.

Lolotte had had the dueling pistols after the murder. She had come in from the porch, not down the stairs, carrying them. Yet her explanation was given to Rev with a swift, feminine impatience which was convincing. Suppose it was an adroit lie! No, no, she must not put Lolotte's name—anybody's name—to the faceless shape of murder.

A day or so later, on the porch again before supper, George was laboriously learning to write with his left hand, while Lolotte, her dark head bent, sat beside him and steadied the paper. It was a leaf torn from the blank pages of some book, for paper was short in the Confederacy. Maude came out and eyed him coldly. "What's the use of that, Cousin George? You're going back to the army. You can shoot better with your left hand than most men with their right and that's what is important right now."

Lolotte said softly, "Cousin George can shoot mighty straight and fast."

George finished the word he was writing and looked up, his plain face hard. "Reckon I can still get me a Yankee or two."

Ben chuckled and tossed a silver half dollar in the air. "Get that, boy."

Instantly, it seemed to Sarah, there was a shot and the acrid odor of powder drifted across the porch. She looked in astonishment at George who now had his gun in his left hand.

Ben trotted down to get the half dollar and held it up, neatly drilled. "Good work."

"I hope that half dollar is still good," Maude said, sourly. "They're not too plentiful these days."

Was there meaning in it, or was there none? The men began again to talk of Vicksburg.

Sarah had thought so many times of her talk with Emile, late in the afternoon before he was killed, that every word which she could remember was now like the memorized page of a book. Sometimes it seemed to her deeply significant; Emile had attempted to trade upon a bare and empty threat, something his mean little mind had conceived as a way to get money from Sarah. Suppose then he had nosed around and dug out something that was in fact a secret and an ugly secret, which threatened someone so urgently that that person had taken the law and a gun in his own hands and killed Emile.

It seemed a reasonable surmise. What was unreasonable was the existence of such a secret, any secret, in that family which seemed to know everything there was to be known about each other.

Lolotte watched for Lucien's coming. She watched even more intently and constantly than Sarah watched, for Sarah was in the office or about the sheds while Lolotte kept close to the house or strolled down the long driveway to the road. Whenever there were the hoofbeats of horses along the avenue under the oaks, Lolotte was the first to flash to the door.

There were few visitors though. Maude said irritably that people couldn't go visiting as they used to; what horses had not been taken for the army were needed for work. That week Maude got an old-fashioned spinning wheel and a loom down from the attic and after that there was the constant thud-thud of the treadle as Maude, Lolotte, Miss Celie or Rilly took their turns at weaving. Later they dyed the material a muddy walnut stain. Sarah took her turn, too, and thought of the mills in the North turning out hundreds of bolts of good, solid material for uniforms. She began to admire her new relatives, at least for their stubborn courage.

That week, too, Sarah learned with a shattering sense of shock that Honotassa was heavily mortgaged. The discovery came about one morning when she was in the office with Rev and he got out the ledger to mark the fact that during the night past, three more field hands, their wives and children, had simply, quietly disappeared. "That leaves"—he scanned the pages, frowned and said, "just exactly five men to work the fields. We used to have and need over a hundred."

She could see the plantation as it must have been in its full production, the wide fields, the white bolls of cotton which Rev had told her would not mature for picking until fall. She said absently, "But there are still about twenty slaves. Enough for you to be exempt from army service."

He turned to give her a swift, hard look. "Did you think I intended to take advantage of that?"

"No, I—that is, Lucien said—"

He came back to the table, leaning on it. "What did Lucien say?"

"He didn't say it exactly. I only got the impression—and then you—well, I don't see how you can walk far with that leg."

"I can still ride a horse," he said shortly. "Why do you think I've been working you so hard? I told you I'd be leaving soon."

"You still limp from your accident . . ."

"That was no accident. I was fool enough to get in the way of a Yankee Minié ball at Sharpsburg."

Stupid, stupid, Sarah cried in her heart, where were her wits? She felt her face grow pink. She said "Sharpsburg?" in a small, shamed voice.

"I reckon you read the Yankee newspapers. They called it Antietam. God knows why. Sharpsburg is a town. Antietam is a creek nearby. The Yankees called Manassas Bull Run, too. They seem to have an affection for the names of creeks. . . . I was carted off and had the good luck to wind up in Miss Sally Tompkins' hospital in Richmond. Damn near lost my leg. Actually I think creosote saved it."

"Creosote!"

"They kept water dripping on my leg, creosote in the water. I got out in time for the fracas at Fredericksburg in December." He went to the cupboard and put away the ledger. "That was a bloody fracas too, but it was worse for the Yankees than for us. They say that General Lee and Old Jack were purring like kittens when they saw the point of attack Burnside chose." He came back and sat on the edge of the table, his gaze drifting out the vinelaced window as if he saw something very far away.

"Old Jack?"

He gave her an astonished look. "Stonewall Jackson. The Yankees certainly know that name."

"Oh, yes . . . And after that . . . ?"

"After Fredericksburg my leg began to kick up again." He grinned. "And I don't mean a bad pun. I went back into the hospital. Was given a furlough this spring and came home."

She thought that over. Lucien was certainly wrong somewhere in his estimate of Rev's fighting courage. She said suddenly, "Why, they really could have hung you that night in New Orleans. You weren't in uniform."

"I told you it was dangerous," he said with another grin.

"But why did you take such a chance?" she asked sharply, and remembered that she had asked that question before.

She received the same answer. He looked out the window again for a moment, his face blank, and then said, curtly, "Business."

"What business—" she began and Rev got off the table and stood with his hands shoved in his pockets.

"Something I had to do," he said shortly.

She couldn't probe further against the smooth blankness in his face. "Well, you nearly were caught," she said. "The Union officer—or whoever it was who came to the hotel—"

"That was no Union officer. That was a New Orleans banker. He lives at the St. Charles Hotel now; he's hoping to get his Louisiana place back from the Yankees. He'd have seen your name if he looked or questioned the clerk. He'd have insisted on seeing you. And if he saw me—"

"But he wouldn't have reported you!"

"This one would. For one reason he has prudently turned Yankee. For another reason he holds the mortgages on Honotassa."

"Mortgages!" To her New England bred mind, a mortgage was a devil with horns and a tail.

He gave her a serious, rather troubled look and said, but lightly, "I told you we needed your gold at Honotassa."

"Why—Lucien owns Honotassa! Who borrowed money on mortgages? Who had the right to—"

He broke in. "Don't look so scared! Everything mortgageable in the South is mortgaged to the hilt. So is Honotassa."

"Lucien didn't tell me," she said slowly.

Rev went to the door and stood for a moment, his back turned toward her. "Men don't like to talk business with their women. Lucien will explain it to you when he gets here. And when Lucien comes," he said softly, almost to himself, "I can leave."

CHAPTER NINE

There was something in his voice which caught her attention, yet if there was a subtle meaning she could not analyze it. Her heart sank though; when Rev left and then Lucien, too, returned to the army, she would have not only the responsibility for Honotassa but a mortgage to deal with. She said, "I want to know now. Why was Honotassa mortgaged? It's a rich plantation . . ."

"It *was* a rich plantation. Times now are bad."

"Well, but—then the New Orleans banker can't foreclose, he can't force us to pay interest, he can't do anything till the war is over and then—"

"And then what?"

"Why, then I can get my father's money and pay the mortgage."

"You are so sure that the North will win."

She was sure; she bit back the words but Rev came back to sit on the edge of the table.

"Sarah, you're happy here, aren't you?"

"Yes. Oh, yes! That is—" She looked away from his direct and too observant dark eyes, down at her hands on the table, with her wide wedding ring catching a golden gleam. "I'd like to be sure that Lucien is safe. I wish he'd come."

"Yes. Of course. He'll come. Times like these—but he'll come. You do like Honotassa, though."

She looked up and he was smiling.

"I love Honotassa."

"Yes, I thought so. In spite of—" He checked himself.

"In spite of Emile?" she said.

But instantly the blank, cold look of reserve came into his face. It was like a barrier, forbidding her to go further.

She closed that inner door of suspicion which had given itself an unnerving little jar.

"This New Orleans banker. It wouldn't have been of any help to him to get you arrested or—hanged."

"It would have done his soul some good," Rev said dryly. "Actually he'd have expected me to tell him just what Lucien is going to do about the money and when. It seemed a good idea for me to avoid so much as a word from him—

and save my neck. So I posted old Jules Lamoreux to warn me. If he'd found me there, with the place jam-packed with Yankees, I'd have been in jail before you could have given me a farewell kiss." There was a dancing, teasing light in his eyes.

She laughed. She had now no sense of embarrassment at the memory of her rush to Lucien's arms, which had proved to be Rev's arms. "You should have taken that kiss when you had a chance. . . . What did Lucien do with the money he had to borrow?"

He rose and ended their talk. "I'm trying to teach that Yankee horse to pull a plow. Don't worry about the mortgages. There's nothing that can be done now."

After he had gone, she went to the cupboard and got out the big, shabby record of accounts. She searched through columns of figures dating back three years. She found no record of a loan of any kind and no records of any interest payments.

She returned the ledger at last, hot and tired, her eyes aching from following the long rows of inked-in figures.

She believed Rev. Yet if Lucien had borrowed money, so much money, she thought with dismay, what had he done with it?

It stayed in her mind, it hovered like a shadow, another unanswerable question, until George unwittingly gave the answer. Lucien had bought Confederate bonds.

The men were talking, always talking of the war and George said, sighing. "God knows the Confederacy needs money. But I used every cent I could beg or borrow to buy bonds long ago. Just as Lucien did."

It was like Lucien. Where were her wits? Sarah thought again. Privately, very privately, she felt that the bonds were likely to be of no more value than so much wastepaper.

The days went on and wrapped Sarah in a kind of cocoon; it was easier and easier to forget Emile's murder for long periods at a time.

It was harder though to wait for Lucien; she had been at Honotassa in fact only two, not quite three weeks. It seemed much longer.

The lingering flame of the azaleas had vanished so gently that she did not perceive its departure. The long purple clusters of wisteria had gone. The roses were rampant now; the honeysuckle overran the place; the vines grew savagely over the wellhouse and the office. There were rains as April drew on to its close. Some were such drenching downpours that the men could not plow and the great trees tossed and murmured as if they had gathered some disastrous news from afar and communicated it to each other. Actually there was no news although once Grandpa Fant came to waggle his white beard over a julep and say that the story was true that a Union cavalry force was loose somewhere in the northern part of the state. He didn't know where.

Ben looked serious. George said that General Ruggles would send them skedaddling, or even Colonel Wirt Adams, if they did get very far.

"Colonel Adams is stationed at Port Gibson," Rev said. "If the Yanks attack Grand Gulf, they'll need him there."

Grandpa Fant said he'd heard that General Pemberton was in Jackson, trying to head off the Yankee cavalry. "Can't seem to pin 'em down," he said angrily. "Looks like somebody could find out where they are. Story is they shot up Starkville the other day."

George gave Rev a startled look. "Starkville!"

"If they're making for the line of the Southern Railroad, there's a good chance to cut them off," Rev said.

"But Rev—the Southern, straight across the state from Meridian through Jackson to Vicksburg! Why, if they get as far as that railroad, they can cut off supplies to Vicksburg!"

"Let's hope Pemberton can stop them."

But after that, Rev and Ben, too, wore guns in their belts; and it seemed to Sarah that Rev was up earlier and worked later.

Owing to the rains Ben did not ride in to Maville once that week.

One day, during the last week in April, Sarah rode with Rev over the entire plantation. She wore her hot black riding habit and a sunbonnet which Miss Celie had forced upon her. "I declare you'll ruin your complexion, running around in the sun. Now wear it, you hear?"

Sarah hadn't the courage to refuse. She caught a gleam of laughter in Rev's eyes and it suddenly occurred to her that it had been a long time since she had caught just that laughing glance.

In some indefinable way Rev had changed. She thought of it soberly as they took the path through the slave quarters. The change in Rev didn't date from Emile's death. It didn't date from any particular time. He was friendly, hard-work-

81

ing, absorbed in doing everything possible that he could do to get the plantation in good working order before his departure. Yet there was a change.

She rode Vampa again but that day with a sidesaddle, which Rev told her belonged to Lolotte. Rev himself rode the horse he had stolen in New Orleans, a big-boned bay, whom they called Rufe; he was too wide between the eyes and, like Maude, he had a stubborn Roman nose; his huge bones had none of Vampa's fine, beautiful lines; he really wasn't very bright, as Rev had said, but he was good-natured and, as a matter of fact, seemed in an odd way interested in his new life. He moved over to poke Sarah's knee demandingly and took the slice of dried apple she gave him with smacking pleasure. She had another slice for Vampa, who took it, but nonchalantly as if it were only his due. Men were hoeing in the fields. Rev pointed out a patch of low-lying bottom land. "It's rich land but tricky. There's a little run in the swamp over there. Sometimes the bottom land floods."

The swamp land was a deep, blackish green with vines interlacing the trees. It looked a little threatening. "If you ever go down there, look out for snakes," Rev said.

They circled the fields and Rev stopped to speak to Stash, who was working on a fence which needed repair. "You'd better start off with the wagon before dawn. It's a right smart piece."

"Yes, Mist' Rev. We'll load tonight."

"Some men from the commissary were here this morning," Rev told her as they rode on. "It was early. Reckon you weren't awake. They took what they could and I promised to send a wagonload of supplies tomorrow to their headquarters, the other side of Maville." He eyed the green fields, frowning. "Reckon we shouldn't have put in any cotton this year. They're going to need food at Vicksburg. You'll need food here, too. Don't strip yourself of livestock and food, Sarah—but let the commissary have all you can. Not that they'll wait to ask for it. Over that way is the spring."

They rode toward another patch of green and he told her that it was the spring from which Honotassa derived its name. "It was an old Indian spring. We're not far from one of their main-traveled roads."

Trees surrounded the spring and two men were working there, too, building a rail fence. Rev hailed one of them and he brought a gourd of spring water for Sarah. It had a brackish taste. She handed it back and Rev laughed a little at her wry face. "What Indians?" she asked.

"Chickasaws and Choctaws mainly . . . Sarah, that fence the men are building back in the trees is for livestock. If the Yankees should come this way they'll want horses—cows, hogs, everything, but mainly horses and mules. They'll look in the barns and then, most likely, down in the swamp because it's nearer the house. If you have any warning of it, try to get the livestock up in those trees around the spring. They'll be hidden there and it's so far from the house the Yanks may miss them. A good mule costs a couple thousand dollars—if you can find a good mule."

He turned the horses along a wagon trail that led up a slight rise and into a stretch of thin, scraggly pines. "There's nothing you can do about this streak of piney woods," he told her. "Only try to keep the seedlings from spreading to the fields. They'll take over everything if you let them. Another thing, maybe Miss Celie told you—salt is a problem. Use it sparingly."

She had already noted the scarcity of salt. The dishes Glendora served up were flavored ingeniously with onion, garlic, herbs, but beneath that there was a perceptible flatness. Rev said as they went on, "Everybody's short of salt. The army needs it, you'll need it. There were some salt licks in Northern Mississippi but by the time the commissary men got there the salt licks were just about exhausted."

"Rev," she said suddenly, "you always say that *I'll* need this or that. *I* must remember this or that. Miss Celie will be here and Maude and Lolotte. They know about all these things."

"You are Lucien's wife," he said flatly. "It's your place to see to things. Besides, Maude is a cousin but she's a visitor. Honotassa is not her home. Lolotte—well, Lolotte is a child. We've all indulged her, too much perhaps. Miss Celie—sometimes Miss Celie—oh, she gets the vapors. I can trust you, Sarah. You have a sense of responsibility."

It wasn't a compliment said like that, dryly and impersonally, yet it *was* a compliment and touched off a warm glow somewhere inside her.

"What do you mean by the vapors?" she asked presently.

"Oh, nothing much. We just call it the vapors. Bear with her."

The sunbonnet ties rasped her chin starchily as she gave

him a swift look. "You don't mean she goes out of her head!"

"Oh, Lord, no." He laughed and then sobered. "It's really nothing, Sarah. She gets over it. There's a bridle path this way."

They circled the piney woods and checked the horses for a moment on a slight rise from which they could look down at Honotassa. The house with its great chimneys, the avenue of water oaks, the rambling whitewashed barns and cabins, the hedged garden, were all spread out below them, clear in the soft light like a picture. She could see the black points of the cedars around the marble cupid.

She didn't look at Rev but somehow she was sure that he was looking at that sinister, pointed black circle, too.

The door of conjecture, the door of suspicion, which it had been so easy during the past days to keep closed, gave itself a kind of tremor. Had murder walked along those green, vinemasked paths below? Did murder dwell now within the serene and gracious house? She said, "Rev, who killed him?"

There was a long pause. When at last she looked at him his face was as blank as a stone wall and he *was* looking down at the sinister dark circle. "There was a Yankee cartridge."

He wasn't going to talk; she was rebuffed again by that stone wall. She looked down at Vampa's head; she smoothed the skirt of her riding habit. Rev's horse moved closer. He put his hand over hers. "Sarah, I didn't mean to hurt you. All right, I had the Yankee cartridge in my knapsack. I'd picked it up just for curiosity somewhere in Virginia. I gave it to the coroner."

"*Why?*"

"Because I thought it was best. I still think so."

"So it was murder."

"It might have been some looter, some—"

"No. You're shielding somebody."

His hand tightened. "I don't know. I'm not certain but if I am, believe me it's better this way."

"Better to shield a murderer!"

He didn't answer. After a moment she said, "Was there any cartridge?"

"No. That's why—you see, Lucien's dueling pistols don't require cartridges. They're French made, made to order as a matter of fact by Gartinne Renette—"

"You took the pistols! You hid them!"

"Late that night I took them out of the clock. One of them had been fired recently. I cleaned it and hid both pistols. Then I hunted out the Spencer cartridge and handed it over to the coroner in the morning."

"Then—then whoever shot Emile did it with that pistol so it was someone who knew of the pistols, who was in the house, who could—"

"Don't go so fast. The pistol had been fired. We heard only one shot that night and it was a quiet night. But that is still not proof that the shot that killed Emile came from that pistol. The pistol could have been fired sometime during the day, away from the house so that no one heard it."

"You said it had been fired recently. Couldn't you tell how recently?"

"Not—that precisely."

"You believe the shot came from that gun! Otherwise you wouldn't have hidden it. Lolotte said she took the case from Lucien's room."

"She may have been telling the truth."

"Then whoever shot him had to get the pistol back into the house, into Lucien's room, after Emile was killed. Only somebody here, somebody who wouldn't be questioned could have done that."

"On the other hand Lolotte may have been lying. She may have found the case somewhere outside."

She thought that over, sorting out the implications. "Do you mean that Lolotte suspected murder right away, thought of the pistols and went to look for them? She couldn't have just happened to find them. If she searched for them and found them, then she knows or suspects—"

His hand lifted abruptly from her own. "Sarah, all of us suspect. You've seen that."

"Haven't you asked Lolotte? Haven't you questioned her?"

"Lolotte! As well try to push back the sea."

"Rev, you must tell me. Who killed him?"

"I have told you. I don't know."

"There's got to be a reason for murder. Why was he shot?"

"I don't know that either. I told you to forget Emile."

Suddenly his face and his voice were hard. But then he pulled up Rufe's head and said in the indulgent tone he always used with animals, "Don't eat that Jimson weed, you crazy fool. Do you want to have colic?"

Sarah took off her sunbonnet and pushed back the damp curls around her forehead.

He gave her a long look. "Sarah, it's best not to question. No, don't ask me why."

So the door was firmly closed again, this time by Rev. "There's no use hitting my head against a stone wall," she said.

A remote gleam of laughter came into his eyes. "None at all. Shall we go on?"

Well, she thought, she'd already been sure that Rev believed it was murder; she'd already doubted the story of the Spencer carbine cartridge. She'd had some uneasy doubts about the disappearance of the dueling pistols. So in spite of getting up the courage to try to break through Rev's silence, she really knew no more than she already suspected.

She said, presently, "Why did you tell me that much?"

"Because I knew that you had some idea of the truth. Your windows are on the garden side. If there'd been anything to hear, you'd have heard it—"

She broke in, "I didn't hear anything. That's one reason—"

"That's one reason why you didn't believe in a Yankee raiding party. Sarah, I don't believe that there's any danger to anybody, now. But a murderer is scared. So don't invite danger."

"Why, do you mean—you can't mean that anybody would—" She caught her breath and cried, "Nobody would murder *me!*"

"I didn't say that. I only said, don't question."

The horses' hoofs thumped slowly along. Vampa shook his head irritably and Sarah leaned forward to brush away a little cloud of gnats around his ears. "And let a murderer go unhung!"

They were approaching the long avenue of oaks. The sun was lower. The shadow of the great oaks fell over Rev's face —that or some other shadow.

"Yes," he said. "Yes."

The horses passed between two of the oaks; the hugely spreading boughs arched far above. A swinging wisp of Spanish moss touched Sarah's face, almost like a warning finger. Unconsciously she gripped the reins so hard that Vampa stopped.

Rev's horse paused, too. The house stood at the end of the avenue, lovely and tranquil in the evening light.

Rev said, looking at the house, quietly, "It's worth fighting for—" and stopped with a quick-drawn breath.

She followed his look and then saw, silhouetted against the glossy greens of a magnolia near the steps, a man and a woman locked in each other's arms.

Rev shouted, "Lucien!" and spurred Rufe so the horse plunged toward the house and shut off Sarah's view of the two figures, like a picture posed against the magnolias.

CHAPTER TEN

She clung to the saddle, for Vampa was galloping along the driveway, almost unseating her. By the time she reached the house she was breathless, and Lucien came, laughing, to hold up his arms. He caught her as she slid down, held her, kissed her vigorously and then George and Aunt Celie, Maude and Ben and the house servants all streamed out to meet him.

It was a moment she had longed for, it had built up in her fancy, she had all but dreamed of it; so naturally it was not like the moment her fancy had supplied.

She stood in her hot broadcloth riding habit, pushing up her disheveled hair, and watched, and all at once felt detached, like an observer, apart from everyone else. Was what she had seen back there by the magnolias true? Considering the girl's story, how did Lucien feel about Lolotte? And for that matter, how did Lucien feel about Sarah, his wife, now? She saw Rilly go back into the house without speaking to Lucien. She caught the flash of Glendora's grin. She saw Uncle Jethro hobbling around the magnolias. She saw George's face glowing and lighted as he pounded Lucien on the back.

Lolotte's face was aglow, too, and very beautiful.

They went into the house. They sat and lounged and talked on the porch. Somebody brought mint juleps. Somebody shouted to a stable boy to take care of Lucien's horse. Sarah was still an observer.

Lolotte knelt on the floor beside Lucien, her wide skirts spreading out like a flower, her lovely face tilted up toward him, like a flower, too. George's pale eyes were shining. Lucien talked, he answered questions, his handsome face was laughing, full of charm which Sarah remembered—and still did not remember.

Lucien had been in Richmond. But first he had been in Nassau. "We got into a little trouble with a Yankee gunboat, after we left Cuba. The Captain decided it was safer to run for Nassau. So go to Nassau we did and it was weeks before I could get on another blockade runner, headed for Wilmington. Finally I got to Richmond—when I left there I had to come home the long way around. I didn't know, nobody knew exactly, the railroad situation in Tennessee. So I finally got to Mobile—left the cars at Pond Bridge, managed to buy that bag of bones I rode home—and here I am."

"Lucien." Lolotte's little hands pounded his arm. "Begin at the beginning. We only heard that you were taken prisoner at Manassas last fall. We hadn't heard another word till Rev went to New Orleans and came back and brought—her."

Lucien glanced at Sarah, his face laughing, his eyes dark and very bright. "Thank heaven for that. Lolotte told me how Rev found you there and brought you home. I was afraid you might be waiting there in New Orleans and of course I couldn't get any word to you."

Sarah wondered fleetingly how long Lucien and Lolotte had talked together there beside the magnolia.

Rev replied, "Jules Lamoreux told me she had arrived. He saw her name on the St. Charles register. He told Cousin Elise."

Rev was sitting on the porch, leaning back against a pillar, a glass in his hand. He spoke quietly, but promptly. Lucien frowned. "Jules Lamoreux! Why, he's that old friend of Pa's. I thought he was dead of old age long ago."

"He's living at the St. Charles."

Lucien stared and then laughed. "Well, he did me a favor, nosing around the hotel register. Lolotte said you stole a horse, Rev. That must have been quite a trip."

"A right smart lot of mosquitoes," Rev said.

Lolotte tugged at Lucien's arm. "Go on, Lucien. Sarah told Rev you escaped the Yankees. We were scared you were dead —or else in Rock Island or some other horrible place."

He touched her cheek lightly. "It takes more than a Yankee bullet to finish me!"

George's plain face was rapt. "Go on, Lucien. How did you escape?"

Sarah had heard the full story of his escape before; she

thought of the moonlit walks with Lucien in Cuba, and looked out across the green lawn, dappled now with blue shadows, and did not really believe that those long walks and talks with Lucien had ever happened.

Lucien was talking. ". . . after they took us prisoner, they put us in a little country jail just to hang onto us till they could send us North. I had a fever there."

"Oh, Lucien!" Lolotte cried.

"Well, it was lucky. They had a new influx of prisoners and the jailor thought I was more or less helpless so he took me in at his house. His wife, I must say, was very kind about feeding me and seeing to me."

"A Yankee!" Lolotte said.

Lucien smiled at her. "She was all of fifty and weighed a good two hundred pounds."

Maude said through her Roman nose, "And how did you get out of her affectionate clutches?"

Lucien put back his head and laughed. George laughed and slapped his knee. Ben grinned and chewed on his cigar. "Oh, that was easy," Lucien said. "Naturally I didn't let on that I was getting well. One night I simply got out of a window and left. Then came the hard part. I didn't know what had happened while I was sick. Didn't know where the Yankees were, and what was more important, didn't know where my own company was. I spent the days in whatever barn I could find. You can't imagine how many haylofts I've slept in."

"How are things in Virginia?" George asked.

"Bad. The main problem is food and supplies. . . . Well, in the end I ran into a scouting party, stayed with them awhile, eventually went with them back to Richmond. And was sent to Cuba to look at some arms—Sarah has told you about that."

Rev looked at the glass in his hand. "Were you detached from your company?"

"To tell you the truth I was still a little bad off from the fever. I reckon they figured I wasn't up to much fighting but I could be of use in Cuba. Old Colonel Wicherly met me on the street one day. He has his nose in everything—"

Miss Celie interrupted, "Colonel Wicherly died."

"Colonel Wicherly! Why, he looked fine when I saw him. When was that?"

89

"Sometime—well, when was it, Ben? Didn't old Judge Hill tell you he died?"

Ben nodded. "Seems to me—well, I don't remember just when. His widow left Oxford and went to live with her sister in Georgia somewhere. Go on, Lucien."

"Surely he wasn't killed in battle."

"Liver complaint." Miss Celie turned her knitting. "I remember that. Then what happened?"

"Well then—first thing I knew I was on a blockade runner out of Wilmington, headed for Nassau. From there I went to Cuba. Same way I got back. . . . Where's Emile? Don't tell me the army finally got him?"

So Lolotte had not told him that.

An immediate silence lapped over the porch, the kind of silence Sarah now felt that she knew. It was like the pond in a swamp, flat and still on the surface with all sorts of things going on beneath it. As usual the silence lasted for only a second or two. Then everybody leaped to break it and tell Lucien about Emile, everybody but Rev, whose face closed in on itself and who wouldn't say: somebody here murdered him.

Lucien didn't see through it; he believed it all. He said, poor Emile. He said it was lucky there hadn't been many Yankees. He said they had scared them out, sure enough, and George's face shone with pride. He asked where they had found the Spencer cartridge.

Everybody told him that Rev had found it in the garden, near the cupid. "When did you find it, Rev?" Lucien asked.

"That night," Rev said promptly, watching a bird in a nearby tree. "I gave it to the coroner."

And you lied, Sarah thought; Rev wouldn't look at her. Lucien shook his head. "Poor Emile. Reckon they didn't give him a chance to defend himself. It's likely just as you say, Ben. They reconnoitered and found Emile—likely he had been drinking a little too much—said something to them— Well, we'll never know exactly how it happened. But I'm sorry about Emile."

While Lucien was still speaking Miss Celie whispered something about supper. Sarah quietly went past Rev, who did not look at her, and upstairs to change her dress. Although she half expected it, Lucien made no move to follow her. She was just then thankful. She thought of Emile. In a way

Rev had bound her to keep the facts of the Spencer cartridge to herself. She hadn't promised though.

Rev had said, almost in so many words, somebody in this house shot Emile. Lolotte? she thought again. Miss Celie? With a wave of panic she went through the short list of names again. Maude, Ben, George—Rev himself.

Lucien would have to be told. Lucien was at home. Now everything would be different. But nothing was different. Nothing was as she had expected it to be.

The fact was that Lucien was a handsome, charming, laughing stranger.

She washed, she brushed her hair so it was smooth and gleaming; she put on her thin green and blue dress and all the time her mind seemed to be running on several tracks at once. Lucien and herself in Havana; she tried to recapture it and could only see herself dimly, like someone seen through the wrong end of opera glasses, infinitely far away.

Danger, Rev had said, a murderer is scared. Would he tell Lucien privately what he had admitted to her only that afternoon?

Lucien was a stranger; Lucien had changed. How Lolotte and George hung on his words! Lucien was different but how had he changed?

She finished buttoning her bodice and thought, why no, I've changed.

It was scarcely more than three weeks since she had come to Honotassa. She had been completely engrossed with this new world.

But of course it was a long time since she and Lucien had been in Havana together. And that was now like a dream half remembered, none of it real.

Have we both changed? she thought. No; the simple fact was that they had known each other too short a time and had been separated for too long a time. Neither of them could have changed fundamentally so therefore it was merely a question of rediscovering each other, getting through these first moments of strangeness, which if she had been wiser she would have expected.

All the same she eyed her reflection in the mirror nervously; there was a kind of stifling sensation within her as if her stays were laced too tightly. For the first time since she had been at Honotassa she touched her cheeks and her lips, very lightly, with rouge. She put dabs of cologne on her throat and wrists. She felt like a warrior going into battle but against an invisible foe.

When she got downstairs, they had already gone in to supper; there were voices and the chink of china and silver from the dining room. A lighted lamp, instead of the usual candle, was on the table beside the grandfather's clock and Rev stood watching her. He came to meet her, limping but moving with Lucien's grace and ease, although now that Lucien was at home she wondered, puzzled, why she had thought they were so much alike.

He took her hand and tucked it in his arm, as if he guessed her need for reinforcement. But he said rather curtly, "No need to paint your face. Come to supper."

"Are you going to tell Lucien about the cartridge?"

"No. That is—not now."

Supper that night was different. For the first time Miss Celie insisted upon Sarah's taking her place at the head of the table, opposite Lucien, the big crystal table bell at her hand. Sarah was too embarrassed in some curious way to resist. Uncle Jethro, who seemed to turn up at what he considered formal occasions, stood behind her chair. There was wine, Lucien's favorite, Lolotte said.

Lucien did most of the talking. She could barely see his face through the flicker and smoke of the candles in the center of the table between them, so his voice seemed different, too, older perhaps than she remembered it. They talked of war and George asked Lucien's opinions as if Lucien were an oracle. Ben asked about Richmond and Lucien said the politicians and even the generals were fighting so much among themselves and doing so much politicking that they hardly had time to fight a war.

"You don't really mean that," George said worriedly.

Lucien laughed and said of course not. Rev stirred. "We're trying to make a new nation and make war at the same time," he said soberly. "There's bound to be a certain amount of friction. But General Lee has no private axe to grind, nor Stonewall Jackson nor—"

"No, no," Lucien said quickly. "Don't fret your mind, Rev. I didn't mean that seriously."

Ben said, "Old man Fant was here the other day and said there were rumors of a force of Yankee cavalry coming down near the Mobile and Ohio Railroad. Did you hear anything of it?"

Lucien's black eyebrows drew together. "Is that fact or rumor?"

"Some of both, I reckon. If they were still around you'd have heard about it on the cars."

"Well, I didn't. Not a word. But then I left the train at Pond Bridge and came cross-country through that long piece of piney woods."

"Oh, well, by now General Ruggles has tended to them!"

Rev broke his silence again. "We don't know that for sure, George. This Yankee cavalry might be coming right on down the state. Looks to me like it could be a diversionary tactic—Grant has got to cross the river."

Ben and George shouted him down. It couldn't happen like that—why, General Ruggles would dispose of any piddling little passel of Yankee cavalry, if he hadn't already. Lucien told Uncle Jethro he wanted more wine and said that if there really was a Yankee cavalry troop within the state it would be suicidal for them. "Why, it'd be like walking into a hornet's nest."

George sighed. "I wish you'd got some news."

Lucien laughed. "All I saw along the way till I got near here was a couple or three cabins. But I wouldn't have stopped for anything. I wanted to get home." Lolotte's soft, dark eyelashes lifted; she gave Lucien a shining look.

After supper they sat in the parlor and Lolotte played the piano and sang. She had a light soprano voice, lilting and gay as a bird's, and Sarah listened as always with a pleasure touched by wistfulness; Sarah's own singing voice was as tuneless as the purr of a cat. She listened also, rather unfortunately, to the words of the sad, war-born and strangely moving songs. Thus when Lucien, leaning on the piano, asked for "Lorena" and Lolotte played and sang the ballad which had taken public fancy to the extent that it was sung in every lamplighted parlor, in every camp and in every barroom, Sarah's mind drifted from the charming and tender tune and fastened upon the words: "It's just a hundred months, Lorena, since first I held thy hand in mine—"

The last soft and tender note died away and Sarah said blankly, "A hundred months—why, that's over eight years."

Lolotte closed the piano with a thump. Sarah felt her face flushing hotly. "I didn't mean—you have a beautiful voice, Lolotte. Please sing some more."

Rev moved into the breach with a low chuckle: "I always

thought he was a rather laggard lover myself. Let's have 'Bonnie Blue Flag.' "

Lolotte pouted for a second. Lucien reopened the piano and Lolotte played. Everybody but Sarah joined in the rousing rhythm: "We are a band of brothers—and native to our soil—"

Sarah didn't know the song, yet something misty, like tears, came into her eyes. They *were* all brothers, North and South, fighting each other and dying, and it's such a waste, she thought, with an ache in her heart.

"Hurrah for the Bonnie Blue flag, that bears a single star," they sang—and Lolotte closed the piano again, this time for good. Ben lighted a cigar and strolled down the driveway, George and Rev disappeared to take their usual last look around the place, the evening was over, candles were lighted. Lucien, singing "Hurrah for the Bonnie Blue flag," half under his breath, went beside her up the stairs and into her room. He stopped singing to survey it, smiling. "Why in the world didn't Miss Celie put you in my room? It's the big one at the corner. Used to be my father's. That's where you belong." He closed the door and turned to her and said, "Did you bring the money?"

Whatever she might have expected him to say, it was not that.

Lucien was impatient.

"The gold! The gold—did you bring it?"

"Oh—of course. Yes."

"Where is it?"

"Rev hid it under the floorboards in the office."

"*Rev* hid it?"

"Why, yes. He brought it from New Orleans when we—"

"Oh, yes. Yes. I'm glad he happened to find you there. I hadn't had time to make any arrangements for you. I hadn't figured out yet who to get hold of or how. I never thought of old Lamoreux. I'm glad he nosed around, without being asked to."

Something was going wrong in the reunion with Lucien which she had longed for; it was as if she were a passenger on a train which suddenly and erratically selected its own destination. She said, "Well, you couldn't let anybody know, not while you were in Richmond—"

"Oh, I was going to sneak a message to some friend there.

94

There are always ways and means. How much gold did you bring?"

"Twelve thousand dollars. It was all I could get from the bank in Havana."

Something flickered across Lucien's face, that or the light of the candle wavered in the gentle night breeze from the windows. "Yes—well. You were a brave girl to bring that much. What was Rev doing in New Orleans?"

"I don't know. He said business."

"Business. I can't imagine what business. Why, if they caught him there out of uniform there'd have been a business of getting his neck stretched. . . . Ben told me that Emile had been in New Orleans, too."

"Emile! I didn't know that."

"So Ben said. Said Emile went to New Orleans the week before Rev went—"

"*Why?*"

"Why did *Rev*—that's what I asked you!"

"No, I mean Emile."

He frowned. "How in the world should I know! What difference does it make?"

Don't question, Rev had said. But this was Lucien. ("Are you going to tell Lucien . . . ?" she had asked. And Rev had replied, "No. . . . not now.")

Lucien was still frowning. "What's the matter with you? You look as if you'd seen a ghost."

And she had seen a ghost, the ugly, giggling ghost of Emile —but the barest shape of murder.

She made up her mind. "Lucien, I had a very disagreeable talk with Emile, the afternoon before he was—killed."

He laughed shortly, "Who hasn't had a disagreeable talk with Emile? What did he say?"

"He was drunk. He thought because you had married me, a Yankee, that—oh, I don't know what he really thought. He wanted money."

"My dear girl!"

"He said you were turning Yankee, he said Rev was, too. My influence seemed to be his idea. He said all three of us had decided to hold onto Honotassa."

"What did you say?"

A light draft sifted across the room, touched her skirts and her face. The door into the hall had not been securely closed; it swung open a little, showing a line of darkness from the hall. She went to close it. "I told him he lied. That doesn't matter, he was drunk." She came back. "But that night—"

He broke in. "I should have warned you to stay away from Emile. I'm sorry, dear. Emile was a sly little rat. Oh, I wouldn't have wanted him to be killed like that. But it really is no loss to anybody. As for going into New Orleans, Emile knew he'd be safe. He was never in uniform; if the Yankees had bothered to arrest him at all, he'd have simply taken their eagle oath and got himself let out. But Rev was out of uniform. . . . Oh well, Rev's business was likely to see some old flame. He's quite a lad with the ladies."

"You're wrong about Rev," she said unexpectedly. "He's none of the things you said he is."

Lucien laughed again, indulgently. "Has Rev been making love to you, too?"

"No!"

"Well, there now—don't get your temper up. I didn't mean it. Although you have been seeing a lot of him, haven't you? Riding, spending hours in the office. Lolotte told me."

Sarah subdued a quick flare of anger; naturally Lolotte had told him. "Certainly. He said I had to learn to manage the plantation."

"Hm. Well, I reckon that's a good idea," Lucien said carelessly. "Somebody's got to see to things after I leave. I hope that gold is still there. I don't like to say this about my own brother but don't trust Rev too far."

"Rev wouldn't—why, Lucien, *Rev* wouldn't steal it! He says I'll need it for Honotassa—and I can see now that we will need it here," she added soberly.

"Oh, but darling, I have a more pressing use for it."

"You mean for the mortgages? It wouldn't go far to pay the mortgages."

"Who told you about any mortgages—Rev?"

She nodded. "And George told me what you did with the money you borrowed. I do understand why you and George or anybody would buy Confederate bonds but—not with this gold. We'll need every penny of it."

He eyed her for a moment, then he sat down on the red settee, his long legs sprawled out. She looked at him, searching for something, anything, that would recapture not only the Lucien she had married but the Sarah who had met and loved and married him.

It was so long ago—too long ago, she thought, with a

kind of cold knock at some inner rampart of her consciousness.

"But you are my wife," Lucien said.

James Salter's daughter replied, "But it's my money!"

Lucien laughed and said easily, incredibly, still laughing, "Darling, it's my money."

CHAPTER ELEVEN

The sweet fragrance of honeysuckle and Cape Jessamine drifted in through the window. The candle flame dipped and rose again with the light breeze.

"Rev told me that," Sarah said at last. "He said that in the South a wife and a husband are one person and the husband is that person."

"Rev seems to have told you a lot of things. For once he was right. But my dear, I didn't marry you for your money. I don't care what you do with that gold. We'll not quarrel about that. Use it any way you like. It's nothing to me."

"Honotassa belongs to you."

"Well, of course. But I must say I didn't expect you to acquire such sudden devotion to—why, just an old house and some acres of land. Is there any particular reason for it? Rev, for instance?"

"Oh, Lucien, be reasonable! Confederate bonds—"

"You're still a Yankee at heart. Naturally, you wouldn't want your money to help the Confederacy. Or is it—why, of course. You saw me, there in the driveway with Lolotte. So that's the trouble."

"You should have broken your engagement to Lolotte before you married me." Again she felt as if she were a passenger on a train which she was powerless to control, headed for some unknown destination.

"How could I? There wasn't time. But darling, I didn't dream you'd be jealous."

"Oh, Lucien, I'm not jealous," she said wearily, and with vague surprise she knew she spoke the truth.

"That explains everything! You've seemed cold and distant. To tell you the truth, I really began to wonder if Rev—but it was Lolotte, all the time! And then you saw me there in the driveway. I was kissing Lolotte. I don't deny it. She was waiting for me, she—well, I don't want to boast but she flung herself at me. She's always been like that with me—I really couldn't help it—"

"Don't be disgusting," Sarah said without intention, without any feeling at all.

Lucien's jaw quite literally dropped. He had unbuttoned his tunic and, lounging like that on the little sofa, he looked flabby and out of trim; his face was handsome—and in the uneven light from the candle seemed slightly puffy around the chin and eyes. A red flush of anger surged up into his cheeks.

She said slowly, "Perhaps I have seemed distant or cold. We haven't had time to—to get acquainted again. Our marriage was so short. We hadn't known each other very long—"

"You were very willing."

Dear God, I'm going to slap him, Sarah thought.

She clutched her hands together behind her back. She forced her voice to steadiness. "Lucien, I am your wife. I want to make our marriage a success. I think both of us need time."

The red flush deepened in his face. He really is fatter, she thought absently. Then he jumped up; he brought his hand down like a blow on the back of the sofa. "You hate the South! And you're jealous of Lolotte!"

"You needn't shout."

"This is my house. I'll shout if I please." Suddenly he laughed. "By this time everybody in the house knows we've quarreled, and why. Lolotte—"

"You'd better leave now, Lucien."

"I'll be delighted." He swung around to the door, turned back, looked her up and down and chuckled. "You'll change your mind," he said airily, settled his tunic with a confident shrug, lifted his black head and went jauntily away.

He closed the door behind him. Sarah sat down in the slippery little chair.

I didn't tell him about Emile, she thought presently. She had tried to tell him, she had tried to tell him many things and somehow the conversation kept taking its own jerky, absurd, unreasonable course.

One fact, however, had unmistakably emerged.

"Why, I've just been a fool," she said at last aloud.

Her own voice roused her. The candle had burned down to a pool of smoking tallow. The house was utterly still.

She rose, undressed briskly before the last wavering little flame of the candle drowned itself in tallow and went to bed. She slept so deeply that when she awoke she realized that Glendora had come and gone, bringing the cup of coffee that stood on the table, without waking her.

She felt refreshed, ready to face the day and whatever it was to hold—even Lucien.

She ought to feel heartbroken.

She didn't feel heartbroken, so there was no sense in trying to work up emotions which didn't exist. Why, she thought with surprised but realistic clarity, I don't even like Lucien!

Sobered by that, she rose and went to the window. A rain was falling, barely a drizzle, shrouding the great rim of oaks. The Cape Jessamines and the magnolias were glossy and wet. It was quiet, indeed strangely quiet as if the whole world were muffled by the drizzling rain. It was almost like a world in a dream, half seen, entirely silent, haunting in its very elusiveness.

But it wasn't elusive; it was her world and she loved it.

All right, she'd made a fool of herself. Lucien hadn't married her because he loved her, so the only reason why he had married her was money. Heaven knows why I married him, she thought. It was a temptation to tell herself that it was because she was lonely, suffering shock and grief from her father's death, because Lucien was so kind, so devoted, so handsome and romantic that he fulfilled to the letter any schoolgirl's notion of a lover. Because the truth was that, aside from one or two young Frenchmen, formally and, she had rather suspected, hopefully introduced by the headmistress of the school, Lucien was her first real admirer, suitor, beau—whatever anyone chose to call him, the first man who had caught her fancy.

But she wasn't a schoolgirl. She had married Lucien because she wanted to. And now she had changed or he had changed or both of them had changed or—she broke off that futile line of reflection. The fact was that she was Lucien's wife.

Certainly she wasn't the first woman to make a fool of herself. She had now to pick up the pieces.

In any event Lucien was going back to the army soon. It was a wry but practical and comforting fact that she would have time to work out some sort of modus vivendi, some sort of basis for their marriage.

Again there was a cold little knock somewhere within her. She wouldn't listen and recognize it, not now.

She went to the table and took up the cup of coffee. It would be cold by now. She lifted it to her lips. Her first taste merely surprised her. She jerked the cup from her mouth and looked at the dark liquid, wondering what new mixture they had arrived at in the kitchen to take the place of real coffee.

Then swiftly, struck by a preposterous notion, she tasted it again. She put down the cup. She stared at it, disbelieving— believing—knowing in her heart that it was dosed with opium.

Why, there's enough opium to kill a horse, she thought numbly. There's enough opium to kill me!

There was a hurried knock at the door. Her heart plunged up into her throat, half choking her. Without waiting Maude thrust open the door and swept into the room. "Well! So you're awake! They've all gone."

Sarah said, past the strangling sensation in her throat, "Lucien and Rev? Back to the army?"

"Oh, heavens no! Why, Lucien just got here. No, it's the slaves. They've all gone now. A mass exodus."

Sarah sat down, her thin nightgown falling around her, her hair over her shoulders, the cup of coffee, full of opium, on the table before her.

"They left somehow in the middle of the night. It was raining. Nobody heard them."

"All of them?"

"All of them except Uncle Jethro, Glendora, one stable boy, Lij, and three dogs."

"But—why? Where did they go?"

She knew that her wits were stumbling, her thoughts in chaos. Maude made a sharply impatient motion with her strong, capable hands. "They went off to fasten themselves on the Yankees, who else? They expect care, food, clothing." She snorted, "They'll get short shrift. Oh, some of them will have the sense to come back. They took two mule teams and two wagons."

"Four mules! *Maude!* That leaves us only two mules and all that plowing." Her mind cleared for a moment and presented her a vision of field after field, already green and giving promise of plenty—much-needed plenty.

"You're a strange woman. You Yankees are fighting to free the slaves—"

"What else did they take?"

"The wagonload of cornmeal and side meat and supplies that Stash was to take to the commissary headquarters this morning. It was loaded last night. Ben said it was likely that gave them the idea."

"Stash couldn't have left!"

"Oh, but he did. And Rilly, too."

"Rilly! She was Miss Celie's right hand."

"Yes, well, she's gone." Maude's eyes roved around the room and fastened on the cup of coffee. "The fact is, Rilly's boy was sold—oh, just before the war. It's never been the custom to sell people at Honotassa. Rilly took on about it at the time. But then Miss Celie, all of us, thought she'd resigned herself. Now it looks as if she was just waiting for a chance to run away. I can't say I blame her," Maude said sourly. "But Miss Celie thought the world of her."

"People have been sold from Honotassa. I've seen the records—"

Maude broke in. "Uncle Jethro is deaf as a post, likely he really didn't hear anything. He swears up and down that he didn't. But that little fool Glendora would have run along after the rest of them if she could and she didn't, so he must have locked her up. She's his granddaughter. . . . I reckon you'll leave now."

"I'll—*what?*"

"Oh, everybody knows you and Lucien had a quarrel last night about Lolotte. And to tell you the truth, if I had all the money you have I'd go straight back to New York and get out of all this. You're a fool if you don't. Can't you possibly imagine what life here is going to be like?"

"It's going to be a lot of hard work. And we didn't quarrel about Lolotte."

There was no use in denying the quarrel, not in that house. Maude shrugged, lifting her shoulders and eyebrows, fatalistically, French fashion. "Seems the door was open and Lolotte happened to be in the hall and you and Lucien were at it, hammer and tongs!" Maude's long nose unexpectedly wrinkled up. "Happened to be in the hall! Happened to hear you quarrel about her! Oh, well, you can't really blame Lolotte. She lost her beau to you."

But she was talking of Emile when she saw the black line

of the open door; Sarah remembered it clearly. Maude went on. "I've got to get busy. Miss Celie's taken to her bed, with the door locked. She opened it an inch and poked out the keys for me to give you. Here—" She thrust a bundle of keys strung on a thick red cord into Sarah's hand. "Not that there's much use in locking up the smokehouse and the storehouse now. Drink your coffee—"

Coffee. "It's—cold." Maude suddenly looked quite capable of pouring it down her throat. "I don't want it," Sarah said, firmly.

"Oh. Well—I'll take it down with me as I go."

Maude swooped up the cup and hiked up her top hoop as if about to take off with a racing start. At the door she turned back, her Roman nose looking very long now and satiric. "I forgot. Ben and Lucien have gone after them. It's just like that book your Northern friend wrote—except there aren't any ice floes to cross and no bloodhounds."

"I don't know Mrs. Stowe. . . . What can they do if they find them?"

"They can't do anything. It's silly, childish, running after them like that. I told Ben so. But of course the patrollers won't be of any help, not with everything so upset and that Yankee cavalry outfit they say is running around, God knows where."

She had swished away, she had been gone for a long time probably when Sarah suddenly realized that she ought to stop her, pour out the coffee, so no one would drink it. But then the so-called coffee was bad enough at best, cold it was all but undrinkable—especially that cup!

She was deeply, horribly sure that Lucien had filled it with opium. She had quarreled with Lucien, she had resisted his demands for money—and if she died, by the provisions of her marriage contract, Lucien would inherit legally not only the immediate sum of gold under the floorboards in the office, but later, when the war was over, her father's entire estate.

She felt cold and hot, sticky and chilly at the same time. Now wait a minute, she told herself, think about it; Lucien is not the only person in this house who could have put opium in that coffee.

She had lost a bottle of opium—but that was on the trip from New Orleans. Or someone had taken it during her first day at Honotassa. Yes, she had missed it after her talk with Emile, after dinner, just before Emile was shot. Rilly or Glendora had entered her room while she slept, bringing back her washed clothes. So somebody else could have come in, too—then or later while she was out of the room. It would have been easy to identify as opium by its odor.

It was not very reasonable to believe that Lucien had procured unprocurable opium and come back to Honotassa with a formed plan to murder her. He didn't even know that she was there. And he certainly couldn't have guessed that she would resist his demand for the gold or that she was not the yielding—yes, and credible fool he had every right to expect. No, he had been surprised, unpleasantly surprised, but surprised.

Then somebody else? Don't question, Rev had said, don't invite danger. Her skin crawled: Lolotte had told Maude that she was in the hall and the door was open. Sarah had begun to tell Lucien of Emile, she had begun to question and a little draft had crept across the room from the bedroom door, open barely enough to show a rim of blackness in the hall. So Lolotte—or anybody—could have listened, and that somebody could have already been supplied with the missing bottle of opium.

That was not reasonable either. The opium had disappeared before Emile's death and whoever shot him could not by any stretch of the imagination have foreseen Sarah's own doubts and suspicions—and questions.

She began to doubt whether there had been in fact a lethal dose of opium in the cup. So suppose somebody only wished to frighten her, so she would leave Honotassa!

That made a certain amount of logic. Added to the argument was the fact that while she might have tasted the coffee if it had been still hot, she might even have drunk some of it, she wouldn't have taken enough to kill her, for she would have been warned by its taste.

No. It was merely an attempt to frighten her.

She wouldn't go back to New York as Maude suggested; she wouldn't run like a scared cat. But—well, she'd be very careful.

She dressed and the accustomed routine restored to her a sense of normal everyday life.

But before she left her room she dug into her big moiré bag, took out the envelope holding her marriage contract and the wax seal had been broken. So somebody else knew what would happen to her father's money if she died.

Rev had known all along. Rev didn't need to break the wax seal, read the contract and find out. He could conceivably have wished to make sure; Rev loved Honotassa, it was like a part of his breath and body; Rev had stressed the need for money. Rev would never have tried to give her poison!

She thrust the envelope back in the bag; there was no point in locking it up in the armoire now, it was like locking the barn after the horse was stolen. And in all likelihood, by now, there was more than one person in the house who knew the terms of her marriage contract. There was no point either in telling herself again what a fool she'd been.

She went downstairs and received another curious shock, for when Glendora flapped into the dining room in her home-made moccasins, Sarah asked her when she had brought coffee to her room and Glendora said she hadn't. "Too much work this morning, Miss Sarah—everybody gone like that—"

Sarah swallowed past another kind of constriction in her throat. "Well, then who brought it?"

"Miss Maude. She come to the kitchen and say she take it up to you." Glendora put down a dish of lukewarm rice. "Not much breakfast this morning. I don't know what we're going to do, Miss Sarah."

"We've got to eat," Sarah said, curtly, because a chill crawled over her again. Maude?

Glendora flapped away. The rice wasn't dosed with opium, indeed it had no taste at all, not a grain of salt. She ate what she could and went out along the covered passageway, with the rain dripping from the vines. In the kitchen Glendora was despairingly picking chickens. "Get a basket," Sarah told her. "We'll go to the storehouse."

Glendora dropped a chicken and a flurry of feathers, and went with her through the drizzle, to the storehouse. Sarah found the right key and unlocked the door.

It was a long, low room, like a root cellar, for it was banked up with soil, and vines had run rampant over that, too. It was dark but dry and cool. She doled out what Glendora vaguely guessed were the right amounts of dried peas, eggs, cornmeal, a little salt. The shelves looked emptier than when Miss Celie had shown her the storeroom, and since the men from the Commissary had called; there were certainly now fewer mouths to feed but there was less to feed them with. She took Glendora to the smokehouse, unlocked it and saw with satisfaction there was still a quantity of hams and sides of bacon, hanging from the smoke-stained rafters.

They wouldn't go hungry, not yet. And the fields were green and growing. "Can't you possibly imagine what life is going to be like, here?" Maude had said.

Maude.

She sent Glendora back to the house, her basket and her apron laden. She stood for a moment, rain dripping from the trees over her head, thinking of Maude.

Maude had the opportunity to take the bottle of opium from Sarah's room. Maude had the cool ruthlessness to do whatever she made up her mind to do. She couldn't see how her death could affect Maude. She couldn't see any reason why Maude would attempt to frighten her. Besides, there was something hysterical and silly, something almost childish about an attempt to frighten her. Maude was neither hysterical nor silly and Sarah rather doubted if she had ever been childish.

Yet Maude had suggested that Sarah return to New York. Maude could have shot Emile—if she'd had a reason to kill him.

There was no use in standing there in the drizzle, trying to find a link between Emile's murder and opium in a cup of coffee.

She started back for the house, saw a light in the office, opened the door and surprised a domestic little scene which was far outside the dark realm of murder or attempted murder. Rev, George and Lolotte were mending shoes.

A lighted lamp stood on the table that dusky, drizzling day. They were all three bent over a shabby riding boot; George had a tack hammer. Lolotte held a patch of leather, Rev steadied something, a tiny brad, waiting for George's poised hammer. George said, "First thing I do when I get to Vicksburg again, is get me a Yankee—"

"With boots on," Lolotte laughed softly.

Rev looked up and saw her. Lolotte looked up and stiffened. George didn't look up at all. There was no way to know, no way to guess whether any one of them was surprised at Sarah's appearance, believing her to be drugged and senseless—and just possibly dead.

Rev said, "Come in, Sarah. Reckon you know the news."

And what news, Sarah thought as satirically as Maude might have said it.

Rev's face was suddenly a little fixed and questioning. He turned to George and Lolotte. "Take your cobbler's shop somewhere else. I want to talk to Sarah."

Everything in the office, the spreading circle of lamplight, the patch of leather in Lolotte's hands, George poised with the tack hammer, the homely, everyday atmosphere, all denied an attempt at murder. A rush of panic caught Sarah. "No. Not now. I mean I've got to—to see to the kitchen. Glendora—"

Her words jumbled together and she all but ran from the office and from the question in Rev's face.

Now why did I do that? she thought as warm, drizzling rain touched her face. She was no schoolgirl, refusing to bear tales.

As she reached the kitchen door the answer presented itself; if she told anyone of the opium it must be Lucien, her husband.

It might be, indeed it had already proved to be a marriage without love, but it was marriage. So she couldn't choose Rev as a confidant; it must be Lucien.

Always provided that Lucien himself had not dosed her coffee with opium, she thought, as coldly and sharply, again, as Maude might have said it.

She paused at the kitchen door, caught her breath, told herself firmly that the opium was only an attempt to frighten her and went into the kitchen, where Glendora was eyeing the chickens dismally and Maude was cleaning lamp chimneys. Glendora gave a gulp. "Miss Sarah, I can't cut up no chicken. Miss Maude say she won't."

Again the homely, everyday details of daily living refuted a vicious attempt to frighten her—or to murder her.

The homely everyday details of living and domestic requirements also pressed upon her with their immediate urgency. No matter what had happened or hadn't happened, somebody had to see about dinner. She eyed the chickens with, if she had known it, something of Glendora's dismal look and thought with a certain fury of the time she had spent on Latin verbs. Much better to have spent the time in learning housekeeping, Glendora detected her weakening and thrust a knife at her.

The door opened again and Rev came in. He sized up

106

the situation, grinned and slid a knife with a big handle from the top of his boot. "It's like ducks," he told Glendora. "I'll show you."

"Will you take these chimneys back to the house, Cousin Sarah?" Maude snapped. "They are still streaky but I don't care."

One small bit of just possibly valuable lore from some class in history flashed up from Sarah's memory: the best defense is offense. She said, "Maude, it was kind of you to bring me my coffee this morning."

"Coffee?" Maude scrubbed away at soot streaks inside another lamp chimney. "I didn't."

"Glendora said—"

"Oh, I took it as far as the hall and put it down and forgot it."

Rev was saying to Glendora, "See—it's easy," but he was listening, too.

Sarah took the lamp chimneys and went into the house. They *were* streaky; Miss Celie wouldn't like that.

The house was quiet and chilly as if Miss Celie's terrors had seeped down through it.

Chapter Twelve

The rest of the day Sarah avoided Rev. Dinner was late; the chickens were underdone; Glendora in a state of daring had essayed floating island for dessert and scorched the milk and overcooked the egg whites on top so they were tough. Sarah had not doled out enough salt, everything was flat and tasteless—but certainly Sarah thought, once, with a sense of unreality, nothing tasted of opium. Miss Celie did not come to dinner.

The drizzling rain went on. Late in the afternoon, when Sarah was sure that Rev and George were out in the sheds or stables, nowhere near the office, she went to the kitchen, took a knife, crossed the dripping stretch of path and grass to the office. There was no one anywhere to be seen or to see her.

She pushed the long table aside, pried up the floorboards with the knife and was not really surprised to find that the bags of gold were not there.

"It's my money," Lucien had said—and took it.

She replaced the floorboards and the table.

Well, she would have to make him give it back, she didn't know how.

It was dusky and shadowy in the little room. After a time she lighted the lamp and took the ledger of slave records from the cherrywood cupboard.

Time passed as she went slowly through the long lines of handwriting and then went back over them. The lamp smoked and she adjusted the wick. Rain dripped in soft monotony outside the window.

At last she closed the book and sat, looking at it. It was perfectly clear now why the remaining slaves had left the night before, the night of Lucien's return.

During the years of Lucien's and Rev's father's life there had been no records of sales, some purchases but no sales. Since the time of his death, since Lucien had owned Honotassa, the records of sales began and multiplied with poignant overtones of human pain and suffering. Calista had been sold almost at once but Calista's life had obviously fallen into pleasant lines. Rilly's boy had been twelve at the time he was sold.

"I can't say I blame her," Maude had said, speaking of Rilly.

Sarah felt chilly and a little sick.

The slaves had not run away before; there had been no place to go. Now with the Union forces so near, and in the unsettled time, there was not only hope for escape but hope of a safe refuge—not from Honotassa and their homefolk but from Lucien.

To be fair Lucien had done no more than any man might do; he had sold property; it was an established economic custom.

Yet she began to wonder, with a sense of something like fright, what kind of man she had married.

A man who could sell people who depended upon him, a man who could separate a mother and her twelve-year-old boy, wouldn't stick at giving his wife, or anyone who opposed him, a real and vicious fright.

Would he stick at murder? He couldn't have had the means to kill her with opium—unless, she thought like a burst of light, someone had supplied it to him!

But she was more valuable to him alive than dead—at least until the war was over and there could be no legal quibbling about the property she would eventually inherit.

She wasn't sure that that was a sound argument; Lucien would be her heir no matter what happened. But he would certainly have to go North to claim an inheritance and he couldn't do that until the war was over.

No; to murder her now would be not only an unnecessary but a dangerously precipitate act.

Murder required an immediacy, a terrific urgency of purpose. Lucien didn't love her, but he wouldn't try to murder her. To frighten her—yes, there could be a reason for that and a simple one. A thoroughly frightened woman will yield to anything, certainly to a demand for money.

Yet that was not a valid purpose now, for Lucien already had the gold. Lolotte, then? George? Maude? It seemed again so childish and spiteful an attempt that she could not reasonably attribute it to anyone at all.

It was almost dusk; there was a light in the kitchen and as she stood at the door Maude came, running ponderously to escape the rain. "I thought you were here!" She came in. She brushed a fine misting of rain from her thick buns of hair and shook her full skirt. "What are you doing?"

"Looking at some records."

Maude gave herself another shake and sat down at the table. "I reckon somebody's got to tell you about Miss Celie. Just pay it no mind."

"Miss Celie!"

"It's like this. Miss Celie's people came from Haiti, fled from there during the revolution. Stars alive, that was sixty years ago but Miss Celie cut her teeth on tales of it, and she can't forget. She's always afraid of a Negro uprising. So today she locked herself in her room."

"But—but the slaves have gone!"

"Yes, but you see she counted on Rilly. She liked her. Now she feels as if—God knows who, Glendora or Uncle Jethro is going to come creeping around with an axe." Maude leaned forward, whisked off the lamp chimney and pinched the smoking wick. "It doesn't mean anything. Don't look so shocked."

"That's what Rev meant by the vapors," Sarah said slowly.

"He calls it that. I call it damn foolishness. The fact is," Maude said flatly, "I reckon all of us have a kind of sense of guilt. But the guilt belongs as much to the slave traders, the manufacturers who buy our cotton, everybody North and

109

South! Not just the South." She brooded a moment, her cold eyes reflecting twin lights from the lamp. "Seems to me Rev said that once. Ben says they are our property and our economy needs them and—of course, though, Ben owned more slaves than Honotassa."

Sarah thought of Miss Celie, locked in her room, stricken with imaginary terrors. Or were they imaginary; there was Emile! "Maude, could one of the slaves have shot Emile?"

Maude's face was a blank. "He was shot by Yankee stragglers."

"But suppose there was some quarrel, suppose one of the slaves had a grudge. And then he ran away last night and—"

"It's against the law for a slave to own a gun. Emile had nothing to do with Honotassa people. For heaven's sake," Maude said irritably, "don't get like Miss Celie."

"But they left. They left last night. Why?"

Maude patted her hair and looked at the windowpane behind Sarah. "Because they got it into their heads to leave. That's a silly question."

It was a silly question; Sarah already knew the answer. Maude, she was sure, knew it too.

Her mind fumbled back to something George and Maude had half said, half hinted. "You said—you told George, that Lucien had settled down."

Surprised, Maude's Romanesque head jerked toward her. "Why—yes! He *has* settled down."

"What did you mean?"

Maude seemed to debate inwardly but not for long. "I meant just that. If you're thinking about George saying that there was a time when I liked Lucien, I did. He was dashing, handsome—still is. But believe me, my heart wasn't broken. Lucien—all right if you must know the truth, Lucien was a gay, young bachelor, going to be rich. Maybe he spent a little too much, maybe he got himself a little too much in debt. That's the slave ledger you've been looking at, isn't it? Well, then you know. Lucien sold some slaves after his father's death. Ben said he had debts to pay. You can't quarrel with that."

"How did he get himself so much in debt?"

"Oh, the usual ways, I reckon," Maude said vaguely.

Sarah had to know. "Gambling? Women?"

Maude rose and gave a suddenly ferocious dab at a moth circling the lamp. It fell without a flutter. Maude said, "Now

I declare, Cousin Sarah, don't get yourself in a state wondering what your husband did before you married him. He was engaged to Lolotte, that's a fact, but that was as much a family understanding as anything else. Lolotte still thinks she's head over heels in love with him but she's stubborn and mad. She'll get over it. The point is Lucien *has* settled down, he's had a good war record, and he's married a woman with money. . . . Now wait, don't get upset. I didn't say that's why he married you but—well, it's this way. We talk a lot about romance—poems, pressed flowers, serenades, a lady's glove next to a man's heart." Maude's Roman nose gave a resounding snort. "It's all poppycock. When we marry it's different. Might be the French in the Hugots—but there it is. If there's anything we're practical about it's marriage. Lucien's marriage to you means security for Honotassa and it means that Lucien has settled down—that's all."

It struck Sarah as an odd argument to accept as proof of a husband's stability and character status but Maude's authority and realism were such that for a moment Sarah did almost accept it.

"What was Lucien like as a boy?"

"Like other boys, I reckon." There was something guarded now in Maude's tone. "Why do you want to know?"

"I was curious."

"Yes. Well—" Maude settled her skirts. "He wasn't like Rev, I'll say that. Rev's always been—just as he is now. You know Rev."

"Wasn't Rev a gambler, a duelist—a ladies' man—"

"Who told you that?"

"I wondered—"

Maude looked at her for a moment. "If I were you, Cousin Sarah, I wouldn't think about Rev. Make up your quarrel with Lucien. I said Lucien has settled down. But Lucien can be right mean when he wants to be. And if you tell him I said that I'll tell him you lied.—I've got to go find some eggs. That little idiot Glendora says she's afraid of hens." She swung back the door, discovered an old coat of Rev's hanging there and swept it around her as regally as if it had been a toga.

"Wait," Sarah said rather desperately. "Maude, you said you left my coffee in the hall and forgot it and—" Words stuck in her throat.

She was discovering that Maude did not require many

words; she gave her one piercing look. "What was the matter with it?"

There was a little silence between them except for the darting flutter of another moth circling the lamp. Lolotte called from somewhere outside, "Maude—Maude, I've got a basket."

Sarah wished she hadn't started it and decided that whoever said the best form of defense was attack was wrong. Maude swirled back to the table, her solid figure as formidable as Miss Celie's, batted down the moth with one efficient slap and said, "Salt? No, we can't waste salt. Mustard—what? You don't want to tell, do you? You said the coffee was cold and you didn't want it." The moth gave a weak flutter and she ended that. "It was a child's trick. Lolotte is a child and she can be a naughty child. Miss Celie indulged her too much. Yes, offhand I'd say whatever there was in your coffee was a mean little trick of Lolotte's."

Lolotte's high, sweet voice called again, irritably, "Maude—where are you?"

"I'm coming terectly," Maude shouted back.

She really did say *terectly*, it would be spelled just like that, Sarah thought in some remote, merely observing layer of her mind. She wondered how her own crisp accents struck their ears, accustomed to their own softly slurred speech.

Maude put both her square hands on the table and leaned over it. "Sarah, I told you to make up your quarrel with Lucien. If you think he's in love with Lolotte's he's not. But he does like to have his own way."

"Oh," Lolotte said from the doorway. "There you are. I brought a basket for the eggs." She came into the office and thrust the basket at Maude. She was smiling contentedly, as smug as a happy kitten. "Go ahead, Maude, I'll catch up. I want to talk to Sarah."

"You come right along with me," Maude snapped.

Lolotte evaded her hand with one graceful sidestep. "Glendora's waiting for those eggs."

Maude hesitated, gave the lamp—and Sarah—a forbidding look as if she might exterminate more moths or Sarah herself if she chose, and marched out into the foggy, wet twilight.

Lolotte giggled softly at Maude's retreat and for a second Emile seemed to giggle again, almost out of hearing, softly and maliciously.

Then Lolotte, her wide skirts swaying lightly, drifted

across to a chair at the table, taking her time, almost blatantly conscious of her own beauty, her own grace of movement, her own utter, complete loveliness. She settled her skirts and looked across the glow of the lamplight at Sarah. Her arched black eyebrows were delicate; her lashes softened her dark eyes, as wide and guileless-looking as a child's—but a naughty child's, Sarah thought.

"Cousin Sarah," she said gently, "everybody knows you and Lucien quarreled about me. So I've come to say—"

"We didn't quarrel about you." Sarah felt a thousand years older than Lolotte; she also felt, contrarily, as if she were twelve years old and about to engage, against all rules, in a hair-pulling, no-holds-barred fight.

Lolotte made a devastatingly charming little face; her lips were literally like a rose. "So I reckon you know how things are between me and Lucien. It's always been that way, you know. It's not your fault," she said softly, watching Sarah under those soft eyelashes, missing no beat of Sarah's pulse, no rise of color in her face. "Lucien didn't tell you about me. I see now that he couldn't have told you. He just *had* to have your money."

There was something coming, something more in this than a vain and childish baiting. "Well," Sarah said, "what do you propose to do about it?"

"Oh, I don't propose to do anything." Lolotte laughed lightly, and musical and feminine as it was it yet reminded Sarah of Emile's laugh. "But surely you see how things are. Now Lucien—well, he's smart and strong and handsome but the fact is he doesn't really look ahead. We need money at Honotassa. All of us need it. Why, even Maude and Ben! What would they do without some place to live till the war is over? And if—well, if the North should win—but the North's not going to win—still they wouldn't have a penny left. Goodness knows what the Yankees have done with their plantation but they're not likely to give it back. Yankees keep things they take. Oh, I see now why Lucien married you, it was his clear duty to marry you. But what he didn't think about is that your money is in the North and there's no way for him or you to get it."

An odd, almost objective curiosity stirred. "But suppose, as you just said, the North wins."

"The North's not going to win! And besides when we win we can—oh, there'd be ways to get that money of your fa-

113

ther's. But look here, Cousin Sarah," she said coaxingly, "you don't want a husband who just married you for your money. Do you?"

"Are you suggesting a divorce?"

Lolotte winced a little too markedly. "Cousin Sarah! We don't have divorces in the South. Nobody I ever heard of has been divorced! Miss Celie wouldn't let a divorced person into the house!"

One phrase enlightened Sarah. "In the South?"

"Well, yes but—of course everybody knows things are different in the North."

"You mean that you want me to go North, arrange some kind of divorce with Lucien and leave him to you?"

The smugness in Lolotte's face almost blotted out its beauty. "But of course I reckon Lucien might feel that he ought to have some sort of settlement. A generous settlement. You've got so much money."

Sarah was sure now; Lolotte had opened and examined her marriage contract, which did not state amounts of money or its source but certainly implied that it existed. It occurred to her in the same breath that Lolotte would have been interested in ornamental, charmingly designed bottles of cologne and scent, perhaps to the extent of opening them and discovering their contents.

"Did you take anything from my room?"

"Why, you—why, how can you say such a thing to me! How can you think that I—"

"I think," Sarah said clearly, "you are a grasping, fighting, clawing little cat."

Lolotte's skirts rustled as she leaped up. Sarah was on her feet, too, without intending to move. But Lolotte's hands were only doubled up, against her slender waist. After a long moment, Lolotte laughed; it was a strained, soft and husky laugh—but it was again Emile's laugh.

Sarah said, "Why did you put that in my coffee this morning?"

Lolotte stopped laughing, she took a quick breath; her face became hard and blank below its soft contours, yet it seemed to Sarah that there was a flash of surprise in it. "What was in your coffee this morning, Cousin Sarah?"

Surprise or skillfully affected surprise? Sarah couldn't be sure. She said, "Just don't try it again, that's all."

"Something in your coffee?" Lolotte said softly. The

smugness came back into her voice. Her lips curved up, gently. "Why, Cousin Sarah! What a dreadful thing for anybody to do. Why, you must have made Lucien good and mad last night. You can see now that things aren't going to be very pleasant for you at Honotassa. But then you'll see sense and go North and—well, I must go and help Maude."

She went out, perfectly calm, moving with delicate grace, and triumphant.

So, where did I get? Sarah thought: nowhere. It was Lolotte who had attacked and enjoyed the triumph of her undoubted victory.

She wished she'd kept her mouth shut. At the same time she wished she had opened it to ask Lolotte where she had found Lucien's dueling pistols. As well try to push back the sea as to question Lolotte, Rev had said.

She sat down; she leaned her elbows on the table. There were, in fact, valid arguments in favor of Lolotte's suggestion. Why not go North, get a divorce, wash out a marriage which was no marriage? Forget it—and Honotassa?

She could get to Natchez, somehow. Rev would take her there if she asked him to. From Natchez there certainly must be ways for Sarah, a Northerner, to get to New Orleans, and then to New York.

Contrary to Lolotte's airy statement, divorce was no more usual in the North than in the South. In Paris, as far as Sarah knew, divorce simply did not exist—but then the French on occasion seemed to make various arrangements in perfect mutual amity and yet clung to the very practical and sensible marriages which were arranged for them.

Divorce? Her mind edged around it. One thing was certain; Lolotte had made no bones about a settlement—a large settlement for Lucien. The meaning behind Lolotte's words was clear; it must be large enough a settlement not only to secure Lucien's willing consent but to provide Lucien, Lolotte, Honotassa, all of them with money. Lolotte really was a little cat, Sarah thought and was glad she had said so, but she was a wily, single-minded and ruthless little cat.

She didn't hear Lolotte and Maude return. The frogs and katydids and locusts began to augment the monotonous volume of their nightly chorus.

If Sarah left Lucien she would also leave Honotassa. The look of the place during the tranquil evening hour with long blue shadows over the grass, the bright clarity of early morning with the birds all singing and the air balmy, the long green rows of cotton, the sounds and smells, the very feel of the house and the great trees, all of it seemed to crowd around her, like a dearly loved presence.

Rev loved it. Rev worked for it from morning till night. He loved every tree, every field, every stick and stone of it. He had entrusted Honotassa to her care. A faint fragrance of rain-drenched Cape Jessamine came in through the window.

No, she would not leave Honotassa. What Yankees take they keep, Lolotte had said with conscious cruelty. Well, this Yankee is going to keep Honotassa, Sarah vowed to herself. And since she had married Lucien—well, she had married him.

There was somewhere in her reasoning a deep inconsistency which she was aware of; it stirred uneasily, demanding recognition, and she thrust it away. The immediate point was that she still did not know who had dosed her coffee with opium, but she believed now that it was Lolotte.

"You can see now that things aren't going to be very pleasant for you at Honotassa," Lolotte had said smugly.

Sarah was vaguely conscious of sounds in the distance, a kind of stir muffled by the rain, out toward the barns.

She rose, cramped and numb. A myriad of small flying creatures was now darting in and around the lamp. She took the ledger with its tragic records and went to the cherry-wood desk. Her skirts rustled as she moved. At the very edge of her consciousness she was aware of some slight shuffle, Some little whisper of sound behind her, at the door.

She put the ledger into its place and turned. The door stood open upon the wet, rainy twilight; it was almost dark. No one was there. But something thin and black like a whip lay as if flung on the floor, stunned or lethargic from cold. It stirred, it moved sluggishly, yet in a second it slid under the chest in the corner.

In that slow second she saw it, too clearly.

She was afraid, she was saturated with fear. She was stricken and paralyzed and couldn't move—and did move, for she clutched up her skirt, jerked a chair toward her with a loud rasp across the floor, climbed onto it and screamed.

She took a gasping breath and had the faintest whiff of something sweet, yet not sweet, in the air, like a flower that still was not a flower. Nothing moved in the corner below the chest; nothing slid out with curious deliberation across the floor. Well, then stop screaming, she told herself and screamed again.

Somebody came running heavily along the path. Ben flung into the office, stared at her and she pointed.

He said something and got a gun from his belt. His clothes were wet and soggy, his boots splashed with mud, his rabbity face glistening. He shouted, "Don't move. I'll get him. . . ."

He moved though with a caution which seemed, too, curiously deliberate and slow. He advanced to the chest, his gun aimed at the shadows below it; then he pulled out the chest with one quick thrust and two shots filled the room with shocking crashes and the smell of powder.

Then Ben looked carefully, slowly put his gun away and kicked something like a twisted thin and wiry black reed out the door.

"Lucky I had on riding boots," he said and wiped his arm across his forehead. He shoved his gun back in his belt. In the lamplight his face was not rabbity at all; it was suddenly pointed and sharp as a ferret's. "That's a water moccasin. Nobody's playfellow. Funny—as a rule they won't come up from the swamp. But you can't tell in weather like this. Have to look out for them. Nasty things. Let one of them get near enough to bite you and that's it." He sniffed. "That's a queer smell. What is it—must be the lamp. There was news in Maville. That Yankee cavalry is headed this way. Nobody knows where they are now but they're too close." He came to her and offered his hand, which was moist, and reeking of gunpowder. "Better get down from the chair, Cousin Sarah. Time for supper."

CHAPTER THIRTEEN

Whoever put the water moccasin in the quiet little office where Sarah sat alone, it was not Ben Greevy. That was her only thought as she took Ben's hand, got down from the chair, remembered to blow out the lamp and went out into the misty, wet darkness, drawing her skirts aside from what seemed to her a dark, still faintly squirming coil beside the door.

But nobody would have put a water moccasin in the office;

it was far too dangerous. There had been opium in her coffee, but the water moccasin had to be accident.

The house was lighted. Water dripped from the trees. George came jogging up, his face a pale blur in the twilight. "Ben, you say they're at Union Church?"

"Postmaster at Maville said they were there yesterday. Nobody knows where they are today. . . . Is my horse all right? He cast that shoe on the Maville road and I reckon I rode him too hard."

"Didn't hurt him, the road was muddy and soft. We'll get him shod tomorrow. Where's Lucien?"

"Oh, he rode toward Natchez. We divided, I took the Maville road. No signs of the runaways but everybody's too worked up about this Yankee outfit to pay any mind to a wagonload of slaves. God, I'm hungry and tired."

Sarah's knees felt as if they didn't belong to her; she clutched Ben's tired arm. George cried, "Why don't they stop them? Who is commanding this Yankee cavalry? How many of them are there?"

"Now how in the world should I know that?" Ben said testily. "Some say five hundred, some say five thousand. The point is they're skyhooting all over the country. Nobody can stop them. Hell, nobody can find them. Where's Rev?"

"Last I saw he was trying to milk that cow that's got a calf and she kicked over the bucket." Something like an un-George-like chuckle came weirdly out of the dusk beyond Ben. "Rev was speaking his mind right powerful. What's General Pemberton doing?"

"What's he not doing?" Ben said sourly. "Flapping around like a chicken with its head off, seems like. But I can't say I blame him."

They came up on the porch and light from the hall streamed pallidly out. George put his hand on his gun. "Reckon I better be getting back to Vicksburg."

"Reckon we all better be stirring our stumps." Ben opened the door. Maude was bringing a lamp into the hall, its light gleaming upward onto her fine face. Lolotte came in a rush from the dining room. "Ben! did you find them?"

He stared at her for a moment as if he couldn't remember what she had expected him to find. Then he shook his head. "Nary hide nor hair of any of them. Maude, I want a toddy. I'm plumb whupped."

"*Rev?*" George shouted up the stairs. "*Rev—*"

Sarah's knees were still wobbly; she sank down in the nearest chair. Ben sagged wearily to a bench and began to tug at his muddy boots.

George's face was white with excitement; his pale eyes blazed as he questioned Ben over and over; how many Yankees, why hadn't they been stopped, where were they?

"I've told you all I know," Ben grunted. In the middle of it Rev came running down the stairs. The cow must have delivered a telling kick, for Rev had evidently just changed clothes, he was buttoning his clean white shirt, his face was shining from soap and water, his hair was still wet and crinkly from water. "What's that about the Yankees?"

George went over it all, appealing to Ben for such few details as Ben had gathered, while Ben tugged away at his boots.

Rev's face went instantly sober and hard but his black eyes snapped. And then, in the middle of it he saw Sarah, and abruptly came to her. "What's the matter, Sarah?"

Ben glanced up. "Only a water moccasin. Crawled into the office and scared her. I shot him."

"I didn't mean—it surprised me . . ." Sarah began.

"Water moccasin's enough to scare anybody," Ben said. "I was passing the office and heard her scream. Wasn't much of a scream though. Reckon she was too scared to give a good yell."

"A water moccasin," Rev said slowly. "How'd it get there?"

Sarah didn't trust her voice to reply even if she knew the answer. Ben said, "Well, it was there. Where's that toddy, Maude?"

"Wait, Maude," Rev said. "Bring some brandy for Sarah."

"Rev, for God's sake listen!" George cried. "The Yanks crossed the Southern Railroad!"

Maude disappeared into the dining room. Ben got off one boot with a plop and stared wearily at it before he tackled the other one. Lolotte said softly, "Poor Sarah! She's just not used to a plantation. Such an unpleasant thing to happen!"

"Things aren't going to be very pleasant for you at Honotassa," Lolotte had said. Her dark gaze was now sparkling and triumphant. But Lolotte couldn't have transported a water moccasin from somewhere, the swamp, anywhere; she'd have risked her own life. Nobody could safely discover and transport a water moccasin and let it loose in the quiet

119

office where Sarah sat alone; no, that was accident.

Maude thrust a small glass in Sarah's hand.

Rev said, "Drink it."

Maude snapped, "Go on and drink it, Sarah. You look like death!"

George cried, "Rev, I wish you'd listen! What are we going to do?"

Ben dropped his other boot. "I told you I want a toddy, Maude."

"Well, I've got to get hot water for it, haven't I?" Maude started for the dining room again and Ben grunted after her, "And no sorghum for sweetening. I want real sugar."

Sarah swallowed some brandy and the hot liquor traveling down her throat made her gulp.

George was shouting, everybody was talking. Maude came back with a steaming mug which she gave Ben, and joined in.

"Where is Lucien?" Lolotte cried. "What does he think about all this?"

George explained. "Lucien and Ben took different roads. Reckon Lucien hasn't heard about all this—unless he met somebody on the Natchez road."

Rev was so close to Sarah that she could have touched him; she looked up and he was watching her. His face seemed hard and rather white in the wavering, smoking light of the lamp.

Glendora said dolefully from the doorway, "Supper's ready."

They went into supper, still talking. The tallow candles smoked, too, and smelled. Glendora had brought in what apparently had been intended as a corn pudding. Maude took one bite and turned a piercing gaze at Glendora. "What is this mess?"

Glendora twisted her apron; a tear suddenly rolled down her pretty cheek.

Sarah said, "Never mind. Take it out and bring us some cold ham and milk."

Rev winced. "No milk for me, Glendora. I've just had a bath in it. . . . Ben, who is the commander of this Yankee outfit?"

Ben sipped his steaming toddy in a glum and brooding way as if he had some secret and troublesome thoughts. "They said that somebody had said it was a Colonel Grierson. Nobody's right sure of anything except that that bunch of cavalry is raising merry hell."

Rev said thoughtfully, "Well, I think he's got more than five hundred men—five hundred men couldn't do much damage. But I don't think he's got five thousand men either. That's a right smart passel of men and horses to manipulate. They must be going like greased lightning."

George got the stub of a pencil out of his pocket and began to draw awkwardly on the worn but glistening white damask tablecloth. Maude said, "Oh, George—" remonstratingly.

"Now then." George studied his rough sketch. "They must have started about here—up at the Tennessee border. Then they came down this way."

Rev took George's stubby pencil. "You said Union Church yesterday, didn't you, Ben? That looks as if they're making for Natchez but—"

Rev frowned at the penciled map and shook his head. "I think they've got to head for Baton Rouge. This Colonel Grierson must know by now that the whole state is stirred up. He can't retreat to Tennessee. He's got to make for Baton Rouge—looks to me like this is a feint. They can't do much good tearing up the railroad. . . ."

"The Southern's Vicksburg's main supply line," George interrupted.

"But still, if this Grierson's got only a brigade and I don't see how it can be more than that—" Rev thought for a moment and then said soberly, "No. Looks to me like it's an attempt to divert Pemberton, because Grant intends to make an attack. Did anybody know anything about what Grant's doing, Ben?"

Ben seemed to come out of a brooding abstraction. "Huh—oh, Grant. Well, now old Judge Hill did say he'd heard that some Yankee boats got past Vicksburg. He figured he was about the middle of April. But then Judge Hill's always got a heap of ideas. And what news he gets is so late that it doesn't mean much."

"This may mean something, late or not," Rev said. "Grant's got to have transports to cross the river."

George exploded. "I tell you, Rev, he can't make it! The guns at Vicksburg, the guns at Grand Gulf will stop him. . . ." George slapped the table and argued. Rev leaned his black head on one hand and studied the map. Glendora had brought in ham and some beans, cooked so long with side meat and a little brown sugar that they were brown, and cold from waiting. Nobody paid much attention to what they ate although Maude looked at the beans and muttered direly, "Next time I go out in the rain to get fresh eggs for a corn pudding, I won't."

Eggs, Sarah thought, and remembered Lolotte with her basket. She wondered, queerly, whether anybody could induce a water moccasin to enter a basket and decided that nobody in the world, certainly not Lolotte, could possibly engage in so dangerous an enterprise.

The candle flames reflected themselves in gleams from the array of silver on the sideboards. George insisted that Rev was wrong. "I tell you Grant can't get men or supplies or artillery across the river."

"Grant's a fighter," Rev said soberly.

George pounded the table so hard that the glasses danced. "Rev, I swear you act scared."

"I am scared. If we've pulled out men from Vicksburg, from Grand Gulf, from God knows where, to chase this Yankee brigade, it looks to me as if that was what Grant planned and he's about to make a move."

George started eating ham which Lolotte, sitting beside him, had cut for him. "Well, one thing's sure. I'm off tomorrow. Might be that Rev's right. If he is we need every man and every gun we can get at Vicksburg."

"George!" Maude's nose lifted. "Do you mean to say you're going to leave us women alone here with the Yankees coming?"

Rev replied. "If they do come this way they'll take horses, unless you can hide them. They'll take corn. They'll take food for their men. But a raiding party can't be burdened with plunder. And they're not likely to start shooting women—"

"*Rev,*" Lolotte screamed. "You know what they've done other places! Bayonets and women and little children and—"

Maude broke in. "Oh, now Lolotte, what's the good of their shooting women and bayoneting children; I never believed any of those wild stories. Rev, are you leaving, too?"

Rev, his eyes on the map, nodded.

Where was Rev going? Sarah thought. To Vicksburg—no, he'd go back to Virginia to his company.

Maude snapped, "When?"

Without looking up, matter-of-factly, Rev said, "Tomorrow, I reckon. Maybe next day. Something is brewing in Virginia. General Lee can't send help to Vicksburg because he needs or is going to need every man and gun he can get. That's sure."

Ben said, "Get me another toddy, Maude."

"If Lucien's heard about this Yankee cavalry, he'll know where they're going," George said. "There's not a better officer in the whole Confederate army than Lucien."

"Why don't they make him a general and end the war?" Maude said tartly and vanished toward the kitchen.

Lolotte put up her pretty head with its heavy black chignon and listened. George looked up from the map and listened, too. Then Sarah heard the heavy thud of hoofs along the driveway. "There's Lucien!" Lolotte ran for the door, her wide skirts like a fan below her slender waist. George cried, "Now we'll get at the truth." But he had a gun, like magic again, in that deadly able and adroit left hand.

It was Lucien—tired, his uniform soggy, his boots muddy —but Lucien in an exuberant, excited mood, his black eyes shining, his face red from the long ride, the weather and the news. He hadn't found the runaways, no sign of them. But he'd heard about the Yankee cavalry.

The news, the danger seemed to go to his head like the toddy he asked for at once and Lolotte flashed away to prepare. He came around the table, his boots clattering on the floor, gathered Sarah up hard in his arms and kissed her vigorously.

It didn't matter about the slaves. He'd stopped at Grafton. ". . . It's just a wide place in the road," he said to Sarah. "Nothing there but a general store but it's on one of the Natchez roads. Everybody around was there, swapping news. Lots of it was talk but—thank you, Lolotte." He took the steaming drink and went on. "It's a cavalry force, about a brigade some say, some say more, under a Colonel Grierson. They've been playing hell with the Southern Railroad."

"We know all that!" George cried. "Where are they heading?"

"Back to Tennessee, if they're smart. Give me some of that ham."

Lolotte fluttered to bring the big platter of ham; she called to Glendora to heat up the beans. Maude was back by then and Ben had another toddy in his hand.

The argument began again. Lucien scoffed at Rev's belief

123

that the Union cavalry would make for Baton Rouge. George listened and nodded, approvingly; Lucien was always right.

The Yankee cavalry wouldn't come along the Honotassa road; why should they? Lucien shouted to Glendora to get him some of that stuff they called coffee. He looked at the awkwardly lined map on the tablecloth and chuckled. "If they do come this way, we'll give them a dose of lead poisoning."

Lolotte, sitting beside Lucien now, her elbows on the table, her face cradled in her white hands, said with a soft-drawn, admiring breath, "You and George act as if—why, as if you'd heard battle bugles."

Maude snorted resoundingly. "I don't reckon that's a very fine sound for men who have fought."

George's face flushed. "Reckon Lucien and I have done as much fighting as anybody, Maude!"

Ben stirred at that, as if there were a not too well concealed insult. "I'd have been in the army long ago, George, if it hadn't been for this heart of mine."

"You'd have been in the army if you hadn't spent so much time figuring out how to save your plantation," George flashed back, quick as an adder.

Maude started to rise; it was sheer chance that she was carving more ham and had the sharp knife in her hand but it caught ominous glints from the candles. Ben said, "Now, now, Maude, George doesn't mean that. He's all worked up."

And at that very moment Miss Celie, whose empty place at the table nobody had questioned, came in from the hall. Her black wrapper was loosely tied; her thick white arm came out from it, pointing straight at the glass of milk at Sarah's place. Her face was stony white, her black hair was for once untidy, falling from its thick knot. She whispered piercingly, "Don't touch that milk. It's ground glass this time."

CHAPTER FOURTEEN

Sarah quite literally could feel the color drain away from her face. She thought of opium in coffee, first. Then she expected outcries, commotion, something. There was nothing but a tired, half-bored, certainly accustomed acceptance. Lolotte made a little face. Maude's lips tightened. Lucien said, "Oh,

124

for God's sake, has she got one again?"

Rev rose and went to Miss Celie. He put his arm around her. "Now, Miss Celie. There's no ground glass anywhere."

"Then it's poisoned. It's all poisoned." Miss Celie looked like a sleepwalker.

"It's not poisoned," Rev said. "Haven't you had anything to eat today? Then you've got to eat. Now I'll give you exactly what we've had. There's nothing in it, Miss Celie—"

She pulled back against his arm. "No, no! You won't listen. You don't understand."

"Miss Celie—now I tell you—"

Glendora solved it. Suddenly her immature body, her round little face were full of authority. She took Miss Celie's hand; she led her to the table, murmuring gently, saying something, anything, Sarah didn't know what. She put her down in a chair. "Now, Miss Celie, you just got a silly spell. You know I ain't going to hurt you. Here—" Glendora had been bringing coffee for Lucien when Miss Celie came into the room. She picked up the cup and began to spoon it, as she might have fed a baby, into Miss Celie's mouth. "Take another spoonful now—you hadn't ought to be saying things like that, Miss Celie. You just make it bad for yourself—now take another—"

Miss Celie's eyes were fastened on Glendora's gentle, worrying little face as if she couldn't look anywhere else; she swallowed the coffee, she swallowed more; presently she took the cup and drank the whole of it, and then queerly as if she were awakening from a nightmare gave herself a kind of shake and glanced around the table. "It's not poisoned," she said firmly.

"Sure enough you do give anybody the creeps, Miss Celie," Glendora said matter-of-factly. "Now you eat some good old ham and corn bread."

Obviously it was over; the vapors had ended. Without more ado the men went back to their argument.

Ground glass, Sarah thought, and there had been opium in her own coffee only that morning.

There was no connection but she wondered how many women in the South, how many men and women everywhere suffered, as Maude had realistically said, from a deep sense of guilt. It struck her suddenly as hopeful, promising an end to that ancient guilt and struggle, that of them all Glendora, in

125

her childlike honesty, her pitying and suddenly mature kindliness, had been the one to restore Miss Celie's sense of reality.

Glendora matter-of-factly again began gathering up plates. George said that somebody ought to stand watch that night. Rev said he didn't think the Union cavalry was likely to do much night riding along strange, winding roads. Ben stirred and told Lucien that he'd met a friend of his in Maville. "John Rader. He was wounded; he's been at home on furlough."

"Oh," Lucien said, "good old John. Hope he rides over here to see us."

Rev took Miss Celie to the stairs and Miss Celie whispered, "I'm sorry, I can't help it. It's over now—" as if she'd had an attack of migraine.

That night they locked up the house, they closed and bolted shutters. That night George and Rev made a long reconnaissance of the whole place out around the barns, down the driveway.

Once the house had settled to a deep silence, with only the sounds of frogs and katydids around it, Sarah went to Lucien's room. The hall was dark so she took her bedroom candle, which cast wavering shadows as she passed the closed doors and the open well of the stairway. At the end of the corridor a faintly lighter patch outlined the small door to the steps that climbed along the wall outside; the door was open, for a misty breath of air touched her face. It had stopped raining but there was still a steady drip from the vines. She knocked at the door of Lucien's room, the southeast corner room, the choice room for the master of the house.

She heard him give a startled exclamation; then he opened the door and laughed softly. He drew her into the room, still laughing. "I said you'd change your mind. I knew it wouldn't take twenty-four hours—"

"What did you do with the gold you took from the office? I want it back."

His face changed. "The gold! You fool! I told you not to trust Rev."

"Don't lie to me, Lucien."

He caught her shoulder so hard that she dropped the candle and it rolled on the carpet, sending up a swift smell of burning wool. She pulled away from him, scooped up the candle and trod out the tiny sparks with her slipper. He caught her arm again. "We'll go to the office. I'll see for my-

126

self! For all I know you are lying to me—covering up for Rev! Come on—"

He took the candle and put it down on the table. He gripped her wrist, pulled her out into the hall and then, instead of going down through the sleeping house, he drew her outside onto the little stairway. It was dark; the fragrance of honeysuckle was sweet in the night; the steps were soggy with rain and uneven but Lucien led the way, sure-footed as a cat, down the steps and around the house. The lawn was wet. Not a light showed in the dim bulk of the house.

Once in the office he released her, groped around for the lamp and lighted it. He asked her what floorboards were loose; he thrust the big table aside, got a knife from his pocket and pried up the boards. The lamplight fell upon his big, squatting figure; his white shirt was rumpled from the day's ride and half unbuttoned. He had changed his riding boots for house slippers. He groped into the empty space with such singleminded intent that it convinced Sarah. Whoever had taken the gold it was not Lucien.

But only Rev, besides Lucien, knew that it was there.

At last Lucien thumped back the floorboards. He rose and shoved the table back over them. Then he sat down in one of the straight chairs, wiped his soiled-stained hands on his shirt and looked at her. "So Rev did take it," he said heavily at last. "Or did you give it to him?"

"I didn't give it to anyone."

He eyed her for a moment; she had no idea what thoughts and speculations were racing behind that bright, fixed gaze. Finally he wiped his forehead with the back of his hand. "I told you that I wondered how Rev dared to enter New Orleans, I even said he might be turning Yankee. I didn't believe it, then. But now—did you pay him to turn Yankee?"

"No!"

He might not have heard her. "Well, he's not worth that much. But Rev went to New Orleans, out of uniform. They'd have hanged him and he knew it—unless he knew, too, that he was safe. If he's made some kind of deal with the Yankees—"

"He hasn't!"

"Oh, you Yankees. You pretend you despise deserters. That's to save your hypocritical self-respect. Actually you'd get anybody to turn Yankee you dared approach—"

"That's not true. You know that, Lucien. I've never said a

word—we agreed not to try to change each other's beliefs." How long ago that seemed: a different woman and a different man.

"Rev went to New Orleans out of uniform. You can't deny that. He's got away with that gold of yours, with or without your consent. You've got to make him give it back to you."

"I don't believe Rev took it."

"Oh, I can see that Rev's got you wrapped around his little finger. He's already got that gold. But he—why, yes, he figures I may get a bullet! So that's why he's been giving you all that sweet talk about seeing to Honotassa. He figures I may not come back—but he'll come back because he's going to make himself safe in some Yankee bombproof job till the war is over. Why, whether I live or die he'll be in clover— with that gold of yours to give him a start. But you wouldn't give it to me to buy Confederate bonds."

"I didn't give it to Rev. Lucien, where are the bonds you bought?"

"They're not here in the office. I reckon you've looked—"

"No, I haven't looked but—"

"Then do you doubt whether or not I bought bonds with the mortgage money?"

"I don't know what you did with it."

"How else would I spend it!"

"Debts—"

His face flushed; then he laughed. "Who's been talking to you? Rev? Or Maude? It was Maude. I can tell by your face. Maude once set her cap for me. She's hated me ever since. Sounds like she filled you up with stories of me."

"She said that you had settled down," Sarah said dryly, remembering Maude's reason for approving, now, of Lucien; he had sensibly married and married a woman with money. "Lucien, I can't get any money from my father's estate until the war is over."

He was still half laughing. "The war may not be over for a long time and when it *is* over—darling, I didn't marry you for money you may never be able to get from the North. Rev took that gold—I wanted to buy bonds with it. You said you wanted it for Honotassa. But that isn't important. What is important is my brother, Rev—turning Yankee."

She remembered a cogent argument in Rev's defense. "He can't have any friends among Union officials in New Orleans!

He was out of uniform and he was afraid they'd arrest him. He knew they'd hang him if they caught him—"

"He's a good liar and a good actor."

"No—the banker who loaned you money came into the hotel. Rev was afraid he'd discover that I was there, he'd see my name—that is, your name and he'd demand to see me and if he caught Rev he'd report him—"

"But Rev wasn't caught," Lucien said. He rose. "I may be wrong about Rev turning Yankee. I hope so. My brother— the Hugot name. No, I can't believe that, not really, in spite of his trip to New Orleans and—no; Rev's got that gold but I don't believe that he'd desert to the Yankees. He couldn't do that. I'm sorry I spoke as I did."

"I don't think Rev took the gold," she said stubbornly.

He shrugged. "Let it go. I'm not going to quarrel with you again. I want to talk to you about something else. . . ."

"I want to talk to you. There are things here that you don't know, Lucien. I tried to tell you last night." She hesitated, then came out with it baldly. "I believe Emile was murdered—"

"Of course he was murdered! A Yankee shot him."

"No. I think—I'm afraid it was someone else. And this morning there was opium in my coffee—"

"*Opium!*"

"I brought some medicines with me from Havana. The bottle of opium disappeared the day I arrived here, the day Emile was shot."

He stared at her. He sat down heavily, still staring. "Do you realize what you are saying? Why—why—" The red flush surged up into his face. "You have the—the—why, you're standing there accusing one of my family of—murder! Opium!"

"Rev knows about Emile. He gave a cartridge—"

"*Rev!* This settles it, Sarah. You are still a Yankee at heart. You hate my family. Oh, it may be that they haven't given you the attention you wanted, the admiration, all that."

"Lucien—"

"I'll grant you that Lolotte may show her jealousy in naughty little ways. Of course, George hates any Yankee. But murder! Dosing you with opium! You've gone too far—"

"Lucien, I'm telling you the truth. You must listen—"

"This settles it. Now we'll not quarrel. I'll tell you what's been in my mind, what I wanted to talk to you about. I couldn't help seeing that you are not happy here. I thought you would be; obviously you are not, or you wouldn't make such accusations. So I'll take you to Natchez in the morning. You can get to New York by way of New Orleans and wait for me there—"

"That's what Lolotte wants me to do. And then get a divorce from you but first giving you a generous settlement."

"Did Lolotte say that? I'll wring her little—oh, that's nonsense. I don't want a divorce. I don't want a settlement. I'd never think of such a thing. I only want you to go where you'll be among friends, happier than you are here, until the war is over. Wait for me there. Now pack your clothes, we'll start early."

"I have no clothes to pack and I'm not going."

"Oh, but you are going." He rose; the disarming smile was on his handsome face; he came toward her, his arms out to take her in his embrace. "Now we'll say no more about all this talk of murder and opium and—why, darling, I'm your husband. I intend to make you happy and protect you and—"

She was not afraid of Lucien. But she clutched at the chair near her and thrust it so hard against his knees that, taken off balance, he staggered. She slid past his still outstretched arms, his still half-laughing yet astonished face, and ran out of the office along the path, past the dark, sleeping house. She remembered that the door from the porch was locked. She ran around the house, found the small stairway and fled up through the murmurous blackness and the night scent of flowers.

It was easy to find her own room, for the door was open. She then gulped for breath and felt like a harebrained, panic-stricken fool. Running from nothing. Lucien would be angry. Lucien would be furious. Lucien had every right to be furious.

When she had got her breath and her heart had stopped its thudding she went to the window. After a long time the pale gleams of light from the shrubbery around the office vanished. She heard Lucien's footsteps, crunching leisurely along the path. There was the small red glow of a cigar and the scent of tobacco.

He strolled along the lawn; she could follow him by the moving, tiny circle of red light.

That, too, gave her a sense of absurd anticlimax. While she had fled up the stairs as if she'd taken leave of her senses, Lucien had calmly lighted a cigar and smoked it, and then as calmly returned to the house.

Her candle was in Lucien's room. Finally she went to bed in the dark. At least she had spoken her mind, or part of it. She did not intend to leave Honotassa. She did not believe that Rev had taken the gold.

That was the night of April twenty-ninth.

CHAPTER FIFTEEN

Many things happened the night of April twenty-ninth. The drizzling rain blew away; the fog dissipated itself; the night turned warmer.

Across the rolling, twisting, muddy Mississippi, Grant's army prepared to move again after a Union attack had been repulsed the previous day by the guns of Grand Gulf. A new approach was found. Transport by boat was already at hand. Port Gibson, a few miles from the too well defended Grand Gulf, offered an initial point of attack after landing —Port Gibson from which Confederate cavalry had been drawn in a pursuit of Grierson's brigade.

General Pemberton, in command at Vicksburg, was distracted, as he was meant to be, by Grierson's brigade, wreaking sporadic havoc within the state, here today, gone tomorrow, only to turn up where they were least expected the next day.

The government in Richmond could not send men to Vicksburg's aid; there were not enough men and arms to send. If Vicksburg went the Confederacy would be cut in two; the control of the river would be lost. But if Richmond went, the war would be lost.

The night of April twenty-ninth was a fateful time: It is always possible, in the hindsight of war, to discover some particular night or day, some particular hour of decision, which seems to mark in its own way a turning point of destiny. If so, the night of April twenty-ninth was such a night and such an hour.

But if so there were no signs and portents. That night Grierson's cavalry rested some eight miles south of Brook-

131

haven, far nearer Honotassa than anyone there could have suspected. Perhaps some men, camping under the night sky, were restless and touched with secret doubts as to whether or not they would spend another night under the soft Mississippi stars, so they turned in their sleep and murmured.

But at Honotassa it was quiet. Yet at Honotassa, too, another kind of decision was made during some dark and wakeful moment.

Dawn was never more beautiful. The sun streaked softly over the green-striped fields. The green lawns sparkled with dew. The birds sang their hearts out in the golden morning hours. The rain-wet honeysuckle and Cape Jessamine flooded the balmy air with fragrance. The roses in the untended garden began to lift their rain-heavy heads.

That morning Glendora brought no coffee, with or without opium. When Sarah went downstairs a stir of imminent departure was already in the air and in the hall there were rolled-up blankets, small parcels, odds and ends which George or Rev or both had gathered together. Maude was savagely cutting out a hole in a battered piece of oilcloth, making a poncho-like garment. "It's for Rev," she said. "He's got the longest trip to make. There's enough left to make one for George, too."

Sarah looked at the worn, shiny oilcloth and thought of long rides, or longer nights under pouring rain, and did not think the oilcloth, which showed cracks and patches of bare threads, would keep out much rain.

Miss Celie was moving swiftly about, ordering Maude, ordering Glendora, ordering everybody. She told Sarah the exact amount of supplies to measure out for the day and when Lolotte appeared told her there was a cobweb in the corner of the parlor and directed her to wrap an old towel around a broom, brush it down and then clean the lamps. There was not the faintest sign of the woman who had cowered behind a locked door the previous day, alone with terror, or who had said, "It's ground glass this time."

Sarah started along the passageway to the kitchen, her keys in her hand, and saw Ben through the curtain of lilacs. Ben was behaving in a peculiar way. He trotted a few steps toward the office, turned around as if he had a string tied to him, pulling him back, then brought himself to a stop, sneezed and wiped his face with his handkerchief, whirled around, started for the office—and as Sarah reached the kitchen door seemed about to repeat the whole performance. Clearly he had caught a cold during his rainy ride of the previous day; he sneezed dismally as she went into the kitchen.

Glendora gathered up baskets. When they went out toward the storehouse Sarah saw that Ben had given up whatever his erratic purpose had been and was settling himself, still sneezing, in a sunny corner of the porch.

As they reached the storehouse Rev came along the path, took one look at Sarah and said, "Glendora, you can get out the supplies." He reached for the bundle of keys, put it in Glendora's hand, turned Sarah to stroll with him along the path, out of Glendora's hearing, and said, "What's happened? You look—I reckon Lucien found out that I took the gold."

"You took it!" The earth under Sarah's feet seemed to waver.

He nodded. "I've got it hidden. I'll tell you where before I leave!"

"Why did you take it, Rev, why? Lucien said it was you; I didn't believe it—"

"Reckon we'd better talk to Lucien. He's in the office."

Lucien, standing in the door of the office, saw them coming. He opened the door politely, and there was no trace of anger, no slightest apparent memory of Sarah's absurd flight of the night before. She felt pink flames come up into her cheeks when she saw the chair she had flung at him, still on its side, in the middle of the floor.

Rev said, "I took the gold, Lucien. No need to get in a state about it. I've got it hidden where you can't find it and I'll tell Sarah where before I leave. If you want to know why it's because I figured you'd want it and I know that Sarah will need it."

Lucien's eyebrows went up but he was still incredibly good-natured. "Well, now that's a fine thing to say. What did you think I'd do with that gold?"

"Oh, Lucien, you know what you did with every penny of cash you could ever lay your hands on."

"I bought Confederate bonds."

"You paid debts and you got yourself further into debt. You spent money like water before and after Pa died. If you were determined to gamble why didn't you learn the difference between a straight and a flush—"

That drew a spark from Lucien. "I don't need you to teach me how to play cards!" But then unexpectedly he laughed. "I'll admit I had some debts to pay when Pa died. I was young and foolish and—but that gold doesn't matter. He'll give it back to you, Sarah." He looked at Rev. "Reckon you took my dueling pistols, too."

"Yes, I did. But that's another thing, Lucien. Emile was shot—no, wait. I'll tell you all I know. I had a Spencer cartridge so I gave it to the coroner and told him a Yankee straggler shot Emile. But the fact is, I believe that somebody had used one of your dueling pistols. So, I put them away. Ben's got a gun, George has got a gun and so have I. But that's all the guns there are on the place except your pistols and there's no sense leaving the pistols around."

"I see. Yes, I see. I'm sorry, Sarah. I really thought you were having a brainstorm. Well then, Rev, who shot Emile?"

"I don't know. Might even have been some stranger, somebody happened on the place and managed to get hold of your pistols or—but whoever it was, I didn't see any use in telling the coroner—"

"And having a murder investigation." Lucien was frowning. "Miss Celie—Lolotte—Ben and George. Why even you, Rev!"

"I didn't shoot him. But I'll tell you this, Emile gave me considerable bother. I reckon I've got to apologize to you."

"Apologize!"

"Emile was in New Orleans a while ago. He hunted around for some of his old chums and came home with the story that—well, the fact is, Lucien, that one of them had seen you in New Orleans, hand in glove, on the friendliest terms, with some Yankee officers. So I went to New Orleans to get at the facts, if I could."

Sarah's mind leaped back to Emile, giggling and threatening. "Why, that's why Emile asked for money! That's why —Lucien, he said you were in cahoots, that's what he said, in cahoots with the Union and that Rev was, too. I told you—"

"Do you mean to say," Lucien asked Rev, "that you believed this? Coming from Emile?"

"Coming from Emile, no. And I didn't believe it of you. But I had to prove it or disprove it. I just had to," Rev said simply. "And I found Sarah in New Orleans and she told me that you had been in Cuba and why. So I knew Emile was lying. But then—then I got to thinking—" He turned to Sarah. "I got to thinking that you, being a Northerner, just might have—"

"Tried to influence me?" Lucien broke in and put back his head and roared. "Not Sarah!"

"No. No, I decided that. And she said you were in uniform in Cuba and—so that's why I've got to apologize to you. Matter of fact, I stayed over my leave hoping you'd get home. So—" Rev said soberly, "that's off my mind."

Still Lucien was almost fantastically good-natured. He slapped Rev on the back. "I can't say I blame you. It wasn't very brotherly of you in one way. But still I can't say I blame you. Why, the fact is, when Sarah told me that gold was gone, I—we might as well have it all out in the open—the fact is, I got it into my head that maybe *you* were going to desert and take Sarah's gold with you. You see, you had gone into New Orleans, out of uniform, and I couldn't see why you'd take such a risk unless you had some good Yankee friends but—yes, I reckon I've got to apologize, too. And there's another thing, Rev: it's been on my mind. This business of Pa's estate wasn't fair."

A slightly puzzled look came into Rev's eyes.

"Oh well, that's the way it is."

"No, it wasn't fair. I'll admit that when I was younger I—yes, I did spend too much. I liked life in New Orleans, you liked Honotassa. When Pa died I did use up every cent of money I could get hold of. I sold some slaves, I—but I did use that mortgage money for bonds. The point is, I'm older now. Maybe war sobers a man. Anyway if we both come out of this war, Rev, I'm going to make it right with you. You'll have half of Honotassa."

Rev's face closed in. Sarah wondered again how she could have thought the two men so closely resembled each other. They were both tall and broad-shouldered; they both moved with a certain ease and grace, in spite of Rev's heavy limp. They both had dark hair and eyes and a swift gaiety of manner when she least expected it. Yet they were as different as two men could be.

Rev said shortly, "Reckon I can make my own way."

"Now see here, Rev, I don't care about that gold. I was good and mad when I knew you had taken it. But Lord, if you don't trust me enough to tell me what you've done with it, I don't care."

"Sarah is going to need it."

"I admit I was going to use it. But I admit now that she's right, she'll need it here. I'll not even ask where it is." Lucien gave Rev's still face a long look and laughed again. "You still don't trust me."

Rev shrugged. "It's Sarah's money."

Now Lucien would be angry; the red, ugly flush would surge up into his face. It didn't. He clapped Rev on the back again. "I told you, I don't care. Keep your secret. Now then —what about this business of Emile being shot? I think you did right, mind you, not to report it as murder. In the first place, you've got mighty slim evidence."

"Oh, there was evidence. That pistol of yours had been fired. I couldn't say the hour and minute but I think it was that night."

"Where did you find it? Near Emile?"

"No." Rev said flatly. "Lolotte said she took your pistols from your room, intending to hide them from the Yankees. That was just after Emile was shot, maybe fifteen minutes or so."

Lucien frowned; then his face cleared. "Why, then you're barking up the wrong tree. Nobody would have taken the risk of bringing my pistols back to my room after shooting Emile, if that's your notion. Besides—no, I can't believe that —why, nobody here would murder anybody! But you did right, just the same. If anybody did lose his head and shoot Emile—no, it's better to let sleeping dogs lie."

There was a curious small silence. Outside, the door of the storehouse closed with a bang. A bird rustled in the vines over the window. Sarah had a certain knowledge that somehow there was communication between Rev and Lucien. Both of them silently agreed to shield Emile's murderer.

Rev said, "That's settled then. . . ."

Glendora came to the door. "Miss Sarah. Reckon Miss Celie aims you to keep the keys."

Sarah took the bundle of keys. Suddenly Glendora's head jerked up, she stared toward the kitchen, through the covered passageway and shouted, "*Somebody coming—horses and men—*"

Rev said something and ran past her, past Glendora's suddenly still and stricken little figure in its faded calico.

Lucien cried, "It's the Yankees—" and brushed past Sarah, running, too.

A lonely dog, sunning himself on Uncle Jethro's door-step, lifted his head, howled and shot for the front driveway. There was the jingle of bridle bits, the thud of horses' hoofs, a man shouting. "Halt—dismount."

Lucien and Rev plunged through the shrubbery bordering the open passage to the kitchen. Ben jumped up from his chair and trotted heavily along the porch toward the door and Sarah ran, too, thinking, as Lucien had shouted, it's the Yankee cavalry.

It was not Yankee cavalry; it was a detachment of men from Major John DeBaun's force, out to intercept the Grierson cavalry, and they had been sent north from the main force to get information; they also wanted water for their horses, they wanted food.

The women, everybody, crowded onto the front porch. There was only a handful of men, in butternuts, on horses, looking tired. Down at the end of the driveway others waited; through the veils of Spanish moss Sarah caught a glimpse of horses, more butternuts, pistols and harness rings gleaming in the sunlight.

No one had information for them; no one knew where Grierson's cavalry was then; George and Lucien theorized but they had only theories. Rev told them the well was back of the house and shouted to Glendora to get out food.

Sarah went to the storehouse; Maude and Glendora went with her. Maude muttered angrily as they got out cornmeal and dried peas, and more angrily when they went to the smokehouse and got down two huge, crusted hams, hanging from the smoke-stained rafters.

"This keeps on, we'll have nothing left. That's enough, Sarah. It's not an army!"

The haste of the men in butternuts communicated itself to all of them. They built up fires, they sliced ham; Maude, still muttering, stirred up big batches of corn pone.

The men seemed to surround the house, yet there were really only a few of them. The well bucket trundled up and down, up and down, the windlass creaking, as they watered their horses. "There won't be any water left," Maude snorted and peered at the steaming pot of peas.

They fed the horses, and Rufe and Vampa wickered and snorted from the barnyard as disapprovingly as Maude. The men sat around below the trees; they washed their grimy faces and hands at the wellhouse. They gulped down water, and milk and clabber from the great crocks along the well-house shelves. Sarah began nervously to think that Maude might be right; would anything be left to them? The smell of frying ham filled the kitchen.

Lucien moved among the men, and talked with a bearded young lieutenant. This was Lucien at his best, gravely listening or pleasantly joking, tall and handsome and as gracious and hospitable as if he had invited each one of them as a guest at Honotassa. This was the Lucien who had listened that morning, who had held no grudge, who had come to friendly terms with Rev, who had offered Rev his fair half-share of Honotassa. Uncle Jethro emerged and made rather a to-do about the well and the buckets of water for the horses but actually did very little. George and Rev saw to their feed.

Lolotte didn't help in the kitchen but she, too, moved among the men and smiled and talked, and they snatched off battered hats and their eyes lighted as she passed, her wide skirts swinging as gracefully as if she were on a dance floor.

"Lolotte is so hot for the cause," Maude said grimly, her nose very long and red with heat from the stove. "Why doesn't she come in here and fry some of that ham?"

Sarah said slowly, "I think she's doing more good out there," and wished that people were consistent, either bad or good, no bewildering shades to try to understand.

"Listen to you talk!" Maude jeered. "I never took you for a sentimentalist." But she went savagely back to the stove.

The noon sun had passed its peak when the men and horses, fed and rested, started off again. Their thanks were varied. "Sure thank you ladies." "We do appreciate your kindness, ma'am." "Best corn pone I ever ate—mighty near as good as my old woman's." "Madam—Madam," with bows to Sarah, to Maude, to Miss Celie, to Lolotte, "we are deeply grateful for your hospitality."

One of them, small, with sparkling black eyes in his swarthy face unerringly picked Miss Celie, kissed her hand and thanked her with charming, polite French compliments.

The bronzed young lieutenant spoke to Lucien. "Thank you, Captain."

"I hope you get them."

"Yes, sir!" The lieutenant grinned wearily. "We'll do our best. Trouble is to find the damned"—he checked himself with a glance at Miss Celie and said, "find them." He saluted. The men, already on their horses, gave a kind of ragged but warmly admiring cheer as Lolotte, standing beside one of the white pillars, waved at them.

They jogged off then at a trot, down the long avenue and disappeared. Rev watched them go, soberly. George, his face already triumphant, said they'd get the Yankees, sure. Lucien nodded.

Miss Celie took a hairpin from her sliding knot of jet black hair, secured the knot with one swift jab and whispered suddenly and piercingly, "Good heavens, what are we standing around here for, like simple-minded idiots? *Yankees are coming!*"

CHAPTER SIXTEEN

She trundled into the house, her little feet carrying her vast bulk with lightning swiftness. Maude and Lolotte followed her, their wide skirts swaying; suddenly there was another kind of hubbub all over the place.

It was like a repetition of the night after Emile's murder but it was, this time, organized. And this time it was all too likely that Union cavalry, hungry, needing fresh horses, was actually somewhere in the vicinity.

Miss Celie directed affairs in the house. She sent Sarah to the smokehouse; from there she heard horses snorting as Rev and George and Lij, the stable boy, drove them toward the spring with its fenced enclosure for just such an emergency. Uncle Jethro, helping Sarah, made her carry most of the hams and sidemeat. Their hiding place was under the bed in his cabin and he draped blankets to cover them. All the time her mind pursued a kind of inner track: Lucien and Rev, whatever their old-time differences and whatever their mutual doubts, had cleared the slate and made peace, Lucien with a forbearance which she could not have expected of him.

That was good; if Rev left the next day and Lucien left soon, too, they might never see each other again. With a kind of chill, that hot day, she refused to let her mind dwell on that.

A chilling thought of another kind was that when Rev and George, and then Lucien, rode away she would be alone with her nagging, sure knowledge of Emile's murder and

139

with his murderer. Let sleeping dogs lie, Lucien had said. Rev obviously, from the first, had taken that stand. What did they both believe, what knowledge or suspicion did they share? Or had she only fancied some silent communication between them?

She went back and forth between smokehouse and Uncle Jethro's cabin, carrying the heavy hams until her arms ached; she was hot and sticky as the sun began to edge down toward the highest oaks.

When the smokehouse was empty and Uncle Jethro retired, tottering, his hand at his back, she went back to the house and met Lolotte on the porch. Her face was pink with heat and exertion; moist tendrils of black curls had fallen from her heavy chignon; she had gathered up her skirt to hold silver. "Help me, Sarah."

Spoons and a small silver pitcher clattered to the floor of the porch. Sarah scooped them up and then held up her own skirt to receive silver platters, a claret jug, ladles and serving spoons, as Lolotte divided her load.

They hid the silver in a hollow, obviously prepared and used before, below Stash's cabin. Lolotte had already made one or two trips to the hiding place, for Sarah caught a flashing glimpse of a gold-framed miniature, sparkling with garnets, and more silver, pushed way back into the dusky hollow. They carried two more loads from the house, including the array of objects d'art (many of which were by no means art but all of which were certainly loved) which as a rule stood on the shelves of the breakfront in the parlor.

When they had finished Lolotte took up rough boards, splintery and damp, and wedged them tightly over the opening.

She looked up at Sarah. "Now you know where it's all hidden. You can tell your Yankee friends when they arrive!"

"They may not get here. And they are not thieves."

Lolotte laughed, the scornful, soft Hugot laugh. "They act like thieves. Didn't you read any newspapers in Paris? Don't you know what they've done in other places?" She sucked at a splinter in her soft, pink palm and tried to dig it out with a fingernail.

Let her dig, Sarah thought crossly but said, "Here—let me."

She pried out the splinter cautiously; a tiny red drop followed it. Lolotte sucked at it again and said, her eyes veiled, "Thanks."

By the time they trudged back to the house through the lowering sunlight, the barnyard, the hen coops, the whole place was remarkably silent. There was then the kitchen to clear up, the litter around wellhouse and lawn, the empty crocks, the buckets. "Looks like the Yankees had already been here," Maude said sourly. "Glendora, if you don't get busy with dishwashing I'll hit you a lick you'll not soon forget."

"Can't do it all myself," Glendora replied mutinously.

"Many hands make light work," Miss Celie said but trundled swiftly away herself. Maude glared after her and reached for the soap.

It was nearly dusk when Sarah at last went to her room, washed her hot face, changed to a fresh dress, Lolotte's pink muslin by chance, and for coolness returned downstairs. The big basket of mending which Miss Celie had assigned to her stood in the hall with Lucien's gray broadcloth jacket folded on top. Obviously Miss Celie had placed it there for mending; she looked it over, found a snag on the sleeve and some gold buttons loose, and took it and her basket out to the porch.

Ben was sitting there, lost in thought. He stirred, watched her for a moment as she fumbled for thread, and then came to her.

"Thought we might have a little talk, Cousin Sarah," he said softly. "I'll be leaving one of these days, too—some things I want to tell you before I go—I might stop a bullet, you know, and Maude—well, I want to talk to you—we might walk this way—I don't want everybody in the house —Maude—to hear me."

He sneezed and looked so miserable she hadn't the heart to put him off, although she didn't think it likely that Ben would put himself in the way of a bullet if he could help it. Still Ben had come to her rescue when she needed it the night before, promptly dispatching the water moccasin. She went with him across the lawn and didn't realize that they had entered the path leading to the circle around the cupid and the black cedars, below which Emile had been shot, until the shadows of the hedge closed around her. She half turned back but Ben said, "It'll take only a minute, Cousin Sarah."

"Well, then—what do you want to tell me?" The sun was in her eyes; it seemed to her that Ben's face was ferrety and intent.

"You know I'm a good friend of yours, Cousin Sarah. I shot that water moccasin last night."

"Yes, you did and I thank you. . . ."

"Yes, well—reckon you don't know much about me, cousin. Fact is, I'm a self-made man—came up the hard way —no family to speak of, no help in that direction, but if I do say it myself I made money."

"Yes. Yes, I know." She moved so the shade of the hedge protected her from the low, dazzling sun. The move brought her around a curve in the path, within sight of the smirking, weather-beaten cupid.

"Well, what I'm trying to say is, I know the value of money. Now to tell you the truth, Cousin Sarah, I think the Yankees are going to win. Oh, I'm a loyal Southerner and I wouldn't say this to anybody but you—but I'm not all Southern, if you understand me."

"No," Sarah said bluntly, "I don't understand."

Ben wiped his moist face with his arm, sneezed and peered at her. "Put it this way. You're a Yankee. I understand your sympathies, all for the North. And I won't say that I don't agree with you, in some ways. Wait now—I'll put it plainly. When the war is over I'm going to need some money—quite a lot of money," he said, his eyes small and peering, "so I reckon you might find it in your heart to help me."

Instead of finding it in her heart to promise him help, her heart sank with a thud.

Money again. In some odd way she felt that she was living through something that had happened once before. "Ben," she said, "I'll put it plainly, too. I cannot possibly come into my father's estate until the war is over. And if or when that happens, how can I possibly know or guess what obligations I'll have, what the circumstances will be? I can't promise you anything, Ben."

"Oh, now, Cousin Sarah, I don't ask for money right now —but think it over. Just think it over," he said, and suddenly, unexpectedly gave her a sly, almost a conspiratorial grin. "Remember, I've been your friend and I'll *be* a friend, no matter what happens."

Now she knew in a sickening flash why the little scene had

142

seemed familiar; it was almost a repetition of her talk with Emile.

She turned, her skirts swishing against the overgrown box-wood, and almost ran along the brick path. Ben, contentedly smiling to himself, followed.

She hurried across the lawn to the porch. Ben strolled after her.

Now just why had he said that? she thought. She applied herself to searching out the one precious needle Miss Celie had given her; she tried to find gray thread which would match Lucien's gray broadcloth coat, failed and resorted to black thread. Why had Ben said just that? Because he had come to her aid when she needed it? Something in her rejected that as an excuse for an immediate call upon her for money she didn't have, and didn't know when if ever would come into her possession.

Ben settled down in a chair at the end of the porch but she felt that he shot sly glances at her, as she bent over her sewing. She was about to gather up her basket and go into the house merely to escape his presence there when Miss Celie came out with Lolotte and Maude. They brought stacks of mending; they had all changed to clean dresses which rustled starchily.

Rufe gave a loud whicker from the barnyard and Vampa gave an aristocratic snort, much like Maude's. So they hadn't hidden Rufe and Vampa in the enclosure around the spring. She thought that idly, still aware of Ben, still puzzling over his manner as much as over his appeal for money. Then abruptly she saw the significance of Vampa's presence still in the barnyard; Rev intended to leave the next morning so he hadn't taken Vampa to the spring.

The sun seemed to dip down lower; the evening sky seemed to have a slight shadow, changing its color.

Abruptly, with shocking suddenness, sounds arose again from the front driveway, a wagon creaking and jouncing, the galloping thud of hoofs.

Sarah dropped Lucien's coat, the basket, her needle, and ran with the others to the front door. It was Stash, standing up in the wagon as it rocked from side to side, lashing his lathered mules. Rev and George came running, from around the end of the house; Lucien came running down the stairs; Uncle Jethro and Glendora appeared like magic. Stash reigned in his glistening mules. "Mist' Rev, the Yankees crossed the river this morning! They on this side, Mist' Rev. Whole army of them—"

So it was Stash who brought the news of Grant's landing in Mississippi. The steaming, trembling mules heaved while he told them.

He had delivered his wagonload of supplies to the commissary headquarters beyond Maville; there he'd heard that there was a passel of Yankee cavalry in the neighborhood, nobody knew where. He'd reckoned that if he ran into any of them they'd take his mules and wagon so in the hope of avoiding them he'd taken the long way around, which brought him out on the Natchez road. He was late by then; he knew they'd be in a state about him, so he was going right smart even though the mules were tired. . . .

Miss Celie interrupted, "When did you start out to the commissary?"

"Why—why, right early, Miss Celie. Fact is I started long about two o'clock in the morning. It's a right smart piece and I knew the sun would be hot and—"

Miss Celie sighed. "You're a good boy, Stash." Her face was warm, her voice had a kind of pride, indulgence and firm affection. Sarah thought, surprised, "I don't understand her; I thought I knew so much; I'll never understand people."

"Yes'm." Stash looked puzzled.

"The rest of the people ran away, after you'd gone," Rev said. "Go on, Stash—what about Grant?"

Well, he'd met a man on the Natchez road, lashing his horse and going like a bat out of hell—beg pardon, Miss Celie, he meant going right fast. The man had checked his horse and asked Stash where he belonged. "I tell him Honotassa. He say to come home fast as I can and tell you the Yankees landed this morning."

"Where?" Rev's hand gripped the side of the wagon.

"He say below Grand Gulf. That little wide place in the road they call Bruinsberg. He say the whole army is crossing, thousands of them."

Lolotte gave a soft scream. Lucien came to the wagon. "This doesn't make sense, Stash. How could they land?"

"Don't know, Mist' Lucien. That's what he say."

"Where are they heading?" Rev asked. "Did he know?"

"He say they're heading for Grand Gulf—maybe Vicksburg. Going to shoot from this side. But he say to tell you he

144

don't know for sure. They might come this way, they might do anything. He say to hide all the horses and mules and burn the cotton and—"

"They're going to attack Vicksburg from the east," George cried.

"How did they cross the river?" Lucien asked.

"He say they had boats, slipped them down past Vicksburg to Hard Times or somewhere on the west bank of the river. They're here, though, Mist' Lucien. That man know. He say to tell you and hide everything—"

"Sounds to me like a crazy sort of rumor," Lucien said. "I don't see how Grant could have crossed the river."

Stash wiped his face. "Reckon it's true."

"Well—we've already got everything done that we can do, Stash," Rev said. "Give those mules some water and corn. When did you last eat, yourself?"

"Reckon I didn't think much about eating," Stash said soberly.

"Well, think about it now. Here—I'll see to the mules."

"I hadn't ought to come in this front way, Mist' Rev. But—"

"You did just right. Glendora, fix him something to eat." Rev sprang up into the wagon beside Stash and took the reins.

There was a wagon road, parallel to the front driveway, which led from the public road straight to the barnyard, but instead of backing the mules around and driving them back along the avenue, Rev turned them across the grass and through the magnolias, toward the end of the house.

It was the shorter, the far more sensible way to take but Miss Celie gave a sharp hiss as a wheel caught in some azaleas and the wagon cut sharply through the grass. George slid the gun in his hand back into his belt and galloped after the wagon.

Lolotte caught at Lucien's arm. "Lucien, they'll not come this way, will they?"

"Now, sweetheart, no need to get yourself in a state. Stash has likely got things all mixed up—"

"Uncle Jethro," Miss Celie called, her voice for once shrill and high. "You go milk those cows."

Uncle Jethro was sliding rapidly away behind the magnolias. He peered out, caught. "Miss Celie, them cows way down at the spring. I can't carry no more buckets—"

"Get Lij to help you. Now mind—Sarah," Miss Celie whirled around. "There's some ham left for supper but we'll need something else—Glendora, get the basket!"

Glendora, however, had vanished. Sarah went through the house to her mending basket where she had left the bundle of keys. Maude and Ben, Lolotte and Lucien were still gathered together at the front door, talking. She had a feeling that Miss Celie had disappeared into the dining room.

The evening shadows were long but it was still light when she made her way again along the shady path past the office and the kitchen, from where there came again the smell of frying ham for Stash's supper.

There were sounds from the barns and sheds, men's voices, the creak of wagon wheels. She felt curiously detached from herself. So Grant had landed. Vicksburg would fall, she hadn't a doubt of that.

She paused at the door of the storehouse; the vines growing over its rounded, cavelike top sent out a sweet and heavy fragrance. She felt as if she were moving in an important, a crucial moment of history.

She wondered how many other women, all over the country, North and South, had felt its touch like that.

Probably every one of them.

Her own problems, her own perplexities, her own inner doubts, her own uneasiness, all seemed trivial, dwarfed and put into their proper and insignificant proportions.

War itself had come almost to the doorstep of Honotassa. Rev would leave the next day. There was nothing she could do, nothing—yes, she could keep and care for Honotassa as Rev trusted her to do.

She unlocked the storehouse door and swung it back. The cavelike, narrow room was dark; the mingled smells of vinegar and spices and sorghum sifted out from the dusky interior. Somewhere she had seen a lantern.

She groped around on the shelf near the door and found the lantern but no matches. Her eyes though became more accustomed to the gloom. She hunted out the huge jar of rice. Dried peaches; she could find them by their almondy scent. Dried peas which rattled softly; she had almost filled her basket when there was a rusty creak behind her. She whirled around as the faint light in the storehouse was quietly cut off and the door closed. The last crack of light vanished. There was a hoarse rasp as the key turned in the door.

CHAPTER SEVENTEEN

She dropped the basket. Peas and rice and peaches rattled around her feet in the sudden blackness; she ran to the door and beat upon it, shouting. The door didn't open. There were no sounds from outside.

It was an accident. Someone had come along the path, had seen the door open with the keys on the outside and simply closed and locked it. Anyone could have done so, almost automatically. The water moccasin had been accident, too. The opium was not an accident. The darkness around her seemed shot with dancing, flashing little lights.

She took a long breath. She leaned against the door. The thing to do—yes, yes, the thing to do was—well, to wait.

There was no sense in beating at the door and screaming. Her hands already hurt from that senseless pounding; her throat was dry. But it was really an accident, perfectly clear and comprehensible. And someone would come soon to release her. Glendora would inquire for rice and peas for supper. Miss Celie would come to find her or send someone.

Even if Glendora and Miss Celie managed to find enough food already in the kitchen, still someone would miss her. Even if she waited until suppertime—why, then Rev would say, where is Sarah?

Someone would say, where is Sarah? They would look for her and Miss Celie would remember that she had sent Sarah to the storehouse and whoever locked the door would remember and—it was silly to let her heart thud like that, stupid to let herself imagine hands coming out of the darkness of a deserted storehouse.

She sank down by the door. The air was dry and cool; she wouldn't suffocate. She didn't like the darkness. She struggled to her feet and groped around on the shelf near the lantern again. After what seemed a long, long time she found an empty cup, with its handle broken, where there had been matches. There was now the splinter of a match with its head broken off.

Again she fought off a senseless fear of the darkness. All she had to do was wait. The hard-packed earth of the floor was damp; she wadded her skirts below her like a cushion and sat, her head at the keyhole. There was a faint streak of light from the keyhole which gave her a small sense of comfort; it was not so comforting when it slowly, inexorably vanished.

In the darkness her thoughts began to dart around her like bats, frightening yet elusive, darting in and darting out again. The talk between Rev and Lucien that morning, interrupted by the approach of the detachment of cavalry, repeated itself—in snatches, but it was revealing. It explained Rev's presence in New Orleans, dangerous though it was to him; he'd had to prove that Emile was lying. It explained his curious words to her, after her ugly little talk with Emile; he had still been a little doubtful of her own purpose and her own influence upon Lucien—and thankful when she denied Emile's accusation and he knew she was speaking the truth. He wouldn't let Lucien have the gold and Lucien didn't care; Lucien and Rev had made peace.

Glendora might have locked the storehouse door, when she called Stash to supper. Stash might have seen it standing open like that and locked it. Anybody could have locked it, even Rev or George, returning to the house from the barns. Who had known that she had gone to the storehouse? Miss Celie. Maude and Ben might have heard Miss Celie send her there. Lolotte and Lucien had been talking, but they could have heard it, too.

Locking the door could be—just *could* be another move, a sequel to the opium in her coffee, merely an attempt to frighten her so she would do—well, what? Leave Honotassa?

Lucien had wanted her to go North. But he had yielded to her refusal; he hadn't mentioned it again.

Her feet and legs were numb; she rose and made herself walk until the stinging prickles stopped. She felt her way back to the door again. There was no faint ray of light from the keyhole. She huddled her skirts below her again; she leaned against the door.

The black bats of fancy and fear darted back again. Why, if she died, and if sometime her father's money came to Lucien, then everyone in that household would profit from it. Ben liked money. Ben had asked for money. Maude openly

148

declared she liked money. All of them liked security and money would bring them that. But Lolotte, lovely Lolotte, really hated her. If Lolotte had in fact read her marriage contract—no, no, she thought. Lolotte could not murder anybody!

If Lolotte knew something about the dueling pistol, then she must be made to tell it. How could anybody force Lolotte to do anything!

Murder.

Don't question, Rev had said. A murderer is afraid. Another black bat of fear sought to entangle itself in her mind.

Time passed and more time. The ugly darting questions resolved themselves into three. Who had given her opium and why? What exactly had Ben meant? There emerged in the stillness and darkness some sense of threat in his smiling, almost conspiratorial words. Who had killed Emile and why?

And then abruptly another question edged itself in upon her but with a kind of numb acceptance; she didn't even feel surprised because it had not occurred to her sooner; a bottle of opium had disappeared and also a bottle of chloroform. Chloroform was as easily identifiable as opium. But then she jerked her cramped body upright. Chloroform—and a faint whiff of something sweetish and yet sickening, in the office along with the strangely sluggish water moccasin!

Panic caught at her again; she had to get out of the storehouse, she had to do something, anything, and in the same instant the key turned stealthily in the lock beside her.

She had not heard footsteps; she had no warning of it. She scrambled to her feet in a surge of thankfulness, she fumbled for the latch—and then choked back the cry rising in her throat and instead of pulling open the door, instead of running out to meet whoever it was who stood at the door, she ran, stumbling, groping along the shelves to the very back of the storehouse. Wait and see, something seemed to tell her; wait and see.

The door opened, for she could see a lighter rectangle, marking it. She thought she could see a figure standing there —but like a mirage, like nothing that had ever existed, without a sound, it was gone.

She waited, her heart thudding, trying to listen.

There were footsteps, loud now, running along the path, thudding as loud and fast as her heart. Rev called, "Sarah— Sarah—"

A figure again loomed up dimly in that lighter patch and she ran toward it. "Rev—I'm here—wait—"

He swore and lighted a match and by its wavering, red flame she caught a glimpse of his face, which looked white and strained. Then he dropped the match and she reached his arms, which closed around her.

She clung to him. She was out of the storehouse. The night air was fresh upon her and his arms were like a wall around her.

She felt his head bent over her own; she felt his hard, warm cheek upon her face, she felt his lips and in that moment of release, of freedom, of safety, she gave him her lips with no restraint, no consciousness of her own act, no thought of anything.

Presently she opened her eyes. She saw only the night stars which were misty and far away and yet seemed so near that she could have plucked them down with her hands and kept them in her heart forever.

"My dear love," Rev said, low, against her face.

There were lights in the house. The great oaks of Honotassa stood above their heads.

Rev put her gently away from him, yet held her, as she stumbled and nearly fell. She said, "My feet have gone to sleep."

Rev, steadying her with his arms, gave a sudden, low chuckle. "A Sarah-like statement of fact. What happened, Sarah? Who locked you in there?"

"I don't know." But someone had come, just the same, someone had unlocked the door and stood for a second in the doorway and then vanished. "Somebody was here! Just now—before you came—"

"*Who?*"

"I don't know. I couldn't see." She thought he was leaving her, to look for that vanishing shadow, and she held hard to his arms. "Don't go. Don't leave me here. Not yet."

"Sarah." His voice was low, yet it had a deadly softness. "Has anything like this happened before? Something went wrong yesterday morning. I knew it when you came to the office. I followed you to the kitchen. You asked Maude about your coffee that morning and I wondered why—but then you wouldn't talk to me. You seemed to avoid me—"

"It was opium. I had it in my bag, the one you brought from New Orleans. I brought some medicines. A bottle of

150

opium and a bottle of chloroform disappeared the afternoon before Emile was shot."

There was a long pause. A lantern flashed dimly across the lawn, down toward the garden. Finally Rev said, "So that was what clinked in the bag. I thought it was cologne, something like that."

"There are lights in the garden."

"Yes, they're looking for you." She could see his face dimly in the shadowy, starry night. He glanced around them; they were still close to the storehouse, close to the heavy shrubbery on either side of it, close to the heavy roof with its masking vines. "Let them look," he said, put his arm around her, supporting her still unsteady feet, and drew her across the path and into the office. It was dark there but the smoke smell from the fireplace, the musty smell of old wood, rose familiarly in the darkness. "I'll not light the lamp," he said. "Opium in your coffee?"

"Yes—oh, yes." All the black bats of fear came swooping out as if they had lives of their own; she couldn't have stopped them. "Rev, could anybody catch a water moccasin and bring it to the office?"

"No! No, they are fighters and dangerous. Oh, long ago when George and Lucien and Stash and I were boys, we used to try to get hold of one with a long, forked stick. Just sheer deviltry. Pa caught us at it once and nearly licked the daylights out of us. It was the only time I ever saw him hit a Negro a lick but he turned Stash up and whaled him, just the same as the rest of us." He paused and said after a moment, "It did strike me as unusual that one would come so near the house. Usually they stick to water, that little run down in the swamp. But nobody could possibly risk bringing one, let alone finding it—"

"There was—I'm sure now that there was an odor of chloroform."

"Chloroform!" Again he thought for a moment, then he said slowly, "It could have been done—yes. Dangerous but it could have been done. But then it wasn't Lolotte."

"Lolotte—"

"Try to understand, Sarah. Emile laughed at Lolotte that night you came. We've spoiled her, she's like a child. But she—"

"You think—you always thought that Lolotte shot Emile! That's why you gave the Spencer cartridge to the coroner."

151

"What good would it have done to accuse Lolotte? And even if I had wanted to accuse her as God knows I didn't, what proof was there? She had Lucien's dueling pistols and one of them had been fired—but she could have taken them from his room to hide them as she said. Someone else could have taken one of the pistols, shot Emile, returned it to its case. I didn't have proof, but I didn't want any proof. Lolotte —no. She's like a child—she's got a woman's power to hate and a child's recklessness in action. A murder accusation couldn't have brought Emile back."

"You were shielding Lolotte."

"Yes, I had to."

"But suppose it wasn't Lolotte! Suppose somebody else—" Another of the black bats darted out. "Ben talked to me to-day. Down in the garden. And it was like Emile. He said— he said he was my friend and he wanted money. Not now but later and—it was like Emile."

"*Ben!*" His voice tensed; he caught her hand. "Tell me exactly what he said."

She told him, word for word; she told him how Ben had looked, his smiling air of conspiracy. She told him every-thing.

"Ben," Rev said at last. "That changes things, doesn't it?" He didn't say what it changed. His voice was far away, lost in thought.

Sarah took a long breath of relief; she had let go every dark fancy, she had told Rev as if there were no barriers be-tween them.

But then she thought, there is a barrier. Her hand was still in Rev's. She drew it away. She drew away from him. Oh, yes, there was a barrier.

Rev sensed her movement away from him. "Don't go, Sarah. I love you," he said simply. "I've loved you from the first. But don't draw away from me. I've had—a moment and that's more than most men get."

"We had a moment," she whispered, without intending to, in spite of herself.

She could hear his quick breathing, she could almost hear his heart. He didn't move, he didn't put out his hands, he didn't take her in his arms; yet the truth was shared so com-pletely that it was like an embrace.

A light wavered at the door, sprang into being, and both Sarah and Rev turned to see George's face glimmering above the yellow light of the lantern, which he lifted high. "So—so there you are!"

His pale eyes surveyed them; they were cold yet bright with suspicion. He put the lantern down with an air of decision and in the same motion he drew out his gun. "Get your gun, Rev. Lucien's your brother. Reckon I'll have to do this for him."

Rev moved lightly between Sarah and George; his tall body cut off her view of George's hard, accusing face. "Oh, don't be a fool, George," he said quietly. "I'm not going to fight any duel with you, or with Lucien either."

"It's wrong to fight with Lucien. He's your brother. But I'll fight you for him. Get your gun—"

"Go ahead and shoot if you feel like that."

"I'll not shoot an unarmed man."

"You might as well." To Sarah's amazement there was the hint of a chuckle in Rev's voice. "Anybody that fights you is as good as dead anyway."

George sucked in his breath with sharp surprise. "Why, I never thought you'd be afraid of anything!"

"Anybody that's not afraid of you with a gun in your hand and in a killing mood is a damn fool. No need to be an idiot, George. Whatever you're thinking—"

"I'm thinking plenty. Here you are with Sarah—alone—everybody's looking for her—"

"Tell Lucien about it."

"Why, you're out of your head, Rev! If I tell Lucien—"

"By the way, just what would you tell him?"

"Why—why—" George gave another splutter. "All right. I didn't see anything if that's what you mean. You heard me coming. But I can feel. I know there's something between you and that little—"

Rev's arm tensed and moved. George caught back whatever word had been on his lips and said, "—that Yankee Lucien married."

Rev's arm slowly relaxed. "Will it make you feel any better, George, to stop and think that she's Lucien's wife? I'm leaving tomorrow, it's not likely I'll come back to Honotassa again. I have no place here, George, and I know that. You know it, too."

The truth in his words and in his voice was like a farewell to Sarah.

George slowly slid his gun in his belt. He picked up the

lantern. "Reckon we'd better go to the house," he said.

Sarah walked between them, the lantern light dancing around them. As they approached the lighted porch, George shouted, "Here she is! Lucien! Ben! Here she is."

Another lantern came, bobbing from the hedge of the garden. Lolotte and Maude were suddenly on the porch. Ben held the lantern high and Lucien's face came out of the darkness. "Sarah!"

There was all at once a hubbub and commotion: Where had she been? The storehouse? How had she got locked in? They'd been looking everywhere. Miss Celie's black dress blended so completely with the night that her white face seemed suspended, like another lantern.

If anyone came from the shadows around the storehouse or office, Sarah did not see a stealthy approach among all the other bewildering shadows.

Nobody knew who had locked the door. Nobody knew who had discovered the keys.

"They were in the door of the storehouse," Rev said. "I found them there and opened the door. The door was already unlocked."

"Why, do you mean somebody found the keys and unlocked the door and then ran away without even opening the door? Or looking for her?" Maude's Roman nose looked stern and magisterial.

Nobody said, yes, I did that. No one said, I found the keys; no one said, I had the keys all along. Certainly no one said, I unlocked the door and then heard someone—Rev—coming and slid away into the shadows.

They were by then in the hall; there were lights everywhere.

When Sarah hadn't come to supper Lolotte or Maude or somebody had thought a moment and said that Sarah was in her room.

"Why, child, we just reckoned you didn't want your supper," Miss Celie said. "We didn't even look for you till somebody—it must have been Rev—yes, it was Rev—said I'd better go and see if you felt all right and then you weren't there and—dear me, Sarah, you've got cobwebs all over you."

"I said she'd gone to the storehouse." Maude eyed Sarah piercingly. "If anybody came along and locked you in there it was a mean trick! You left the keys on the outside of the

154

door, Cousin Sarah—so now, who came along and locked the door?"

"Why, nobody did it on purpose," Lolotte said softly. "That would be a—why, nobody would do that to Cousin Sarah!"

"Oh, Glendora did it," Miss Celie said impatiently, "or Uncle Jethro, or Stash or—didn't you and George come past the storehouse on your way to supper, Rev?"

"We went to the spring," Rev said. "Saw that everything was all right there, and came back that way to the house. We didn't pass the storehouse."

Miss Celie ended it. "We can question Glendora and Stash later. It gave Sarah a fright but no harm's done. The thing to do now is get her some supper—maybe a toddy, Maude. Yes, a toddy."

Maude started to say something; her long nose was lifted as if she smelled battle; but then she bit her lip and turned around, heavily, like a figure on a pedestal and went to the dining room.

"Here, darling." Lucien smiled down at Sarah. "I'll take you upstairs." He brushed her hair, his fingers touched her face. "Why, darling, Miss Celie's right. Come along—and get those cobwebs washed off."

She went upstairs, his arm tight around her. Over the railing she caught a glimpse of Lolotte, watching them. Rev stood there, too, his face unreadable. George lifted the lantern he still carried and blew out the flame.

The lights and faces below them vanished as Sarah and Lucien turned around the landing. In the upper hall, Lucien said softly, "Something happened between you and Rev. You'd better tell me the truth about it."

CHAPTER EIGHTEEN

He led her through the night-dark hall to her own room. He found and lighted a candle.

"Now then," he said, "let's have it. Is Rev trying to steal my wife? He was always jealous of me. What happened?"

She sank down on the hard settee. It was directly opposite the mirror in the door of the armoire so she saw herself reflected, her hair loose, streaks of grime on Lolotte's pink

155

dress, her eyes luminous in the wavering candlelight. Her cheeks and her lips were pink. She looked excited, she looked triumphant, she looked loved.

George had felt it in the air, in the packed silence of the dark office. Lucien, whose perceptions were much quicker than George's, could not have failed to see it, once he saw her.

He came up suddenly, in the mirror, beside her. "There's no use denying it. I've got eyes in my head. You look like a girl who's been kissed for the first time. What did Rev say?" Unexpectedly he laughed, his big body moved away from the dusky depths of the mirror. He sat down, his long legs sprawling out, and surveyed her. "I'm sure it was all very noble. Did George interrupt the big moment of renunciation? Let me see now, what did Rev say? He loves you devotedly but you are his brother's wife, so therefore he will give you up. He's going away to war. He will cherish his love forever. He'll never come back to Honotassa, he'll never see you again. Oh, you don't need to tell me, it's written all over you. Duty and the army call him. The warrior rides away." He put back his dark head and laughed again. "No woman ever forgets the man who loves and rides away to war. All from noble motives. It's the best way to a woman's heart."

She only wished that he would leave. He felt around in the pockets of the black long jacket he was wearing, he drew out a cigar and lighted it. The odor of tobacco filled the room.

"So you won't talk. Can it possibly be that you fancy yourself returning Rev's passionate devotion? You have an impulsive nature, my dear. Cold and prudent, yet impulsive, too. I advise you to let your Yankee nature rule. You'll never see Rev again."

"You told him, you promised him you'd make it fair, you'd give him his share of Honotassa."

"I did. And I meant it. But—" he looked thoughtfully at his cigar and said, "Rev won't take it, now. There have been times when Rev and I have not seen eye to eye. But he'll not take property from me after he's made love to my wife. I'll give him credit for that."

She looked at him with an odd kind of objectivity. She could not blame him; he had tried to be fair; the fault was hers. Yet it struck her in a half-formulated way that whatever it was that had convinced her once that she loved him was merely a foreshadowing of her love for Rev. It was the difference between a pinchbeck gem, glittering and brilliant but made of glass, and the real jewel.

Lucien flicked ashes from his cigar on the carpet.

"Oh, well, it doesn't matter really. I felt rather like a fool. A man expects certain things of his wife. I lost my temper. Now—" he said kindly, "you'd better forget all this. I intend to."

"Lucien," she said suddenly, "where were you when Rev found me in the storehouse?"

He smiled and shook his head. "Not near enough to hear your fine and noble scene with Rev. I didn't need to be told any of it."

"Someone unlocked the door and then just—disappeared."

"I didn't, if that's what you mean. Why should I? Don't be childish. It was Stash. Or that little fool, Glendora. Even old Uncle Jethro, he's in his dotage. One of them locked you in there simply because the keys were on the outside of the door and then got scared when we were all looking for you, unlocked the door and made himself scarce, afraid of a whipping."

"What did you do?"

"Why, I looked for you! We took lanterns—hunted all over the place."

"You and Ben?"

"Everybody. Even Miss Celie."

"Where did you look?"

"I told you. All over the place—the garden, the driveway, clear down to the road—all over the house." Lucien puffed out a cloud of blue smoke. "Why did you ask about Ben? I saw you talking to him this afternoon. I was in my room. You looked as if you didn't like whatever he said. What was it? Money?"

"How did you—"

"I know Ben. So he wanted money. Why?"

"He said he would need it. He—oh, he hinted that he was really on the Union side—a friend of mine, he said. No, I didn't like it. He reminded me of Emile." A small memory and an explanation flashed to her. "Ben—I think he tried to ask you, first. This morning he started for the office, turned around, then started toward the office again as if he couldn't make up his mind."

"He wouldn't have asked me for money. He knows I don't

157

have any money! Is that all—"

Maude called from the hall. "Open the door, Lucien. My hands are full."

Lucien sprang up from his chair, opened the door and Maude came in, carrying a tray. "Here's some supper. And here's a toddy. Now drink that and—oh, for goodness sake, Lucien, don't drop ashes on the carpet. Miss Celie will have a fit."

She put down the tray, gave the toddy a brisk stir with a spoon and said, "That's hot. . . . Now then, Cousin Sarah, what is all this about being locked in that storehouse? Who did it?"

"I don't know."

"Well then, what *was* in your coffee yesterday morning?"

"Opium," Sarah said wearily.

Maude's eyes widened. "Opium! Why, there's no opium on the place—"

"Oh, yes," Lucien said, "Sarah brought some with her. She knew we were short of medicines. It disappeared."

"But then—why, then—where was it? *Who took it?*"

"She doesn't know that either."

"But it might have killed her!" Maude began with the effect of Vesuvius beginning to erupt and stopped as Lolotte swirled into the room like a spitting cat, upon Sarah.

"You told Rev that I killed Emile! You told him I put something in your coffee! You told him that I locked you in the storehouse! You hate me. You know Lucien's still in love with me! You know he only married you for your money, you hate me—"

Maude put out an arm which was solid as a rock and fended Lolotte and her small, flaring hands away from Sarah. "Don't knock that toddy over," she said calmly. Then she gave Lolotte an ice-cold look. "What did you say about Emile?"

"Oh, you don't think any Yankee shot him either! You know you don't. Everybody in the house knows that—" Lolotte stopped with a swiftly drawn breath.

Lucien said, "What does everybody in the house know, Lolotte?"

She backed away a little. "Why—why—well, you know how mean Emile was. And then—well, I found your dueling pistols, Lucien. The case was on that little stairway at the

158

end of the house near the garden. So right away I knew—
that is, I thought—but I didn't care who killed him. I told
Rev that I got them from your room because I just wasn't
going to get anybody into trouble for shooting Emile. He
was so mean! Besides it wasn't what they call evidence. I
didn't *see* anybody shoot Emile. I didn't *see* anybody touch
those pistols. I just did what I thought was right and I'd do it
again."

It sounded true. But her air of impatient truth when she
told Rev that she had taken the pistols from Lucien's room
had been convincing, too.

"Lolotte," Sarah asked suddenly, "How did you happen to
find the pistols? Were you looking for them?"

"Certainly not! Rev asked me that, too. I reckon you put
him up to it. You'd like to make people think I shot
Emile!"

"Lolotte," Maude said, "That's no answer. How did you
happen to find the pistols? Did you just stumble over them?"

Lolotte flashed her a beaming smile. "Why that's exactly
what I did! But don't ask me why I went down those steps
because I don't know why. I don't know why I did anything
that night. I was scared out of my wits."

Again it sounded true.

There was a moment of silence, so still that the murmur
of the frogs and the steady rasping of locusts outside seemed
to take over.

Finally Lucien said, "Lolotte, tell me the truth. *Did* you
find some opium anywhere and try to give it to Sarah?"

Lolotte's eyes flared. "Opium! No! I never heard of any
opium or—oh, there were some bottles here on the table!
Fancy bottles. I thought Cousin Sarah had brought them
from Paris. Cologne and stuff to put on her face and—don't
look at me like that, Lucien. Of course, I came here to her
room, just as soon as I could, and looked at everything she'd
brought with her. I found her marriage contract, too. I
opened it, of course I did, why not? And I read it." Her dark
eyes had garnet lights in them; she glanced at Maude. "Do you
know that if Lucien—if anything happens to him in the war
Honotassa and everything he's got goes to Cousin Sarah?
Not a thing to any of us! It wasn't fair, Lucien. It wasn't fair.
You've got to change it."

"Why, now, Lolotte," Lucien said softly, "I hope I'll not be
killed."

"Oh, Lucien—" She ran to him, her face distressed. "Lucien, I didn't mean that! I only meant—well, can't you see that that's all Cousin Sarah wants from you? She wants a husband and a home. Why, she just snatched you—and then she got you to agree to that silly marriage contract and—" She caught his arm. "Lucien, you've got to change it."

He looked down at her; he put his hand over her hand. Sarah said, "Lolotte, how many people have you told about our marriage contract?"

"It doesn't matter," Lucien said. "Lolotte, is that why you gave Sarah that opium?"

"Why—but I *didn't*—"

Maude said, "Cousin Sarah's got no money here. God knows when if ever she'll get her father's money. Good heavenly days, Lucien, if you mean that Lolotte tried to kill Cousin Sarah—what earthly good would that do for anybody?"

"I've got to leave tomorrow," Lucien said. "Lolotte, if you shot Emile—well, it's done—"

"*I didn't—*"

"Nobody's going to let you be accused or—charged with murder."

"*But I didn't!*"

Maude smoothed her hair in the only distracted gesture Sarah had ever seen her make. "But—murder—who took the pistols? Who shot Emile?"

"How should I know?" Lolotte shrugged. "Most anybody. Why, Cousin Sarah could have done it, easy as anything. She had some kind of quarrel with Emile, that afternoon. I saw her and Emile strolling along, thick as thieves, toward the garden. And then I saw Rev come out of the office and go after them, running. And in a few minutes Cousin Sarah and Rev came out of the hedge and—and I knew something had happened. They were talking and—why, Cousin Sarah could have just got mad and shot Emile, that night."

"And how did she get hold of my dueling pistols?" Lucien asked softly.

"I—there they were in plain sight. Anybody could have taken them." Lolotte flashed around toward Maude. "And you know perfectly well, Maude Greevy, that everybody in this house has been wondering about it. Everybody in this house has been thinking, who really did kill Emile? But nobody cares. Why should we? It's good riddance. Why—why for all I know, you killed him, Cousin Maude. Ben or George killed him. Why—why, maybe Rev did it himself, even if he has been asking me all those horrid questions! Emile," she said with utter, incredible dismissal of the whole situation, "Emile was right mean. What does it matter?"

"It matters that you have accused Sarah," Lucien said. "I won't have it, Lolotte. And I'll not have any more of this—opium in coffee, locking up the storehouse—"

"Why, Lucien!" Tears, real tears, came into Lolotte's eyes. Her face was all beauty again, all pleading, all reproach. "I'd never, *never* do such dreadful things."

No, Sarah thought, I'll never understand people. She believed Lolotte.

Maude gave a sigh. She jerked her hoops, settled her skirts, put both her hands up to smooth the two great buns of hair over her ears. She gave the impression of having emerged from a tornado, but not quite unscathed. She said, "Well, Emile's dead and none of us can do a thing about it. Drink your toddy before it's cold, Cousin Sarah."

Lolotte clung to Lucien's arm. "Lucien, come and tell Rev he mustn't talk to me like that ever again. Cousin Sarah put him up to it. She said I'd done all those dreadful things—"

"No," Sarah said, "I didn't."

"You did, too! You're jealous of me—" The spitting little cat was back again.

Maude made one stride to Lolotte, took her hands in a grip that made Lolotte give a little scream and literally pushed her out the door.

Lucien came to Sarah; he bent his head; he put his arms around her. He said, "She'll behave now. . . . Goodnight dear." He kissed her.

Maude stood aside as he opened the door and went away, jauntily again, settling his coat and his broad shoulders.

For a moment the two women eyed each other across the room which still seemed to echo with Lolotte's furious attack.

Then a wry half-smile touched Maude's mouth. "I will say this is a fine state of affairs."

"You thought Emile was murdered."

"I'll not say it didn't enter my mind."

"Maude, is there anything—any secret, anything Emile could have used to—to threaten somebody?" But Maude's face was now as uncommunicative as if it were in fact carved

161

in marble. "Every big family has its skeletons."

"What?" Sarah asked bluntly.

"Oh, this and that. Old Grandpa Hugot was nobody's saint —if the stories are true. You can't tell me he built that stairway at the end of the hall for any good purpose. But mostly we are pretty honest and decent people. There was a cousin who drank herself to death. Cousin Faustine, that was. To tell you the truth, my father wasn't everything he should be but thank heaven he's in Italy and likely to stay there. But don't you ever tell Miss Celie I said that! And there was Aunt Maude—I was named for her—she ran through three husbands and they do say—but the fact is, in our family, everybody knows everything about everybody else. There've been skeletons," she said flatly, "but I can't think of anything that was Emile's private skeleton. Reckon somebody just had enough of him and shot him. I never did quite believe that story Rev told about the cartridge. What difference does it make? Better men than Emile are dying every day. But honestly, Cousin Sarah, we don't go around shooting people. No need for you to get worked up. Now you eat your supper. You've taken quite a lot of whiskey on an empty stomach. We don't want another Cousin Faustine in the family," she said with a flicker of grim humor, and went away, stately as a dowager; she closed the door after her with a firm bang.

She left Sarah feeling as battered as a shuttlecock. No, she thought after a while, I'll never understand people; I don't understand a single one of them. But she understood Rev and herself far too well.

She left the candle burning that night. Its wavering light on the armoire, the settee, the whole room, promised to tie her with the force of physical vision alone to a sense of reality which forbade dreams.

All the same she must have dreamed, for she thought that Rev was speaking to her. It was so clear a dream that she awoke.

The candle had guttered out. The mosquito netting was like a dim veil around her but Rev *was* speaking to her, whispering from the doorway, "Sarah—"

It still seemed so much like a dream that she heard only snatches of his whisper. "Sarah—I want to show you where it is—I'll get a lantern. Sarah, do you hear?"

"Yes. Yes—"

"Be quiet—"

She thought she could see his tall figure move away. It was like the night he had come to her room and removed the gold. Her mind cleared; he intended to show her where he had hidden the gold. In the confusing, dreamlike darkness she found her wrapper and her slippers. Rev would tell her where he had hidden the gold and leave Honotassa the next morning. But she knew, too, that nothing could have prevented her from taking this one last moment that fate had offered her.

The house was quiet. She edged close to the banister. She groped her way along the hall downstairs; he had unfastened the bolts of the door and it stood open.

The porch made a band of shadow but beyond it faint starlight outlined a stretch of lawn, blackly rimmed with trees and shrubbery. She waited a second or two, thinking Rev would come to her. Then she saw the pale glow of a lantern above the garden hedge.

Why, of course, he'd hidden the gold in the garden! It was an obviously safe place, deserted and untended since Emile's murder. She ran across the lawn. The faint light moved ahead of her, showing in intermittent flashes above and beyond the curves of the brick path.

The light stopped, it seemed to grow brighter. The bitter fragrance of boxwood pressed around her. She came out into the circle around the cupid. The lantern stood on the bench.

The cupid was in the shadow; the roses looked pallid and strange and a man lay sprawled like an empty sack at the marble feet of the cupid.

She took one step nearer and stopped as if she, too, had been struck into marble and would never move again.

In fact though it was Ben who would never move again, Ben who lay there at the feet of the cupid, Ben whose ferrety face was agape in the dim yellow light. The handle of a knife was starkly black in the wavering light, against his light shirt.

There was no sound; there was only a sense of movement somewhere near her and a swift, sweet, penetrating smell, as something like a black blanket closed over her face, around her throat, shutting off air, shutting off everything except that cloying odor which she fought against and still had to breathe. She went down, struggling against something that was too strong. It eluded her, down and down into dizzy blackness.

163

After a long time, after a short time, after no time at all she was vaguely aware of movement again, somewhere near her. There was clean fresh air on her face; she took great gulps of it. The smothering, woolly blackness was gone.

After another space of time, she opened her eyes. The stars were misty, far above her. The circle of cedars still enclosed her. The lantern stood on the bench—and Ben still lay at the feet of the smirking cupid.

There was a difference though, for the knife lay now in the shadow of the bench, but so near her that she could have touched it.

Then she heard, dully and far away, a kind of turbulence, a remote blending of small sounds. Off in the distance a horse snorted and was quickly silenced. Feet were pounding along the brick path. She grasped at the bench to pull herself up; the hedge shook and trembled and Stash ran into the circle. He looked at Ben and said something. He whirled around and came to her. "Hurry—hurry—Miss Sarah."

His voice, his helping hands were urgent.

She was on her feet, stumbling over a woolly, dark shadow on the grass; she was on the brick walk, hurrying—hurrying with Stash. They reached the porch and stopped for there were now other sounds; she listened this time with sharp attention. A horse was galloping hard, along the back lane from the barns to the road. "Who—" she whispered.

"Mist' Rev."

"Where did he go?"

"Don't know, Miss Sarah. He say for me to find you and —now go in the house, Miss Sarah."

The thud of a horse's hoofs was already diminishing, already gone.

"What did he tell you, Stash?"

"He wake me. He tell me Mist' Ben dead. He tell me to take you to the house. That's all, Miss Sarah," Stash said firmly.

"Yes—well, you'd better go and tell them about—"

"Yes, Miss Sarah."

She sank down on the porch; she leaned back against a pillar. Stash went into the house.

So Rev had gone, without another word, without another moment. But Rev had found her, Rev had come in time, Rev had pulled off that suffocating blackness. Rev had gone and they would say that Rev had killed Ben.

164

CHAPTER NINETEEN

They did say it, almost at once.

She heard it all. She saw patches of light fall upon the lawn from swiftly lighted lamps and candles in the house. She heard a woman—Maude?—scream. She saw Lucien, George and Stash come out of the house, all together. They ran past her, there in the shadow, and down to the garden.

She heard Lolotte and Miss Celie's voices in the house; she heard Maude. She wouldn't go into the house; she wouldn't listen—but she did listen and she did go into the house, for Lucien and George came back, running. "Sarah!" Lucien called. "Stash says—*Sarah*—"

"I'm here."

He came; he caught her up in his arms. "Sarah, what happened? Stash said Rev came and woke him and told him Ben was dead and told him you were in the garden and he must bring you to the house and—then Rev left. What happened?"

She moved with him, as he spoke, into the lighted house. She told him flatly, "Rev came and said he'd tell me where the gold is. I followed somebody with a lantern—I thought it was Rev—to the garden. Ben was there. Something came over my head—there was chloroform. Then—then it was gone and Stash came for me. Rev sent him."

"Dear God," Miss Celie whispered. "Rev killed him."

"And he killed Emile!" Lolotte cried shrilly. She was wearing her pink silk wrapper and its laces fluttered as she ran to Lucien. "Rev killed Emile and he killed Ben."

"He saved my life," Sarah said and might as well not have spoken.

Lolotte gave her a swift look. "Gold—you said gold? What gold?"

Lucien replied, "It doesn't matter. Some gold Sarah brought with her. Rev—took it."

"Oh," Lolotte said. "Oh. How much?" Nobody answered.

"Rev," Maude said dully from the stairway. "Rev did that."

"Stay here, all of you," Lucien said. "George—"

He and George went back to the garden.

Maude sat down on the stair steps and put her head in her

hands. Miss Celie went out to the porch, where her black hair and black wrapper blended completely with the night. Lolotte stood at the door.

Finally the men came back. They had found a black shawl which belonged to Miss Celie; it still reeked of chloroform. They had found the knife and it was what they called a Bowie knife. Rev had had one—and Sarah remembered suddenly the knife Rev had taken from his boot top when he said to Glendora, "It's like ducks. I'll show you."

George said, though, that almost everybody had a Bowie knife. Lucien agreed.

The senseless thing was the chloroform.

"Why would he give Sarah chloroform?" George said, his face taut and white and his eyes very bright.

"He didn't," Sarah said. Again nobody listened.

"Why would he kill Ben?" Lucien said. There was no answer to that.

Suddenly the tap, tap of hammers began again, off somewhere in the night. Lucien said, "Stash said there are some good pine planks in the carpenter shop. He got Uncle Jethro to help him."

"No." Maude rose, holding to the banister. She would not have Ben buried at Honotassa. She was going to take him to Natchez and bury him on his own place.

She would hear no argument. It was Ben's home and he loved it. If there were Yankees on the road they'd better look out for themselves! "But they'll not bother a woman taking a man to be buried. Stash can go with me. We'll take the wagon."

Lucien's face darkened. "Stash knows more about this than he lets on."

"Let him go with me," Maude said. "I want to start with the first light."

"You can't do that." Lucien had dressed hurriedly, in a ruffled white shirt, which had seen better days, and his gray uniform trousers. All of them were dressed haphazardly, but George had a gun at his belt.

"You can't do that," Lucien said again. "He was murdered. I've got to report it to the coroner. George, send the stable boy, Lij—tell him to go to Dr. Raymond's place—"

"There's no use in that," Maude said. "All these Yankees around, goodness knows where Dr. Raymond is—likely hiding under the bed."

166

"She's right." Miss Celie put her hand on Lucien's arm, commandingly. "The doctor can't do anything now. Let Maude go."

"We've got to tell him. We've got to report it—it's murder—"

"You can't accuse your own brother, Lucien, and that's what you'll have to do if you send for the doctor. Besides, what good would it do? Rev is gone. He'll never come back."

Sarah said, "Rev didn't kill him. I told you Rev came and —why, he saved my life. He pulled off that shawl. He sent Stash to see to me. The murderer—it wasn't Rev!"

Miss Celie shook her head. Maude listened without a quiver of feeling in her face.

Lolotte said, "She's protecting Rev. She's trying to make us believe it wasn't Rev—"

"Well, God knows I'd like to believe it," Lucien said.

"He was going to tell me where he'd hidden the gold—" Sarah's voice fell flat as George took out his gun, turned it over and examined it as if he'd never seen it before. He said, "Reckon she'd lie for Rev, any old day. Shall I send Lij for Dr. Raymond?"

"I'll not have it!" Miss Celie's black eyes flashed. "I'll not have it, Lucien."

"He's taken that gold away with him," Lolotte said, suddenly. "And Ben—Ben knew it! So he tried to stop him and Rev killed him! Ben was always hunting around, listening, watching—"

"Shut up!" Maude's hands doubled up. "You just shut up, Lolotte Hugot."

"Rev's gone and he took the gold with him and Ben's murdered—"

"Lolotte," Sarah said, "Rev thought you had shot Emile but he tried to shield you. Now because he questioned you about Emile you've turned on him!"

"I didn't shoot Emile! You hate me, you're jealous—"

Lucien tried to stop her. "Be quiet, Lolotte. There's no real proof that Rev did this. Sarah says he didn't—"

"How could she know—with that shawl over her head? That is—if she's telling the truth. Maybe Rev told her he'd killed Ben. Why yes! She knew he'd killed Ben and she had let him have that gold you've been talking about. Rev put just enough chloroform on that shawl so it would look as if somebody else had tried to—to kill her! They made up that story, Rev and Sarah, to protect Rev!"

To Sarah's horror, George and Miss Celie both gave Lolotte a long, thoughtful look as if considering, half accepting her version. But Lucien shook his head. This time his voice was hard. "Stop that, Lolotte. George—"

"No," Miss Celie said, "I'll not have it. I'll not let you accuse your own brother. Oh, what difference does it make? Rev's gone back to the army, that's where he's gone. He'll never come back here."

"Lucien," George said suddenly, "maybe Miss Celie's right. Don't send for the coroner. Nobody's going to question, ever. We'll just say Rev left for the army—"

"And what will we say about Ben?"

"We'll say Ben went back to—to Natchez. No, we'll say he found some way to get back to his plantation, across the river. Lucien, times like these with the Yankees breathing down our backs nobody's ever going to question anything. And I reckon nobody in this family's ever going to spread the fact that Rev killed a man—I reckon he killed Emile, too. Yes—I reckon he did. That Spencer cartridge always seemed a mite too handy, to me."

There was no use in saying no; no, he didn't kill Emile. One of you killed him, Sarah thought, and then swiftly added and one of you killed Ben!

Yet when she had said that Rev hadn't killed Ben, with its clear implication that, therefore, someone else had killed him, there had been no exchanged glances, no slightest hint of question, nothing.

George ended the argument. "I'll go help Stash."

Maude moved, she put her hand on Sarah's arm. "Help me dress. I've got to pack a few things. Miss Celie, can you fix a little basket for us, something to eat? If we have to take back roads to get around Yankees we'll be a right long time on the road."

But Lolotte cried suddenly, "Chloroform! Where did Rev get hold of any chloroform?"

Maude turned slowly; her hand with its broad wedding band was on the banister. "He got it the same way he got the opium. Those medicines Sarah brought—and Rev knew it, he had plenty of chance to take it. I wouldn't have thought it of Rev." She stared down at her wedding band. "No, I wouldn't have thought it of Rev. Emile needed shooting. Nobody would have blamed Rev much for that. But I wouldn't have thought he'd kill Ben."

A question, unuttered until then, all at once hovered over them. Miss Celie cried, "Maude, why did Ben go to the garden at all? How did Rev get him out there?"

Maude stared at her wedding ring. After a long moment she said, "I don't know. I just don't know. I was asleep. I didn't know anything about it till Stash came hammering at Lucien's door. Maybe Rev did it the same way he got Sarah to come out there. Likely came to the door and whispered to Ben and told him—oh, told him anything." She sighed. "I sleep like the dead. I—" She heard her own word, gave a kind of gulp and went up the stairs.

"She does sleep like the dead," Lolotte said, coolly. "Except nobody dead ever snores like that."

"Well," Miss Celie said unexpectedly, "what can you expect with a nose like that? Just like her father's."

She spoke absently, as if automatically. Sarah caught a glimpse of Glendora hovering in the background, pop-eyed and her hand over her mouth. Miss Celie saw her too and made for her. "Glendora, I want to fix some lunch for Miss Maude—"

But Maude had heard; she turned and said dangerously, "Just you keep your own nose out of my affairs, Miss Celie."

In spite of shock, emergency—murder—the old feud still operated; it gave an odd touch of something lasting, something fantastically real and normal. It was something that would continue to endure within that house in spite of murder, in spite of anything, as long as the house stood, sturdy and strong beneath its great and solid oaks. It was strangely friendly.

Miss Celie looked for once a little taken aback. Sarah thought she whispered a word or two by way of, not retraction, but apology. Maude went on up the stairs and Sarah followed.

So they were not going to tell the coroner that there was again murder. No one had the effrontery this time to put the blame on nonexistent Yankee stragglers.

But this time Sarah was thankful. It would give Rev time to make his way back to the army. As things stood the evidence against him in the matter of Ben's death was overwhelming. Later, perhaps the evidence would clear away. If, for instance, they found the gold. If, for instance, the murderer were discovered.

She went slowly up the long flight of stairs. Someone had put that shawl over her head. But she'd have known it, yes, she'd have known it if that someone had been Rev.

The knife? Suppose whoever had put that shawl over her head had intended an easy and simple murder by way of chloroform, and then had found that there wasn't enough chloroform, that Sarah still struggled, and that the knife which already had been used to kill Ben would make it final. More difficult, but final.

Perhaps, too, murder was not intended; the chloroform was to be only another move in a campaign of terror. No; it was to have been murder, for the knife lay near her, so close in the shadow of the bench that Rev had not seen it.

He had come, she was sure of that. He had almost certainly stopped murder and the murderer had escaped because —why, because Rev had waited to make sure that she was unhurt. Then he had sent Stash—and had gone, galloping furiously along the back lane. She was as sure of all that as if she had been the marble cupid, witnessing the whole thing.

Yet something she couldn't so much as surmise, had happened between the time when Rev woke her and she had followed that faint glow in the darkness between the hedges, moving like a will o' the wisp, and when she found the lantern placed on the bench.

A will o' the wisp—well, of course that was what had been intended! She had followed, believing Rev carried the lantern, thinking how sensible it had been for him to hide the gold in the garden where nobody ever went now. She had let that will o' the wisp of murder lead her to the circle of cedars where the shawl and bottle of chloroform—and a knife if that failed—were waiting for her.

But something had happened in that short interval of time, something which alarmed Rev so he came through the darkness, following her, or hurrying to her rescue. Something had happened which then sent him hurrying to Stash's cabin, waking him, telling him to see to her, and then on to saddle his horse and ride in frantic haste along the back wagon road, away from Honotassa. Leaving murder behind him.

So, then what had happened?

His departure alone put a load of guilt upon him. Maude called from her room. "I'll wear a muslin dress, that old blue one, it'll be hot. I'll take my black silk in a box—"

Maude had lighted two candles; she was already at the mirror, unbraiding and brushing out her thick light hair.

"There's a box in the armoire. There's no tissue paper but fold up my good black silk. I'd better take an extra set of underclothing, there in the drawer."

"Maude," Sarah said, "did Ben know something about Emile's murder?"

"He didn't know who killed Emile. He didn't believe in the Yankee raiders but, no—Ben didn't know who killed Emile. And I'll tell you this—whoever killed Emile, it wasn't Ben and it wasn't George and it wasn't," Maude said coldly, "me. I was right here in this room when I heard the shot. You can see, the windows are right above the front driveway and Ben and George were out there, walking along, smoking. Ben had given George one of his cigars and I could see the two cigars, red as stars. It wasn't Ben and it wasn't George." Maude started to roll up a big bun of her hair.

"Maude, why do you think Ben was killed?"

"I tell you I don't know. But—" Maude took a hairpin out of her mouth and said thoughtfully, "Ben's been different. Ever since that day he went to Maville in the rain, chasing the runaways. He—he's been different. As if he had something on his mind." She secured one loop of hair and started in on the other. "And then he kept writing down figures and calculating, just as if he expected to get some money from somewhere."

From me, Sarah thought.

Maude gave an expert twist to the bun of hair over her other ear. "But he was always fighting about money. Ben— well, he came from people who didn't know where their next cent was coming from—didn't care—but Ben was different. He made all his money himself. Built up his plantation and built his fine house in Natchez, and he loved it and was proud of it. Maybe he had to make money in the beginning in some ways that—but all the same he made it. And I'm going to bury him where he'd want to be buried. Don't forget a nightgown, Cousin Sarah."

Sarah bent over the open drawer. She folded up the long, batiste nightgown, mended, its ribbons faded. Ben had talked to her about money; he as good as said that the Union would win and he wanted to be on the winning side. He had tried to enlist her friendliness and the promise of money to help him get a fresh start once the war was over; it had reminded her, even then, of her ugly little talk with Emile, and Emile

171

had been shot that night, within hours of his talk and his base-
less threats.

Ben had made no threats. But Ben had been murdered, too.

Glendora came into the room. "Miss Celie sent me with
some coffee, Miss Maude." She put down the tray. "Miss
Maude, take me with you."

"Stash is going. And there may be Yankees along the road."

"I'm not scared of Yankees. I'm scared to stay here—"

"You'll stay here," Miss Celie said, coming into the room
behind her. "Now then, Maude, if you're still determined to
go to Natchez—well, I see you are—I don't see why Rev did
it, honestly I don't. He was a headstrong boy, maybe it's my
fault. Maybe I wasn't always fair to him. No—" Miss Celie
said, seeming to look bleakly back along the years, "I reckon
it was my duty to see that his pa fixed it so Rev had his share
of Honotassa. Then he wouldn't have been so jealous of
Lucien—then he wouldn't have done this. But it's right to let
him go. He'll never come back to Honotassa, now."

Chapter Twenty

It was well past dawn, it was far into the morning by the
time Maude and Stash left. There had been delays; it had
taken a long time to make the box, which stood in the back
of the wagon. Miss Celie had given it a troubled look, trundled into the house and come back with a faded paisley
shawl which she put over it, hiding the bare ugliness of the
unfinished pine boards.

And at the last Lolotte had come, running, with a parasol
for Maude; it was a delicate lacy affair, tiny and ruffled, a
prized possession of Lolotte's for it was carefully wrapped in
old newspapers. Maude took it and looked grotesque, sitting
there like a statue, in her faded muslin, her black bonnet, the
frivolous, gay little parasol held over her head—and the long
box in the wagon behind her. Stash held the reins.

Lucien, his hand on the wagon, said, "Look out for
Yankees. Take the back roads."

The wagon started up with a creak. The great oaks and
long wisps of Spanish moss cast glancing shadows upon
Maude sitting erect and stiff, and upon the faded paisley

172

shawl. The dismal little cortege had almost reached the end of the driveway and the turn into the road when Sarah thought sharply, I should have questioned Stash again, made him answer; he must know more of Rev than he told anyone. She almost ran after them—and then the wagon halted; she saw the sway of Stash's body as he pulled back on the lines and a buggy came from the road, around the curve, and stopped beside the wagon.

Lucien stared. "Why, it's Dr. Raymond!" He started down the driveway hurriedly. George went too but both of them stopped as the wagon started up again, disappeared around the curve, and Dr. Raymond, standing in the buggy, touched his whip to his raw-boned old horse and came at a rattling dash toward them.

He pulled up at the steps as Lucien grasped the bridle rein of the panting, speckled old horse. "Yankees!" Dr. Raymond gasped. "They're coming! Get your stock hidden. They're taking everything they can lay their hands on."

"Where are they?" George shouted.

"God knows—they're everywhere!" The doctor drew a breath and took off his battered Panama hat with a flourish of bows. "Miss Celie—Miss Sarah—Miss Lolotte—"

"For God's sake stop that bobbing, man!" Miss Celie clutched the wheel of his buggy. "Where are the Yankees now?"

"I tell you they're everywhere," he said testily. "I came to warn you. I stopped at the Fant place and now I'm trying to make—" He broke off. "I'm sorry about Ben, Miss Celie. Sorry about Rev, too, I'll tell you the truth. As if we didn't have enough trouble on our hands without a duel! And a nasty stabbing duel at that!"

"A—duel," Lucien said.

"Miss Maude told me. Said Ben and Rev had fought and Rev killed Ben and then he lit out."

"Oh," Lucien said. "Yes—a duel—"

"Believe me, any other time I'd have to do something about it, Lucien. I've had my stomach full of duels in my day. No excuse for them—none—against the law, too. But right now, don't know as I *can* do anything about it! First we'd have to find Rev—and besides—" The doctor's withered old face was sober; his thick eyeglasses winked in a ray of sunlight. "Besides," he said, "reckon Rev's mighty likely to get a bullet himself. They say there's likely to be heavy fighting up Vir-

173

ginia way soon. No, sir—time enough to do something about this—this duel when Rev comes home again. If he ever comes home."

"Doctor—" George was at the side of the wagon, too. "Doctor, you couldn't get a coroner's jury together today, could you?"

Is he on Rev's side, Sarah thought; is he on anybody's side, *is he on his own side?*

"Good God!" The old doctor stared at George. "You couldn't get two men together to hang a— Wait," he swiveled around to Lucien, "I knew there was something else —they say the Yanks have got out a passel of scouts. They're not in blue coats, they've got themselves rigged up in butternuts. They say they call them butternut guerrillas! Butternut guerrillas!" Reckless of Miss Celie's presence, reckless of his usual courtesy, he scornfully spat over the side of the wagon. "Yes, sir, that's what they've done. And these butternut guerrillas likely do their share of looting and burning and shooting, too. So look out for them. I've got to get on. Miss Celie"—his courteous manners returned—"I'm right sorry about this. I wouldn't have thought it of Rev—no, I wouldn't." He turned to Lucien and shook hands with him. "I'm right sorry, Lucien. Tell you the truth, I'd have never thought that Ben Greevy would have got up the spunk to fight a duel with anybody, let alone Rev." There was a spark of curiosity in his face. "Now what did they quarrel about?"

Ben and Rev had not quarreled, there had been no duel —but then Sarah thought swiftly, let it go as a duel; it was far better than to start a story in the county, in the whole state, which Rev would never be able entirely to clear up. She stopped words almost on her lips and for that moment joined the closed ranks of the Hugots.

Lucien was saying something in reply. ". . . nobody knows. None of us will ever know. Unless Rev comes back—"

The doctor shook his head, bowed to Miss Celie, slapped his old hat back on his head and clucked to his horse. "If you see anybody be sure to warn them about the Yankees," he shouted above the rattle of the buggy.

The buggy jounced and swayed down the driveway again, in and out of the sun and shadows. The old doctor stood, leaning over to use his whip, jouncing and swaying along with the buggy. Nobody spoke until it turned into the

174

road and vanished. Then Miss Celie said, "For heaven's sake, you girls get in out of the sun. You'll ruin your complexions."

It was so weirdly unexpected, it lent such a touch of fantastic reality to the scene that Sarah felt something like a sob and something like a laugh well up in her throat. Murder might come and murder might go, but Miss Celie went on, fatalistically accepting whatever happened—and determined to preserve the magnolia delicacy of Lolotte's complexion and to prevent Sarah from getting freckles.

"Cousin Maude thought right fast," George said approvingly.

"Yes, she did." Lucien's face was sober. "I never would have thought of a duel."

"It's the best way out," George said.

Miss Celie nodded. "Maude always had her head screwed on the right way. She got it from the Hugots, not from that no good father of hers. Girls, you go and get some clothes on, too. You look downright trashy!"

Lolotte was still wearing her pink silk wrapper with its lace flounces. Sarah glanced down at her own wrapper with a kind of surprise. Miss Celie herded them into the cool, shadowy house. Behind them, Sarah heard Lucien say, "What horse did Rev take?"

George replied, "Vampa. He's the fastest horse."

"We'd better see the stock fed. That boy Lij is scared of his shadow."

"If the Yankees do come this way—"

Their voices faded.

Sarah's eyes felt hot and tired as if she'd never had any sleep.

There was a charged and driving energy about Miss Celie which suggested that she intended to take up living and the remorseless routine she exacted from herself and from others. Sarah saw her big mending basket still standing on the floor near the door upon the south porch. She hurried to take it; she caught up Lucien's gray coat, with its gold buttons.

Miss Celie saw everything. "Be sure to mend that snag in the sleeve. And there may be some worn places in the pockets, there always are. Lolotte—"

But Lolotte had already run lightly up the stairs, out of Miss Celie's reach.

Once in her room Sarah looked around her, half incredulously because nothing was changed yet so much had happened.

It seemed as if years had passed since she had roused and thrust aside the mosquito netting, exactly as it was now, in tossed thin folds, and gone down to meet Rev and met murder instead.

Yes, a duel was the way out. Again a kind of respect for the Hugots caught her. It *was* fast thinking on Maude's part. It was also grimly realistic; Maude believed, all of them believed that Rev had killed Ben; he had taken the gold; he had, as George said, lit out and never intended to return. So, Maude's reasoning ran, nobody could bring Ben back; why accuse Rev of murder? If anybody on that day was likely to bother his head much with a private killing, a personal murder.

Stash must have known more than he admitted knowing. But somebody, she thought, tried to murder me! This time she was terribly sure that it was not merely an attempt to frighten her. It was intended to be murder.

The words were like an echo, which will not still itself. They came again and again, beating at her as if they had wings: *someone tried to murder me.*

Rev had said, don't ask questions; Rev had said a murderer is scared.

She heard Miss Celie downstairs, her voice raised in a thin, silky scream. "Lolotte, get right down here and help me, you hear?"

Presently, from down the hall, Lolotte's voice replied. "Yes, Miss Celie."

In another moment Miss Celie would send for Sarah. Again Sarah was caught up by the pressure of women's affairs. The house must be seen to, meals must be prepared, the household routine must go on.

She made her bed, hoping that Miss Celie could hear her footsteps; she dressed quickly. The only fresh dress she had was her blue and green lawn, washed until by now it, too, was faded.

She took her mending basket and settled herself at the window. She finished the buttons; she mended the snag in one sleeve. She searched for other little rents. She turned the coat inside out; she pulled the pockets inside out, discharging a small load of scraps of paper, the stub of a pencil, the crum-

176

pled remnants of a cigar, extra buttons rolled up in an old envelope.

She found a scrap of material in her basket and was mending the worn place when Glendora came in. "Miss Sarah."

"Yes, Glendora—"

Glendora sidled in and closed the door behind her. "Miss Celie sent me to get the keys."

"I don't know where they are. They must be downstairs somewhere, tell Miss Celie—"

"Yes'm." Glendora rubbed one foot along the thin calf of her other leg, looking like a nervous young crane in faded calico. "I already got the keys, Miss Sarah. I picked them up last night. I—the fact is, I got something on my mind. Seems like I ought to told somebody."

Sarah sat up with a jerk; the clutter of objects she had taken from Lucien's pockets slid to the floor. "Told what?"

"About the night Mist' Emile got shot."

"*What?*"

"Well, Miss Sarah, you know when that dog barked and everybody jump up and think it was the Yankees coming—"

"Yes—yes, go on—"

Glendora came closer; she glanced back over her shoulder and whispered, "Well—that shawl last night, that shawl they find in the garden there where Mist' Ben got killed, Miss Celie give that to me to wash out that stuff that put you to sleep—"

"Chloroform! Yes—"

"I know who took it out of this room."

"*Who?*"

"Yes'm. That night when Mist' Emile was shot, just before we had supper I come up here to fix the beds. Everybody was down there talking on the porch and I come in here and fix your bed and I see some little bottles on the table. Pretty bottles, Miss Sarah, and I look at them—that's all I did, just look at them, except I opened them and smelled them. But they wasn't no perfume, it was something else, like medicine. I put them all back. Didn't do anything to any of them —but Miss Sarah, that shawl smells like one of those bottles."

"Yes. Yes—I know." Yes, she knew, Sarah thought, and the echo came again: someone tried to murder me.

"Yes'm—but—" Glendora's legs twisted. Suddenly a tear came rolling down her round cheek. "I know who took it. I was toting water for the washstands and somebody come out

177

of this room and I see him."

"*Who?* Hurry, Glendora—"

"It was after that dog bark and then they say nobody around and supper was over. Cook say to me, never you mind no Yankees around, you just tote that water to them pitchers upstairs. I had a bucket of water and it was dark in the hall but kind of light too, light enough so I see him. I was at the back stairs and he come out of this room. He run down the hall but quiet, like he was on tiptoes, and when he pass that place at the big stairway where the light comes in from the windows I see he have two bottles in his hand—your fancy bottles, Miss Sarah. I saw them shine and he ran right on, down the hall and outdoors—out to the old stairway, outside the house. It was Mist' Rev."

The room wavered. "Are you—sure?"

"Yes'm. It was dark but I see them little shiny bottles. He put them in his pocket, one at a time—"

"Did he see you?"

"No'm. Didn't see nothing but the little bottles."

"But—but you said it was dark in the hall, then?"

"Yes'm, but there was some light from them windows. I see him. He had on a black coat and light britches and—it was Mist' Rev, Miss Sarah. And now he lit out." She wiped the tear from her cheeks. "He's a bad man. Reckon he shoot Mist' Emile and now he kill Mist' Ben and that why he lit out."

After a long moment Sarah said, "Have you told anyone else about this?"

"No'm. I was scared. But I got it on my mind all this time. I didn't touch those bottles except to look at them and smell them and that shawl of Miss Celie's—"

"Yes, yes! Think hard now. Have you seen either of those bottles, an empty one or—have you seen them since then, anywhere?"

Glendora's small face screwed up anxiously. "No'm. But there's a heap of hiding places around here. No use looking for them. If anybody use that stuff then he throw the bottles away off somewhere—swamp or spring or—nobody could find them ever. No use looking."

"No. No. Well, wipe your eyes. Now you've told me. It was right to tell me."

"Yes'm. Mist' Rev a bad man but"—Glendora gave a strangling sob—"he was good to me. He was good to all of us—"

178

She ran sniffling out of the room, wiping her eyes.

She didn't believe Glendora; no, she didn't believe it! But like a picture she could see Rev, in his ruffled white shirt, his black coat, his elegant fawn-colored trousers, standing in the door of the room in New Orleans, at the St. Charles, smiling at her.

"Sarah," Miss Celie called from the hall below, her thin voice piercing the noonday silence of the house. "Sarah—Lucien's packing. He wants his coat."

She took a long breath. "Yes, Miss Celie."

She picked up the coat, she scooped up the litter she had taken from the pockets. The old envelope had rolled loose, spilling gold buttons over the floor.

She gathered them together in the envelope and so saw the address.

She stood for an endless moment, with the noonday sun hot and drowsy upon the grass and trees outside, hot and drowsy in the room around her. She knew who had shot Emile and why. She knew who had killed Ben and could guess why. She believed she knew what problems her own murder would resolve. She knew too much, and yet not enough, not enough.

It was Mist' Rev, Glendora had said. Her tearful story brought back every small event of the night of Emile's murder, seemingly so quiet a night, supper and sitting around the lamp and—supper!

Lolotte had not come to supper. She had not joined them around the lamp. Sarah had assumed that Lolotte was in her room, sulking perhaps but certainly unwilling to sit at the table where Sarah was now to preside as Lucien's wife.

It was a small fact, perfectly open, no secret about it and it had been lost, forgotten, completely ignored.

It was futile to question Lolotte. As well try to push back the sea. There was no need to question Lolotte.

At last Sarah folded the soiled, wrinkled envelope and held it in her hand. She gathered up the mending basket and went downstairs.

There was a flutter of black in the dining room, Miss Celie busy at something. Lucien stood outside on the front steps, his hands in his pockets. Sarah put down her basket and went out; he turned when he heard her. His smile was never more charming. "Darling, I want to talk to you. I'm leaving this afternoon."

There was a thin clatter from the dining room as if a spoon had dropped. He led her down the steps. Their footsteps crunched lightly on the driveway. "Sarah, I'd feel easier in my mind if you'd go back to New York."

"Why?"

It was hot in the blazing glare of the sun. Sarah moved into the shade of a great thicket of magnolias.

"Why?" Lucien said. "I told you. You'd be safer there."

"That is not the reason. You want me to go to New York and get my father's estate settled."

"Why—why, Sarah!" His eyes were squinted against a ray of sunlight which sifted through the foliage. "What do you mean?" He was going to laugh.

"Oh, Lucien, it's no use. You were not in Richmond. You were in New York, trying to get my father's money—"

"Why—you—"

She opened her hand. She smoothed out the envelope and the address stood out clearly: Mr. Lucien Hugot, The Astor House, New York City. It was postmarked St. Louis and dated March third. She said, "There's a return address on the back of it. Why did you write to Mr. Eads, Lucien? Did you tell him that my father was dead and that you are my husband and—what did you tell him? What did he say in the letter that was in the envelope?"

"Why, that—I didn't—" He snatched the envelope from her hand. He held her away and hunted through his pockets. His coat fell back and a pistol was in his belt. He saw her look and laughed. "I found my dueling pistols. Rev had hidden them in Stash's cabin. As soon as Stash left this morning I went to look. Stash and Rev always stood up for each other and sure enough there they were—" He had found a match. He struck it, held the flame to the envelope and laughed as it traveled up. "Now what can you say?"

James Salter's daughter replied, "You have been in communication with Mr. Eads—trying to renew contracts, perhaps increasing the price. You have lied to us all. Emile said you were a deserter and he was right. You came here that night and shot him and then went away again—"

Lucien dropped the charred scraps of paper and ground them into the grass with his heel. "You saw me in Cuba. You know I'm not a deserter. You're accusing me because of Rev! You'd rather have them say that I'm a murderer than Rev—"

A sound was traveling through the air. A horse was trot-

ting along the avenue. Lucien whirled around. Rev, riding
Vampa, came from the long blue shadows of the driveway.

George came running around the opposite end of the
house, stared as he saw Rev and ran to him. Rev halted.
George said something. Rev said something. She could hear
only the murmur of their voices, no clear word. George
shook his head, he put his hand on the saddle, he seemed to
argue. Rev spoke again and George's hand made a swift motion and came up with a gun.

Lucien had a gun in his hand, too; the long, slender barrel
of his pistol caught dancing lights from the sun. She saw that.
She saw the two men outlined against the glossy green bank
of magnolias, full in the sunlight. Vampa fidgeted and tossed
his head. Rev was talking, slowly now, a few words at a time
as if he had to drag them out.

It was like a pantomime. George lifted his gun and aimed
it straight at Rev.

And then, like a pantomime again, as if they had heard a
significant sound offstage, both men seemed to stiffen and
listen. Rev jerked around in his saddle and looked behind
him. Horses were coming along the avenue at a steady trot.

Lucien pulled her back, hard, into the concealment of the
magnolias, yet she could see through the foliage and she
could hear the jingle of bridles, the creaking of leather as the
horsemen trotted briskly up to Rev and George, who now
stood transfixed, behind Rev.

There were five men on horseback. They were not wearing the blue coats Sarah had half expected; they were wearing odds and ends of clothing, butternuts and homespuns.
The first man threw up his hand and the whole party came to
a halt.

"This the Hugot place?" he inquired. "You Mr. Hugot?"
He spoke loudly, above the shuffling sounds of the horses.

Rev's soft voice was clear now, too. "Yes. What do you
want?"

His saddle creaked as the first rider seemed to relax and
shift his weight. "Sure am glad to find you. I was told to find
you. They told me to find the Hugot place and you'd help
us. We want some food first, want to water our horses—"

Rev suddenly had a gun in his hand, too. "You're not
Confederate men—"

All the men smiled. The speaker laughed resoundingly.
"We're scouts for Colonel Grierson. My commanding officer

told me if I could find you, you'd give us all the help you can. You stand high with our forces in New Orleans, Mr. Hugot. They say they sent you off to Cuba soon as you—soon as you saw the light and decided to turn Union." There was a slight yet perceptible note of contempt in his hearty voice. "The way I hear it you did a fine job getting information about that shipment of arms in Cuba that was intended for the rebels. Yes, sir, they say you certainly fooled them. Guess they're waiting there for some Secesh to buy them." He chuckled. "These clothes we're wearing—I hear tell you wore your Confederate uniform in Cuba. Yes, you certainly fooled them there. Now Captain Hugot—beg your pardon, guess you were Captain Hugot when you were rebel but not now—"

Lucien's dueling pistol pressed against Sarah.

The man speaking seemed to sense something wrong. He leaned forward. "You said you were Captain Hugot. They told me you had turned Union. What's the matter here?"

Vampa had shifted nervously, nearer the magnolias. Rev looked across the now clear space between them and saw Sarah. He saw Lucien. He saw everything in one blazing glance and his gun jerked away from the Union scouts masquerading in butternuts and aimed straight at Lucien.

There was a flash, two flashes—sharp reports, shocking the noonday stillness. Then the air was full of sounds, shouts, gunshots and the smell of powder. Vampa shot off at a wild gallop past the men and horses, down along the avenue of oaks. A Union scout fell from his horse and rolled, doubled up on the grass. George caught the reins of his horse; he got up into the saddle somehow, whirled the rearing horse around in his tracks and galloped off down the avenue after Rev.

All the men in butternuts were turning, whirling, firing. There was a flurry of horses and men, shots and the thudding hoofs of horses. Dust and gravel flew back. They disappeared around the curve of the driveway. For a few heartbeats Sarah could still hear them pounding along the road.

A bird twittered and flew with frightened wings out of the magnolias, past Sarah. Lolotte and Miss Celie stood on the steps. Lucien's dueling pistol lay on the grass at Sarah's feet. Lucien lay there, too.

The Union scout stirred, tried to rise and fell back.

Lolotte's skirt fluttered nearer. Her black head was bent;

then her eyes blazed up at Sarah. "Rev killed him. He killed his own brother!"

Miss Celie had moved swiftly as a black shadow. She, too, looked down for a long moment. Then she lifted her head. "He was a deserter. You heard them, Lolotte. He was a deserter. . . . Sarah, that man in the driveway needs help. Come with me—"

CHAPTER TWENTY-ONE

It was a houseful of women. The only man in the house was the wounded Union scout. Sarah and Miss Celie nursed him but Lolotte took the long night watches and sometimes through the hot darkness Sarah could hear his mumbled delirium and Lolotte's voice as gentle and soothing as a mother bird's. No, Sarah thought again, she would never understand people. Now she thought that it was not important to understand; the important thing was to love and be loved. Thus she made, without knowing it, a long step toward maturity.

One day the Union scout rode away again, toward Baton Rouge, on George's horse. Miss Celie, looking after him, said, "He's only a boy—such a waste—"

It was a house full of questions, too. They were almost tangible, yet none of the women spoke of them. But in the hot, still nights, the questions almost took on voice and sound. Yet Sarah knew only a few answers.

Lucien had been a deserter. She surmised that sometime after the second battle of Manassas he had decided, as Ben had decided, to put himself on the winning side. She was deeply sure that Lucien's motive in so doing was not one of conscience or conviction in the right of the Union cause, but for his own gain.

The Union scout had made it clear, too, that Lucien had been sent to Cuba, in Confederate uniform, by a Union command to pose as a Confederate officer seeking to buy the arms sent there from abroad and intended for the Confederacy. Perhaps the Union intended to buy them, perhaps the Union merely wanted to assess the amount and usefulness of the arms. Perhaps, as the Union scout had suggested, it was only an attempt to confuse the owners of the arms, keep them waiting with false promises for a bonafide offer from the Confederacy which would never come. Whatever the reason, Lucien was a deserter, acting in behalf of the cause he believed would win, wearing the uniform he had deserted.

He had married Sarah for the same reason, his own again. He had gone straight from Cuba to New York and attempted to implement his claim upon Sarah's father's estate. That was clear, too. That was why he had urged her to go back to New York; there was, she was sure, some formality, some stamp of authority that her presence there would put upon Lucien's claims. Yet it wasn't entirely necessary; it was all too clear that he considered his marriage contract with her as binding; perhaps he had already consulted lawyers about it. In any event he had only two choices: he must induce Sarah to return to New York, or kill her and present himself as her legal heir.

She was sure now that Glendora had seen Lucien, not Rev, leaving her room, running to the door of the stairway outside the house. So she was sure that Lucien himself had undertaken the campaign of frightening her into submission, or of accomplishing what would be considered an accidental death, by opium, a water moccasin. What he had intended to do after locking her in the storehouse she didn't know—yet in her heart she did know.

She believed that Lucien had killed Emile because Emile had known that Lucien had deserted. She didn't know how Lucien had learned of Emile's knowledge unless, when Lucien came home by way of New Orleans (not Mobile as he had said), someone, perhaps one of Emile's friends, had told him. But Lucien had known.

She believed that Ben, too, had come upon some knowledge of Lucien's activities for he, too, had wanted money from her; therefore he, as Emile had done, had in fact attempted to blackmail her in the belief that, a Northerner herself, she not only knew but approved Lucien's desertion, yet both she and Lucien hoped to keep Honotassa—yes, and Lucien's place as a loyal Southerner and valiant soldier.

That was all she knew except that Rev had killed Lucien. It always came back to that. May went slowly into June and June into the first hot week of July and it was still a houseful of women, and a house full of muted questions.

The second week of June two more women added themselves to the household, Calista and Rose Tiller. They drove

184

up one afternoon in a buckboard, pulled by a flop-eared and dusty mule. Calista said simply that her old Miss had gone to Texas to live with her daughter and she, Calista, had come home. Rose Tiller said that the Yankees had come too near her home; they were everywhere. She brought the only news they had of Grierson's cavalry for they had ridden past her place "Hell-for-leather," she said wearily, on their way to Baton Rouge and Union forces there. "They had a brush with our men at a place called Wall's Bridge, but got through."

The brush at Wall's Bridge, it developed, occurred the same day that the butternut guerrillas had visited Honotassa; by afternoon the entire brigade was across the Mississippi line.

But still no one knew whether or not Rev and George had escaped. If they had escaped, then George was at Vicksburg and Rev was back in Virginia.

That week, too, Maude returned alone. Stash, she said, had gone North; he had been sure that Rev was going back to his company in Virginia. Vicksburg was under siege by Grant's army.

She brought one of Sarah's trunks. It had been sent by boat to Natchez and Maude had hunted it out. She didn't know what had happened to the rest of the trunks.

The women unpacked it then and there. Their faces fell for it contained the silks and laces Sarah had worn to the opera and rare dinner parties, nothing they could use, everything that reminded them of balls, of carefree gaiety, of times which for them were gone forever. They watched bleakly while Sarah hung the dresses in the armoire.

Miss Celie told Maude of Lucien, and of Rev and George, for that night Maude came to Sarah, when the rest of the house was quiet. "Ben knew something—or guessed it," she said tiredly. "Emile had been in New Orleans not long before Rev took it into his head to go to New Orleans. Emile picked up some news of Lucien there—somehow Ben guessed. That's the way I look at it." She put her hand on Sarah's shoulder. "Rev was right to shoot him, a deserter. Besides, Miss Celie says she saw Lucien's pistol right against you. Rev's got mighty quick eyes. But Rev will never dare come back here, if he lives through this war."

Sarah did not tell Maude, she never told any of them that Lucien had not only deserted, he had clearly intended to profit by his claim to her father's foundry and rolling mills, arms to be used against the people he had deserted.

In the night when Sarah finally slept, she dreamed of the night when the dogs had barked and then, because they recognized Lucien, stopped barking. She awakened, wondering why that had not occurred to her or to any of them at the time. But how could they have conceived of that night visitor being Lucien, who was, they believed, in Richmond.

She thought through the mesh of lies Lucien had concocted, and of how convincing he had made it. Perhaps it was when he was taken prisoner that the idea of deserting to what he felt was a superior and winning force had occurred to him. Certainly he had found his way to New Orleans somehow. All that was conjecture.

Once and only once Lolotte spoke to Sarah of Lucien. The two girls, banded together by necessity but also by a cautious yet increasingly secure friendship, were picking beans. Lolotte pushed back her sunbonnet and said suddenly, "That night Emile was shot I was in my room. I heard somebody come in that side door from the little stairway. Whoever it was went into Lucien's room and then came out and tiptoed along the hall. I was so mad at you that I didn't pay it any mind. I reckon now that Lucien figured you had come to Honotassa by that time and wanted to make sure, so he went hunting along the hall till he found your things in the guest room. Anyway, after quite a while—long enough for him to find and take those bottles of medicine—I heard somebody come back again, very softly but in a hurry, and out the side door. He'd hardly gone when Glendora came with water for the bedrooms. But then after Emile was shot—well, I thought of Lucien's pistols and they weren't in his room so of course I ran down the little stairway and sure enough there they were, on the bottom step. I knew right away that whoever shot Emile had passed the little stairway, running from the garden, and just dropped the pistols there. I knew too, of course, that it was somebody we knew right well or somebody in the family and—it's just the way I told you. I wasn't going to get anybody into trouble for shooting Emile. I never thought. I never dreamed it was Lucien himself. What good would it have done if I'd told anybody?"

"None," Sarah said and would not let herself wonder what Lucien might have done had Lolotte not so definitely and truthfully denied seeing the pistols taken from Lucien's room.

186

No more was said of Lucien. No one visited the quiet, shady plot beneath the old oaks with its mossy headstones. Only Sarah herself went, early one morning and pulled the weeds already springing from the newly turned patch of soil. She dug up myrtles and planted them there. The tiny blue stars reminded her of the stars Lucien had denied. In a few days the myrtle would cover the place that marked tragedy and a blood quarrel between brothers. Wherever Rev was, whatever happened to him, there was and always would be a wall, an insurmountable barrier between him and Sarah.

Several times men from the commissary came and all but cleaned them out of food. They said only that Vicksburg was still holding but avoided the women's eyes when they questioned.

Once, about the middle of May, old Dr. Raymond came driving slowly up to the house and he had news. "Good news," he said. "We won a big victory at Chancellorsville, yes, sir, whipped those Yankees. But"—his face fell—"we lost Stonewall Jackson. They say it was accident, shot at night by our own men, lost his left arm. He was getting better though, everybody thought he was going to live. But then he got pneumonia. Yes—"

Vicksburg, the doctor told them, was still holding; but he seemed doubtful and tired; he rode away again. He said nothing of Lucien, he said nothing of Rev, and Sarah fancied that he knew the whole story.

One day in July Sarah was cutting some early sweet corn, and laying the milky kernels out on a sheet to parch, when she thought with surprise, why it's July fourth, the day of America's independence.

Grandpa Fant brought them the news of Vicksburg's surrender and said that there had been a big battle in Pennsylvania and General Lee's army had been defeated. That was all they knew until, nearly three weeks later, George Osborn came home, walking slowly and with enormous fatigue under the oaks along the driveway. He had been sick; his face was yellow with malaria and he was so emaciated that he looked like an old, old man.

Vicksburg had surrendered, he told them, on July fourth. He, along with what remained of General Pemberton's army, had been paroled. Meanwhile, a battle in Pennsylvania had been fought at a place called Gettysburg, ending in a Union victory on July third, with General Lee's retreat July fourth. There had been crushing casualties among the Confederate forces; the University Grays, he told them, had had almost a total record of casualty, killed and wounded. "Just boys," Miss Celie whispered. "Boys from our own university. Just boys—"

"It's over," George said. "Oh, we'll fight on—but I think it's over. Cousin Sarah, I lived on mule meat at Vicksburg, when I could get the mule meat."

When he was fed, when he was dosed with quinine from one of the gay little bottles which Sarah had purchased so long ago, when his ragged butternuts had been replaced by some of Rev's clothes—Sarah's heart missed a beat when she saw the worn, ruffled white shirt—he sought out Sarah.

He wanted to talk to her, he said; they went across the lawn and along the brick walk with its bitter-smelling boxwood and into the circle of cedars. The cupid had fallen during some summer storm; it lay face down among the tangled vines.

George had a letter for her. "I met John Rader, as I was coming through Maville. He got a bullet at Gettysburg, was given a leave and made his way home, riding his own horse. Somebody gave him this letter to bring you. John Rader is an old friend of Lucien's. The letter's from Rev."

She had known it would be. Her heart hammered. She took the letter which was addressed in pencil, battered and soiled as if it had traveled many miles—as, indeed, it had. George said, "Wait a minute, Cousin Sarah. Reckon there's something I've got to tell you. Right's right. That night after Ben was killed Rev went to Maville to find John Rader. He figured that Ben had something on his mind, he'd been acting queer, different—ever since the day he went after the runaways and met John Rader in Maville. And then Ben asked you for money. So Rev was afraid something—well, he was afraid Lucien—anyway, he heard Lucien come to your room and whisper something and go away again. Rev couldn't hear what he said—"

That was new; that was different; that had never once occurred to her. "I thought that was Rev! He was going to tell me about the gold—"

"No, it was Lucien. He wanted to get you away from the house. He'd already killed Ben, I figure, and—"

"Yes. He was going to kill me."

"Rev followed you when you left the house. He got there,

right here, I reckon it was." George glanced around him. The bench still stood but there was no lantern on it now, no marks of the things that had happened there. "Anyway, Lucien heard him and ran—Rev stopped to make sure that you were all right. Rev didn't have any proof that Lucien killed Ben. But he figured maybe John Rader had told Ben something. He knew Ben had got hold of something that scared Lucien. Rev was afraid that Lucien was a deserter but he—he hated it. The only thing Rev could think of that seemed to have some meaning was the way Ben spoke of John Rader and—anyway Rev went to Maville. He got hold of John—and John said he'd seen Lucien on the Natchez road the afternoon before Emile was shot. So Lucien wasn't in Richmond. He was lying—all that story of his." George passed his hand over his drawn, yellow face. "Well, when Rev told me—that day the Yankee scouts came—I didn't believe him. Besides it didn't prove anything, except Lucien was lying and that he was near Honotassa when John Rader saw him—the day Emile was shot. I told Rev I didn't believe it, I got out my gun—before God I was going to shoot Rev. And then the Yankee scouts came and—reckon you want to read your letter," George said and turned away.

"No," Sarah said, "Stay here—"

He seemed to sense her need; he sat down on the bench.

She opened the letter, tearing it swiftly from the envelope. It was written on a page torn from some book; its edges were faintly marked with gilt. It was dated July third.

"Dear Sarah," he wrote. "The gold is under the floorboards in the office. I put it back there after Lucien had looked for it. I have so much to tell you. I can't now. I wanted to believe Lucien, I did believe him until that morning when he offered me a share of Honotassa. It wasn't like Lucien. It seemed like a bribe but why? I thought it was something about Emile's murder. Then that night you told me some of the things that had happened and you told me that Ben had asked you for money. You must have told Lucien that, too. It was like Emile. There was only one thing I could think of, one possible source of information, a man by the name of John Rader in Maville. You were there by the magnolias so you must have heard what I told George."

She hadn't heard it but George had now told her. She remembered the hot, sunny noon, and read on.

"Sarah, I had to shoot Lucien. I saw everything.

189

"As you see I got away. George did, too. The Yankees followed us for a while but we lost them. I'm back with my old company, at least I was till yesterday when I was sent to report to General Pickett's command. A battle has been going on near a little town called Gettysburg. Word is that we're to go in soon. We're waiting now. The day is hot and sunny and so still that a while ago I heard a church clock or something strike, down in the town. Rumors are flying—always rumors. They say that General Lee gave orders for a charge and that General Longstreet opposes it. I don't know. But if Pickett does charge, looks like we'll make a charge right under the Yankee guns. They have us outnumbered, Sarah. More men and more guns.

"Yet it struck me last night that it's a war between brothers. One of the boys has a Bible and I was reading it last night—this page is torn from the front of it—and I came on this, 'the days of our desire.' It was still and quiet with the stars very bright and I thought of you—and then I thought maybe these are the days of desire, desire for different things, maybe mistaken things, but deep down, under the dirt and blood of war, a desire for peace and understanding between us all.

"Oh, we'll keep on fighting as long as we can—

"I have to stop, word has come that we're to move. I'll give this to one of the couriers. He'll see that you get it. If I don't come out of it he'll put some kind of mark on the envelope to let you know.

"My dear love. Rev."

She didn't read it again, not then. She would never forget a word of it. But she couldn't look on the back of the envelope.

George said, "Cousin Sarah."

She turned slowly to look at him. This time there was no icy hatred in his pale eyes, only sadness. "There's something else I've got to tell you. I shot Lucien—"

"*I saw Rev*—"

"No. You maybe saw Rev aim at him but I shot him. He was a deserter. I'd admired Lucien all my life as I had nobody else in the world. So I had to shoot him. Besides I saw Rev's gun aimed and I couldn't let Rev shoot his own brother."

"George—is this true?"

"Oh, it's true. I'm a better shot than Rev. His shot went wild. I had to do it, Cousin Sarah."

190

After a long moment she heard a mockingbird singing. Perhaps it had been singing all that time.

She thought, I must have this garden cleared, that marble cupid—who has seen so much—taken away. I must make Honotassa beautiful again.

She put the letter in George's hand. "Turn over the envelope. Tell me if there is any mark, any words, anything at all on the back of it. If there's nothing—oh, George, I'm sure there's nothing—then Rev will come back."